LONG WAY DOWN

Also available by Lisa Kusel

Novels

The Widow on Dwyer Court

Hat Trick

Memoir

RASH

Collections

Other Fish in the Sea

LONG WAY DOWN

A THRILLER

LISA KUSEL

NEW YORK

Published in the United States by Crooked Lane Books, an imprint of The Quick Brown Fox & Company LLC.

Crooked Lane Books and its logo are trademarks of The Quick Brown Fox & Company LLC.

Library of Congress Catalog-in-Publication data available upon request.

ISBN (hardcover): 979-8-89242-331-1
ISBN (paperback): 979-8-89242-333-5
ISBN (ebook): 979-8-89242-332-8

Cover design by Lauren Harms

Printed in the United States.

www.crookedlanebooks.com

Crooked Lane Books
34 West 27th St., 10th Floor
New York, NY 10001

First Edition: October 2025

The authorized representative in the EU for product safety and compliance is eucomply OÜPärnu mnt 139b-14, 11317 Tallinn, Estonia, hello@eucompliancepartner.com, +33757690241

10 9 8 7 6 5 4 3 2 1

For Elizabeth Brue

"We live in a silent explosion, Everything is flying away from everything else . . . flying away . . . flying away . . ."

— Jerry Spinelli

PROLOGUE

THE SCENE IS already crawling with officers when I arrive. Before I get too close, I pop a mint into my mouth and switch to mouth breathing. As I duck under the tape and crouch down to get a closer look at the victim, I mutter, "Fucking tweakers," to no one in particular.

She's sprawled out on her back, her blank eyes staring up at the clear sky. I'm guessing she was once beautiful, this one, but given the state of bloating and decomposition, there's nothing pretty about her now. She's wearing a blue dress, but the only color I care about at the moment is the red around her throat, long congealed into a dark red. The dirty brown red of a beet pulled free from the soil. Dirty brown red and crawling with maggots.

CHAPTER 1

THE MOMENT I switch the blow dryer to OFF I hear my father slam the front door. I follow the sound of his heavy footsteps into the kitchen. He's opening the refrigerator door. Pausing. Removing a glass bottle, hitting another one on its way out but not hard enough to shatter it. Another pause. He's considering grabbing two bottles so he won't have to get up again. Then he slams that door too.

One of these days a door in this old house is going to fall off its hinges.

I go out to the hallway and stop in front of his bedroom. It's a mess. His dirty work clothes strewn around the floor emit a stench of kerosene and chlorine and I remind myself to wash them tomorrow. I glance over at Dad's beloved red tool kit in the corner. His prized possession. It's the only thing in the room free of dust.

I step inside and pick up the pink and purple wildflower bedspread from the floor and lay it out across the queen bed, smoothing out the decades-old wrinkles as best I can.

I stand back and admire it then yank down the right corner so it's even with the left side. My mother loved the once-bright spray of colors, the dainty bend of the green stems. She said it made her feel like she was sleeping in a garden. Even after it started to fade and threads began to come loose she refused to replace it. After she died I asked my father if maybe he wanted a new one, something that wasn't so feminine. His head had snapped back as if I'd slapped him. I took that as a no.

As I walk through the hallway into my bedroom I catch the sound of artillery fire coming from the living room. He's watching *Apocalypse Now* again. I block out the explosive squall by humming to myself while foraging through my pathetically tiny wardrobe. It's mid-September and still warm enough for something lightweight. I pull out the blue cotton dress with a scoop neck and three-quarter cap sleeves that my fiancé Cal bought me to wear to meet his parents for the first time. After I do up the tiny white buttons along the bodice, I cinch a brown belt around my waist and slip on a pair of faux-leather brown sandals.

I go out to the living room and stand behind the couch, watching my father watch Martin Sheen shoot an innocent woman six feet from where he sits. I move around to the right side of the couch so he can see me out of the corner of his good eye. "Hi, Daddy," I say. "How was work?" I have to speak loudly to be heard.

He mutes the television and emits a sound somewhere between a burp and a grunt. "It was slow today, so they made me clean the toilets," he mutters without meeting my eyes.

If he hadn't gotten himself fired from his aviation mechanic job at Southwest Airlines, he wouldn't have had to stoop to taking a line service technician job at our small regional airport. I know he was grieving my mother's death, but he never should have gone to work drunk off his butt.

After a 737 landed at SMF, ground crew was notified that some passengers had seen smoke coming up from the floor during the flight. Dad was asked to troubleshoot the issue, and when he removed the floor access panels and activated the air-conditioning units, a cloud of superheated particles flew into his face. A man who was once a stickler for following rules, my father had stupidly ignored safety protocols by not wearing eye protection. Now, instead of maintaining 737s he's been reduced to driving a fuel truck and scrubbing urinals.

"I'm sorry," I say, feeling the sentiment deep inside me, but not knowing what other words to add.

He shrugs. "Why are you wearing that?" he says, noticing my dress. "Where you going?"

"The Coopers' house. Grant's coming home from rebab today, and Jean and Calvin are throwing him a party."

"Yeah, Cal told me about Grant getting out while I was fueling his plane."

"You saw Cal?"

"I did." He takes a swig from his beer. "He said he was flying down to Santa Monica to pick up his brother. He didn't mention anything about a party."

If not for being engaged to their son, Jean and Calvin wouldn't have ever invited me. But inviting Joe Rydell?

Never. "It's just a small dinner party. For the family," I say, trying to make light of it.

"The *family*," he says, looking at the frozen scene on the television as if the Coopers are characters in the movie. "Those people have bad blood running through their veins, Deni. I don't think you know what you're getting yourself into."

"I know exactly what I'm getting myself into," I reply, with as much conviction as I can summon. My father is right not to like Calvin and Jean Cooper. I don't like them either. They're cold, selfish, domineering people, but I'm not about to let that stop me from marrying their son. Cal is not like his parents. He is charming and thoughtful. Kind. "I need to swing by Marvin's and grab a pie. Can I make you dinner before I go?" I ask, wanting to change the subject.

Before he opens his mouth to answer, the monstrous rumble of a muffler-less car engine blasts through the open window. It's coming from Deez Yellen, the dopehead in the rental next door who, when he's not selling or snorting or shooting or smoking drugs, is working on busted cars. Last count there were four piles of metal littering his front yard. The sound is so grating I'm tempted to grab Dad's rivet gun and punch through my own eardrums.

People assume I'm marrying Calvin Cooper Jr. because I'm after his money. They're wrong. Beyond the fact that Cal is everything I want in a partner, it's the silence I want. The kind of quiet where you can hear the sound of insects buzzing past an open window. Where a dog's bark a mile away still reaches you across the shifting wind, as if there's nothing between you and him but space and light.

The kind of quiet only a lot of money can buy.

I rush over to the open window and slide it down, which merely dampens the noise. "I've gotta go," I say, walking into the kitchen to find my keys. "There's some deli meat in the drawer. Are you okay with soup and a sandwich?" I ask my father, who by now has unmuted the television and made it even louder. He doesn't answer me so I plaster myself in front of the screen and wave my arms around like a teacher trying to get her students' attention. "Hello? I'm leaving now, Dad. Are you okay to find food on your own?"

"I'm fine," he says, shooing me away from the screen.

I give him a small peck on his cheek and leave him to his war. Just before I reach the door he yells, "Deni?"

"Yeah?"

He swivels his body around to the right so he can see me. "Promise me you'll be careful," he says. "Don't let them hurt you, honey."

"I promise, Dad," I say, twisting the knob.

* * *

I peer over at Deez Yellen, who's presently leaning against one of his junk piles and staring at nothing. The engine is still running. Still unleashing a load of soot and stink. I unlock my mother's old Honda Accord and get in, being careful not to wrinkle my dress. "Ten more months. Ten more months," I repeat like a holy mantra as I back out onto Wilkins Street and head into downtown Prosperity, an oxymoron if ever there was one. I pass by The Owl's Nest, a foul-smelling bar where I once worked for a grand total of five hours (I quit after a *patron* put his hand on my butt) and see a huddle of men leaning against the wall having a smoke. Down a block next to the shuttered furniture store is Beauty's Best, which sells women's clothes my mother wouldn't have been caught dead in. The kind of candy-colored knitwear that even the yellowed mannequins in the window look embarrassed wearing.

Two more blocks and I'm clear of the city limits. Half a mile after that I reach the Osborne River Bridge, the demarcation line between the have-nots and the haves. On this side of the bridge lies my hometown. On the other side is Gold Hills, my home-to-be.

"Soon," I whisper as I speed over the churn and thrum of the water raging beneath me. "Soon."

* * *

The moment I turn onto Main Street I'm hit with that feeling you get when you walk into someone's warm house after being outside in the snow all day and they tell you to take off your coat and come sit by the fire. I slow to the posted 25 mph and take in the brick and wood storefronts, where from every viewpoint along the way, you can see the changing shadows and hues of the high rolling hills surrounding the small town.

It's quiet today. There are only a few tourists and locals strolling along the wood-planked sidewalks. I pull over to the curb in front of Marvin's and park. Marvin's is only open for breakfast and lunch so I know they're closed, but I also know that Sue Marvin is in there, prepping for tomorrow. I peer in through the glass and knock. I can see the kitchen light on in the back and a second later I see Sue's smiling face.

Sue and Bob Marvin opened Marvin's back in 1990, and it didn't take long for the café to become a Gold Hills institution. I think some of that has to do with Sue's apple custard pies. When Bob died of a heart attack, a year after I started waitressing here, Sue carried on as if he'd never left. There have been times when she's flipping an omelet or rolling out a pie dough when I could swear I see her talking to him, like he's standing right next to her.

Sue walks over, wiping the sweat from her reddened cheeks and chest with a dirty kitchen towel. "Hey, Deni. Don't you look pretty in that dress," she says as she opens the door, breathing hard, as if the twenty feet it took her to cross the dining room was enough to wind her. "You here for your check?"

"Yeah, but I'm also wondering if you have any whole pies left from today."

"Pie?" She raises an eyebrow. "I left the water running. Come in."

I step inside where the smells of bacon grease and bleach duel it out inside my nostrils. Smells that have been a part of my existence for going on five years.

"Since when do you eat pie?" Sue asks after she returns from the kitchen, her hand on her hefty hip. "You hate sweet things."

"I need to bring something to the Coopers'," I say, ignoring her comment. It's not that I don't like sweet things; I just try to avoid them now that my body looks how I want it to. "Grant's getting out of rebab today, and they're throwing him a welcome home party."

"Well, good for him," Sue says with a sharp nod.

"I really wish I didn't have to go," I add, aware of the discomfort creeping into my belly.

"You're about to be part of that family, Deni. In for a penny, in for a pound, even if that pound includes a bruised apple. Speaking of which—" she says, suddenly walking back to the kitchen. She comes out holding an apple custard pie in a cardboard box. "This gorgeous thing will sweeten any sour in that house." She hands it to me and before I can ask her if she minds taking the twenty-five dollars out of my next paycheck, she adds, "This one is on me, Deni."

"Thanks, Sue."

"Anything for my star waitress who I am never going to be able to replace."

"That's so not true," I insist, blushing. "And who says I'm going to quit just because I'm getting married?"

Sue laughs. "Now who's taking drugs?" she says, then quickly slaps her hand over her mouth. "Oh, that was in bad taste, wasn't it?"

"Nah. It was funny."

"Okay. Well, anyway . . ." Sue waves away her faux pas and continues. "Once you're a Cooper, you and your mother-in-law will go out together and you will be a 'lady who lunches,'" she says, air-quoting with her fingers. "Do me a favor and make sure you bring her to Marvin's every now and then."

I picture Jean Cooper and me at Marvin's, sitting at a small table by the window, plates filled with eggs and toast in front of us. I take a deep breath through my nose to keep from gagging. "I'm not so sure about that, Sue. Cal's mother doesn't exactly love me."

"How can you say such a thing, Deni? Of course she loves you." Sue runs the dish towel over a small splotch of grease someone must have missed on the empty table next to her. "Any woman would be proud as a peacock to have you as their daughter-in-law."

I shuffle my feet a little and even though I can feel a splotch of something sticky beneath my right foot, I don't want to alert Sue to the fact. I also don't wish to get into the reasons why Jean is anything *but* a proud peacock.

The Coopers have lived in Gold Hills for six generations, and people think they know everything about them. They don't. Most folks only see their philanthropic side; the money-giving, community-minded family. It's only the few and far between who have been let into their inner sanctum who have witnessed their cold cruelty. I am one of those people.

"Just remember, Deni: you're marrying him, not them," Sue adds.

If only that were true.

CHAPTER

2

GRANT COOPER STARES through the glass at the tarmac, trying to keep his thoughts fixed on the empty blackness before him. "I control my own story," he whispers, touching his right thumb to his right forefinger. "I am enough," he says, moving his thumb to his middle finger. When his thumb hits his ring finger, he recites, "My past does not define my present." With his thumb against his pinkie, he utters a quiet "I choose to be happy today." And then, having completed the ritual, which he finds himself doing about a hundred times a day, he lets his right hand go limp.

He scans the sky, looking again for signs of his brother before turning around to face the small executive lounge at the Santa Monica Airport. The furniture is set up in a rectangle. Six cushy black leather two-person sofas, separated by black coffee tables, make up the sides. At each end is a huge armchair. In the center of the rectangle are three neatly arranged black leather ottomans. Erika has dragged the fourth one over to an armchair. Both her legs are draped across the top and she is staring into her phone.

Grant goes over to the other armchair directly across the room from her and sits down. He is still finding it difficult to believe this woman wants to come home with him.

She looks up from her phone. "When is he going to be here? I thought you said three o'clock? It's three twenty."

"Headwinds maybe? I don't know," he says, standing up and moving over to the couch next to her. It is far less comfortable than it looks and he wants to return to the armchair, but he's not sure if he should get up again. It might make him look antsy, and why does that desk agent keep eyeing him? "What's your hurry?" Grant says, deciding to stay put. He is in no rush to go back to Gold Hills. But his ten months in rehab have ended, and his parents say he needs to head north again and get back to work. If he had his way, he'd call an Uber, grab his bag, and move back into Reflections Sober Living House. In a perfect world, Erika would come with him. He chuckles, thinking how stupid an idea this is and not only because the house isn't coed or that it's against the rules to have overnight guests. Or even that they'd have to share a single bed.

He is definitely going to miss that place. The camaraderie of the other men, the routine. He will even miss the chores they made him do, like cleaning his own bathroom and mowing the lawn. It'd been great to feel included in every part of the household. To sit around a dinner table and talk about what was going on in his head. He's never known what it is like to really be listened to. He will miss that most of all.

The house manager Rick warned him that leaving would be hard, but, as he repeatedly pointed out, Grant wasn't leaving alone. "You've got Erika now, man," he'd said from the doorway to Grant's bedroom, as he watched Grant throw the last of his clothes into his duffel. "She speaks your language. Not to mention she's fucking hot." Grant knows Rick is right. Having a sober partner is awesome.

* * *

Grant watches Erika push her hair out of her eyes. She'd insisted on getting a new haircut for the trip. And a new color. It's light brown now. And cut really short, like a boy's, but with bright blonde streaks and long side bangs she still hasn't figured out how to tame into place. When he first set eyes on the new girl during a coed group session at Malibu Reflections Treatment Center last January, she had stringy, shoulder-length jet-black hair that hung in her face. She'd looked desperate, like a starving cat that had been kicked down a long alley. Whenever anyone was about to speak, she'd shift her gaze and squint her eyes, poised to challenge whatever they said. He felt those eyes on him before he spoke that day. He'd planned to say something about how good he was doing. How, for the first time in as long as he could remember, he believed he could get through a day without needing to snort some oxy.

Though what came out of his mouth was, "I'm feeling pretty okay about myself these days, but I still want to drive a pickaxe through my father's brain."

The room had gone silent. The counselor—what was her name? Polly?—had cleared her throat and attempted to steer the conversation back to the part about Grant feeling okay about himself, but Erika had burst out laughing so hysterically her feet flew up into the air and the chair she was sitting on fell backward.

"Dude!" Erika yelled after standing and throwing her hands up in front of Grant's face. He'd high-tenned her, feeling a wave of warmth pass between their palms. Once the excitement fizzled, Grant zoned out of the conversation, but he and Erika continued to stare at one another under lowered eyes. It was as if they were floating underwater together, the sounds around them a deep, pulsing hum.

During the next few weeks, when Grant and Erika weren't getting acupuncture or massages, when they weren't attending single-sex group meetings or yoga classes, when they weren't meditating or riding horses or sitting through CBT, EMDR, hypnotherapy, art therapy, music therapy, or psychotherapy sessions, they'd meet whenever and wherever they could. They swam in the pool together, took long walks along the beach, played ping-pong. If not for knowing that they were being monitored through their tracking bracelets, they might have been on vacation at a posh resort. Although the fact that they couldn't actually sleep together completely screwed with that delusion.

When his residential treatment ended in February, Grant moved into a male-only sober house down in Mar Vista, which meant he couldn't see Erika anymore, and man, did he miss her. In April, after Erika finished her own ninety-day treatment, she relocated to a women's transitional house only a few blocks away from Grant. That was when things between them got real. Fast. As long as they passed their daily drug and alcohol tests, no one cared what they did outside of their houses. And what they mostly did was each other.

* * *

Erika throws her feet onto the gray-tiled floor and stands up. "I'm not in a hurry," she says, rearranging her denim shirt dress so it hangs right. "I just want to get this over with, you know? So we can get on with our lives together."

"Over with? What are you talking about? It's just the beginning." Grant's stomach tightens. He should have warned his family he's about to show up with an uninvited guest, but he was too afraid. Too afraid of what he knew they would have said: "Take her back where you found her." Like they'd said when he'd carried home a stray kitten tucked inside his parka.

"We have to get this right," he says anxiously. "You have to forget everything I told you about them, Erika, and be nice or I swear to God they won't let you stay." He needs his parents to like her. He needs her to be able to stay. At least until his father sends him back to work. He has no idea which site he'll assign him to, but he knows it won't be the one in Wadsworth, Nevada.

"Relax, Grant. I get it and you don't need to worry. Your parents will love me." She twirls her body as if on display. Grant sees the desk agent looking at them again. "Believe me, I can handle *any* family, no matter how fucked up they are. And darling, no one's is as fucked up as mine."

"Huh," he mutters. He wishes he knew more about this fucked-up family of hers, but that isn't going to happen in this lifetime. Other than confessing that she was raised by faulty humans, Erika refused to share anything personal about herself, either during group or with him. The first and last time he pushed for more of her backstory, they'd been sitting on the beach out in front of the Center. The sun was low in the sky. The wind nonexistent. When Grant said they needed to head back for dinner, Erika uttered, "I hope it's mashed potatoes tonight. Eating them makes me feel like a kid again." Grant figured it wouldn't be a big deal to ask where she'd grown up, a small detail anyone would want to know about the person they were falling in love with. She went quiet for a few seconds, then turned and stared into his eyes. "Has this place not taught you anything, Grant? We're supposed to be living in the now. We are not who we were before. And if you ever again ask me about the old me, you will never ever see *this* me again." And then she'd kissed him hard on the mouth.

He never asked her again.

* * *

Grant clicks on his phone and opens his flight tracker app. Since his brother is only certified to fly VFR (visual flight rules), and filing a flight plan isn't mandatory, Grant guesses Cal didn't file one. He's never known him to file one. But, just for the hell of it, Grant types in the plane's tail number: N9971W.

Nothing.

He should really be here by now.

Grant gets up and goes to the window and sure enough he sees his dad's old Piper Cherokee taxiing off the runway.

"He's here," Grant says without turning around.

"Where?" Within a second, Erika is beside him.

"There." He points at the slowly moving plane heading north toward the tarmac.

When they lose sight of the plane Grant goes back to the couch and sits down, reflexively massaging the phantom pain in his left shoulder. The reality of the situation is making his brain fire in directions he's not liking. He takes a breath and starts doing his finger mantras but only gets as far as his middle finger when Erika interrupts him. "Now what? Why are we still waiting? He's here."

"Relax. He's got to fuel up. It'll take a few minutes."

"Oh," Erika says, falling back into the armchair with a childish pout.

Grant's phone pings. He reads the text and says, "He's waiting for the fuel truck to come, but says we should come out." They both stand. Grant hoists his duffel bag over his shoulder and reaches to take Erika's large black rolling suitcase, but she pushes his hand away.

"No, I'm good," she states, walking down the hallway toward the exit.

They go outside and as they get closer to the plane Grant sees Cal looking down at his phone. There's a fuel nozzle stuck into the right wing so at least they won't have to wait long on the tarmac. The sun is hotter than it looks so late in the day. If there's one thing Grant hates, it's waiting around doing nothing. That's when his brain starts talking to him too much.

When he finally looks up and sees Grant heading toward him, Cal smiles that phony movie star smile of his.

When he sees Erika, he raises his eyebrows. "Hey, big brother," Cal says, pulling Grant into a tight bear hug. Grant is so stunned, he drops his duffel to the ground. He remains motionless, confused, unsure if he should raise his own arms or not. Before he has the chance to do more than breathe out, Cal pulls away and looks Grant in the eye. "You good?" he asks as if he really cares about the answer.

"I am," Grant says, nodding. He wants to ask this guy what he did with his brother Cal, the narcissistic shit who Grant has spent most his life avoiding. Resenting. Sometimes hating. Grant was the firstborn son to the great and powerful Calvin Cooper, but it was the son born two years later on whom his parents bestowed the honorific "junior." Grant often wonders why; what was it they saw in him on the day he took his first breath that made Jean and Calvin say, "Nope, not good enough. Let's wait for the next one."

"Thanks for coming to get me," is all Grant manages to utter.

"Glad to do it. Who's that?" he asks, nodding toward Erika, who is watching them from ten feet away.

"That's Erika." Grant notices that Erika looks as if she's just taken a bite of something that tastes bad, and that's not good. They've gone over this for weeks now. For his sake, for *their* sake, she needs to pretend she's thrilled to meet the Coopers. All of them. She needs to charm her way into the family or they will lose everything. "Erika," he says, beckoning her over. "This is my almost-famous brother Calvin Cooper Junior."

Cal extends his hand, and the moment their hands clasp he asks, "Have we met? I feel like I've seen you somewhere."

"Nope. I'm just a girl who came to Malibu to get clean and ended up falling for this guy," Erika says, poking Grant in the side. "Nice to meet you, Cal. Your brother has told me absolutely nothing about you," she says, smirking, which makes all three of them laugh. Grant lets out a breath. Okay, this is going to be fine, he thinks. Fine. Their cheery reunion is interrupted by the fuel truck driver who taps Cal on the shoulder and hands him a clipboard with a receipt to sign. After Cal hands it back to him, he says, "Let's fly," but Grant doesn't move.

"You're not going to sump some fuel? And you didn't even look at the receipt!" he says, hoping not to start a fight. "What is it with you and Dad not checking to make sure it's the right fuel? Do you not remember what happened at Buchman Regional?" His head begins to fill with worst-case scenarios.

"What happened at Buchman Regional?" Erika asks nervously.

Cal doesn't wait for Grant to recount the story. "It's all good, dude. Let's load her up. You know Mom and Dad hate to be kept waiting." Grant watches Cal pick up his duffel and toss it into the baggage storage compartment. Cal takes hold of the handle of Erika's suitcase and begins wheeling it toward the plane, stopping short when he's right next to Grant. He glances back at Erika before moving his mouth close to Grant's ear. "What the fuck were you thinking, bro?" he whispers. "You know this isn't gonna end well."

Grant shoves past him, walks to the plane and opens the passenger door. "Erika," he yells more forcefully than he intends. "Get in."

CHAPTER

3

THE SMELLS OF apples and pine trees fill my car as I wind up Skottsman Creek Road, taking the blind curves slowly, hesitantly. It's getting close to dusk, and I am afraid of hitting a deer. A few years ago a guy driving way too fast down Skottsman swerved to avoid a huge buck, slammed into a tree and, because he wasn't wearing a seat-belt, missile-projectiled through the windshield. They found him face down in the creek. His injuries were bad, but he probably would have survived if he hadn't drowned first.

When I reach the intersection of Skottsman and Cooper Hill Road I make a sharp right and downshift to first, slapping my hand on the pie box to keep it from crashing against the seat. The road is as steep and scary as the climb up a colossal roller coaster. I'd been a passenger in Cal's silver Ford F-150 the first time I ascended this twisty hill. I remember feeling nervous enough about meeting my new boyfriend's parents, but the way Cal drove had me clinging tight to the grab handle above the door. When I asked him to slow down because he was ripping around the curves as if he believed there were some invisible bumpers that would somehow stop us from crashing into the trees, he'd laughed. "I've been up and down this hill about a hundred thousand times, Den. I could drive it with my eyes closed."

Five dizzying minutes later I reach the top of the hill where the road flattens out and the excessively long driveway for the Cooper compound begins. Before I turn in I press on the brake pedal and wipe my sweaty palms along the fabric on the back of my seat.

I take my phone from my purse and check to see if Cal has returned with Grant yet. He hasn't texted me since he took off hours ago, which means I'll be the first to arrive. I hesitate before stepping on the gas.

I head straight for a while then curve around the circular driveway that rings an enormous cement fountain before finally reaching the side of the house where the pavement ends. I step out of the car and go around to the passenger's side to retrieve the pie. Thankfully it's still in one piece. I smooth out my dress. I check that my hair is behind my ears, off my face. And then I just stand there. Alone. In the silence. I hear the soft ticks of my car's cooling engine. The leaves and needles stirring on the hundreds of young oak and pine trees spread across the property. The birds skittering through branches.

I walk around to the front of the house and am once again awed by the immensity of the structure. By the hideousness of it. In the early eighties, Cal's parents bought fifty acres of sloping land that wound along the top of

Bowman Hill. Instead of building a house that would fit naturally into the rugged terrain, they razed the entire summit and constructed a 5,500 square foot puke-colored brick and lap-sided McMansion. When they first submitted their plans to the city, there had been a fierce outcry from Friends of the Osborne, an environmental group in town, but after the Coopers donated $25,000 to their cause and agreed to place catch basins and plant lots of trees to help stem sediment runoff from the construction site, most of the resistors backed off. Unsurprisingly, given Calvin's connections to three of the members on the Planning Commission, the plans were approved by a three to two vote.

When I reach the top of the steps I can hear Sean Hannity from Fox News shouting past the front door. I shift the pie from my right hand to my left and knock. Nugget, the Coopers' Bichon Frise, immediately begins to bark wildly. Through the tall, narrow stained-glass window at the side of the huge wooden door I see Jean walking toward me. "Hush, Nugget," she scolds. The moment before she extends her hand out to open the door, I see her urge a smile onto her mouth. My heartbeat pounds in my chest and I tell myself to relax.

"Hello, Deni," Jean says without a trace of sweetness. "You're early. The boys aren't back yet and the party can't start until the guest of honor is here." Jean Cooper is a tall, thin, strikingly handsome woman. If you were only looking at her shiny, mostly unwrinkled face, you'd think there is no way she could be in her late sixties. But once your eyes drop down to her chest and arms, mottled brown by sun damage, you'd see the span of time. She's wearing impeccably pressed dark gray slacks and a pale pink button-down silk blouse. Her bony wrists and fingers are festooned with thick gold bracelets and chunky rings with stones of all colors.

"I know they're not here yet," I say, trying not to let the sound of my eyeroll come through my voice.

We stand there together on the large brick landing, momentarily frozen. What does she want me to do? Does she expect me to go wait in the car? I clear my throat and push the pie box toward her. "I brought one of Sue Marvin's apple custard pies," I say with a forced smile.

Jean looks at the box and reconfigures her face so she resembles someone less frightening. "Oh, that's perfect. I bought a cake from Safeway, but you know what I always say about dessert."

Actually, I have no clue what she says about dessert. I barely know what she says about anything, given that every time I've been in the same room with the woman, all she ever talked about were her sons.

"Is that the boys?" Calvin Senior calls from somewhere inside the house. This seems to snap Jean into remembering she invited me to this gathering and she steps back.

"Come in," she demands.

I follow Jean through the brown-tiled entryway into the massive living room. It's furnished with two huge brown leather sectional sofas, the kind with reclining chairs at each end. On the back wall is a large oil painting of a group of men in old-fashioned clothes standing next to the Osborne River holding shovels and axes. Cal said his great-grandfather William Cooper painted it in 1930.

I'd asked Cal about his family's history on our second date and, in his abbreviated version, he told me that in 1850, two years after James Marshall discovered gold in Coloma, California, Cal's great-great-great-grandfather Henry Emmerson Cooper headed west from Taunton, Massachusetts, to see if he too could strike it rich. Henry did make a small fortune in gold-mining, but it was his son, James Cooper, who saw California's building boom shooting up around them. He figured they could make even more money selling the kind of rock that was used for constructing roads and buildings and bridges. He was right. Today, C. G. Cooper & Sons Aggregates owns and operates ten quarries and processing plants all over northern California and Nevada.

I stare at the gold-miners and imagine what it will feel like to tell my children all about our family's rocky legacy. I silently snort at my own pun while trying to avoid looking at the huge deer heads mounted on either side of the painting. Wherever I'm in this house, I can't help but feel their glassy eyes follow me around.

Calvin is sitting on one of the couches watching Fox News on the seventy-five-inch television, a drink in his hand. "How you doing, Deni?" he asks blandly, without actually looking at me. Calvin Cooper is handsome, for an older man. He has thinning gray hair, but it's the kind of gray that is more like silver, not the murky gray of rat fur. He has pale blue eyes, the same eyes Cal has. He's tall and still has the muscular form of a much younger man. Tonight he's wearing what he always seems to wear: faded blue jeans with an elegant blue-and-white striped button-down shirt.

Calvin is a man of few words, and his silence always feels like a storm waiting to break. I assume he's in good spirits at the moment because his oldest son is coming home. Clean. Now he'll have both sons working for him again. Both his boys will be under his thumb, right where he wants them. Right where he can control them.

Cal and Grant know it too, but still they keep coming back to Gold Hills. Keep being dutiful to their father. It's not as if Cal has ever spelled it out for me in words, but I know he's afraid to disappoint his father. I can see the subtle fear on his face whenever his father addresses him. Asks him about how the quarry's running. It's as if there's a charged current running between them, threatening to spark. But still he stays. As will Grant, starting tonight. They stay and put up with their father's abuse because one day, when Calvin dies, everything he and his ancestors have built will be theirs.

And mine.

"I'm fine, Calvin. Thanks." I feel like I should say something more, but he never takes his eyes off the television screen. He's finished with me. I look around for Jean and see she's gone into the kitchen. Instead of standing in the middle of the room trying to avert my gaze from the dead animals on the wall, I make my way over to the floor-to-ceiling windows that look out over the back of the house. There's a large rectangular swimming pool with a square jacuzzi cut like a brownie out of a pan. At the far end of the yard is a grill big enough to cook an entire cow on, three red-cushioned couches, and a glass dining table with those kind of metal chairs you can't sit comfortably on unless you have a big butt. Beyond the cement there's a vast sweep of flat green fields that lead into the forested hillside. Deep inside that forest is a five-acre plot of land where Cal and I plan to build our dream house.

"Deni, could you come in here, please?" Jean calls out. I cross the expanse of living room and walk into the kitchen. It's enormous and as plain as a manila envelope. Laminate wood floors. Pale oak cabinets with generic white pulls. Countertops made of the kind of large white tiles you see in bathrooms. It is as if they bought the entire kitchen off the floor of a Home Depot showroom and transported it up the mountain piece by piece.

A kitchen should be the heart of a house. Even in our tiny 1940s bungalow in Prosperity, the kitchen is a place where I can still find comfort. It's small, with a smooth pine countertop running beneath homey whitewashed cabinets. We have a table barely large enough to fit four people. I loved sitting there while I was growing up, my homework spread out atop the brown and gold flowered tablecloth my mother only washed every now and then. One day it would be clean. The next day I might find a dark spill from my father's Coca-Cola when I closed my algebra book. Once my mother was gone, I let the tablecloth get so filthy, it wasn't worth washing. Now when I'm having my morning coffee at the table, my elbows rest on its cold bare wood.

I'm still not sure how I'm supposed to address my future mother-in-law. Jean? Mrs. Cooper? When we initially met last March, she introduced herself as Jean, but the intimacy of a first-name basis, still, after all these months, doesn't gel with the way the woman acts around me. If not for their almost obsessive love for their boy Cal, Calvin and Jean Cooper wouldn't give me the time of day.

"Can I help with something?" I force myself to ask. Over on the counter next to the sliding door I see a platter heaped high with T-bone steaks, raw and shot through with bone and fat. There's also a wooden bowl with a bag of prewashed salad greens inside, just waiting to be set free so Jean can drown them in Hidden Valley Ranch. I smell the potatoes baking in the oven. Steak, potatoes, and salad. It's all I've ever eaten in this house. It's all I expect to ever eat in this house.

"As long as you're here and we're waiting, I thought we could check off some things from the wedding list," Jean says, opening a drawer and pulling out a black binder.

I stifle the urge to groan.

"Join me," she says as she sits down at the roomy kitchen table. It's covered with a stark white unstained tablecloth. In the center is a tall glass vase filled with multicolored faux flowers. The polyester arrangement saddens me almost as much as the dead deer in the living room. One of the first things on *my* to-do list as soon as Cal and I move into our new house is to buy a flower share from my friend Luna's flower farm. There will be vases filled with live fresh flowers all year long.

I make myself sit tall in my seat as I watch Jean open the binder and turn a page, her bracelets making little tinkly sounds as they slide against one another. Our wedding means a lot to Jean. That's not entirely accurate: it's her son's wedding that means a lot to her. I mean nothing to her.

* * *

When Cal first brought me home to meet his parents, they did not even attempt to hide their disappointment. I'm not sure what sort of person they expected their son to fall in love with, but a woman who grew up in Prosperity and waited tables at the local diner was probably not high on their list.

At the time I wasn't sure whether or not to feel insulted that we hadn't gathered around the formal dining room table and instead ate in the kitchen, as if Jean Cooper didn't think I deserved a place at the better table. As if I didn't deserve to eat her overdone steak off her fine china. Jean had remained mostly silent throughout the meal, slicing slowly into her meat as though she were trying to cut through the hurt Cal was causing her heart. Calvin, who'd already drained his glass of bourbon down to two fingers' worth, asked me if I'd gone to college. When I said I'd attended Chico State for two and a half years but had to drop out because my mother was dying, he nodded once. Then, before I had a chance to tell him I planned to finish my degree after the wedding, he'd turned to Cal and started talking about some new rock washer he wanted Cal to try out at the Truckee site.

During the drive back home I hadn't let Cal see the hurt inside me. I didn't ask him why he hadn't stuck up for me. It was too soon in our relationship to make him defensive. Too soon to scare him off by whining about what jerks his parents were. I'd been majorly crushing on Cal Cooper Jr. ever since the day I saw him slam Tom Natali's head against the lockers after he overheard Tom call his older brother Grant the "R" word. It'd taken me ten long years to get Cal to even notice I was alive. There was no way I was going to let his parents spoil my chances with him.

* * *

"I know the wedding isn't until July," Jean says curtly, "but many of the vendors we plan to use are already filling up."

"Of course," I reply dutifully, as if I am one her company employees. When Cal proposed to me last month I'd pushed him to get married right away. I even tried to get him to elope. It wasn't as if I had more than a handful of people who would come to a wedding. Jean, though, insisted on throwing a large, elaborate wedding for her son. Ever his parents' obedient son, Cal didn't care one way or the other. If they wanted a big deal wedding, he was fine with it.

"What's the hurry, Den?" he'd said once his mother declared that she'd need at least ten months to plan all the details. "We'll have our whole lives together."

I pretended not to care either.

"Let's see now," Jean says, flipping a page. "Thankfully we have the site booked." She grins at her own inane joke. Naturally the wedding will take place here at the Cooper compound. It's a beautiful spot. I'll just have to make sure to ask the photographer to keep the house out of the pictures.

"I still need to finalize the tents," she continues. It never rains in Gold Hills in July, but if the Coopers want to spend a few thousand dollars to provide some shade for their friends, that's great.

"Sounds good," I say absently. Where is Cal? My hands are starting to sweat, and the smell of baked potatoes is making me queasy.

"Now as for the florist, I know Bev at Hills and Dales is going to do an amazing—"

"We're not using *them*!" I shout out before I can stop myself. At the sound of my outburst, Nugget races into the kitchen, barking at the person she assumes is attacking her master. Jean's bracelets ring out as she reaches down and gathers the dog onto her lap.

"Excuse me?" she says, raising her eyebrows.

I wipe my hands on the part of the tablecloth that hangs below the table, knowing they will leave a sweat stain on the fabric. "I apologize for yelling like that, but, it's just that my best friend owns a flower farm over on Greenhorn Hill. Luna Rose Farm and Flowers? I promised her she could do the wedding flowers."

Instead of responding, Jean languidly looks over her shoulder, gazing out to the backyard, all the while stroking Nugget, who's panting, her bright pink tongue flopping up and down like a huge worm. After a few seconds, Jean calls out, "Cal, you should probably put the steaks on."

I wait, silently, my heart thudding. Calvin ambles into the kitchen and grabs the stack of meat from off the counter and walks outside without saying a word. Only when the sliding door is closed does Jean turn to face me again. "Yes, I know who Luna Rose is," she states, narrowing her eyes. There's a brittle edge to her words and I don't understand the vehemence.

Then it hits me like a slap to my face. To Luna's face.

Luna's father, Paul Rose, had been one of the more outraged and outspoken opponents of the Coopers' house plans. He'd joined Friends of the Osborne just so he could help them stop the Coopers from laying waste to Bowman Hill. Even after the hefty donation came in and the other members quietly retreated, Luna's father would stand outside city hall with a SAVE BOWMAN HILL FROM COOPER'S CARNAGE sign.

I cannot believe that Jean Cooper is still harboring a grudge against both Luna's father—long dead from prostate cancer—and even Luna herself. I am so beyond angry, I want to knock the binder onto the floor. Not only does Luna need the money, but she's my best friend and she deserves this! I take a deep breath in through my nose, the air suddenly smelling of something burnt and electric as if a bolt of lightning has just slashed across the room. I open my mouth to say something, to insist that Luna and her flowers have no connection to the past. Then, remembering my promise to my father that I would be careful, I immediately shut it.

"You know, Deni," Jean says, looking at her nails and not at me, "maybe all this wedding planning is causing you too much stress."

"No, I'm—"

"The more I think about it, the more I realize what a mistake we made planning a July wedding. It's far too hot here in July," she says as she smooths down the hair on Nugget's face.

"But we'll have the tents for shade and—"

"We should move it to next December." She smiles to herself. "Yes, a winter wedding will be even lovelier than a summer one."

"What?" I don't want to wait until next December to get married. I don't even want to wait until July. I want to become Mrs. Deni Cooper *now*. "But you've already done all this planning," I point at the black binder as if it contains my entire future within its pages, "and it'd be crazy to start again. July is great. I mean—"

"It's settled then."

As I watch Jean close the binder I get the feeling she's closing me out of her life altogether. Before I am able to utter a single word of protest I hear the sound of a truck engine and my heart leaps.

"They're here!" I shout, running toward the front door. I fly down the stairs and look down the long drive, shading my eyes. It's not until the truck winds around the circle that I see that there's a person in the back seat. A woman with bright blonde highlights in her short hair. I see her staring up at the big house with an amused expression, like she finds the beastly mansion behind me funny. She lowers her eyes until they meet mine. And then her smile vanishes.

CHAPTER

4

THERE ARE THREE shiny helium balloons tied to three fist-sized river rocks in the center of the large pine dining room table. The word *WELCOME* is sprayed in glittery gold on the purple balloon. The orange balloon says *HOME*. Grant's name is printed on the red one. With every shift in the air, they bounce against one another, emitting a soft squelchy sound that Grant finds grating as hell. That his parents thought enough about him to throw a welcome home dinner, even going so far as to buy decorations, is about the only positive aspect of the evening so far. Grant clings to their considerate gesture like a soldier hanging onto a burning slab of wood after his torpedoed ship goes under.

When they'd first pulled up to the house and he stepped out of the car, his mother had walked up to him and said, "We're so happy to have you back," and gave his shoulders a squeeze. Which, for Jean Cooper, was a pretty substantial display of affection. Grant had looked up at his father who stayed fixed on the landing. He'd met Grant's eyes and grinned, a sign that he approved of Grant in some significant way.

As soon as his mother dropped her hands from his shoulders, she turned to Erika. "And who do we have here?" she asked with one of those questionable smiles she slapped on when meeting people at charity events.

"This is Erika," Grant said, beaming. "We met at the Center." Then, as if in a dream, he'd watched the next few harrowing moments unfold in slow motion: Erika taking his mother's hand and saying how great it was to meet her. His mother turning around and exchanging a glance with his father, whose proud expression melted into something like disappointment. His mother giving Erika a not-so-subtle once-over, deciding, for no obvious reason, that she did not belong here. Grant could see it on his mother's face, in the way her posture, rigid to begin with, became more erect, as if she were trying to intimidate this stranger. This intruder.

And then, just when Grant had thought the awkwardness couldn't get any more painful, Cal suddenly appeared next to him and said, "Hey, Mom, we're starving. Can we please eat?"

* * *

Grant's father, seated at the head of the table, is talking about a new state-of-the-art cone crusher some Finnish manufacturer is letting their company test out at the Willits quarry. Next to him, Erika pretends to be rapt, leaning toward Calvin's words as if his pompous exhales hold more weight than they actually do. But then Grant sees it's not so much his father's words that hold her attention as it is his glass. And what's in it. He watches as her eyes follow his father's hand as it reaches for his whiskey. When he raises it to his mouth, Grant sees her lick her lips. Then quickly, almost desperately, she downs her glass of sparkling water. When she looks across the table and sees Grant staring at her, she smiles and gives him a thumbs up. He smiles back.

Erika's tiny loss of resolve makes Grant fidgety. If she is doubting her ability to stay sober within minutes of meeting his parents, how well will he be able to hold on? Hopefully their time in this house will be short-lived. At some point he'll ask his father what his plans are for him. Where he intends to send him. Until he knows what's next, he will lay low. He'll keep Erika close. They will lay low together.

Sitting to Grant's right, Deni Rydell is being quiet as a mouse. He can almost smell the nervous sweat coming through her pores. Deni Rydell. It's hard for Grant to wrap his head around her being engaged to his brother. As Grant cuts into his steak, he steals a look at her. She is pushing her food around her plate with her right hand, but her focus is fixed on Cal across the table from her. Grant can understand Cal's attraction to her, that's for damn sure. Deni has become a stunningly beautiful woman, with cheekbones so pronounced, they seem to almost cast shadows across her dark eyes.

The three of them went to Monroe High together, but the kids from Gold Hills hardly ever mixed with the Prosperity kids. Grant remembers seeing Deni around school, usually sitting alone in the cafeteria. There was something sad about her dark eyes that made Grant feel as if they'd have stuff in common. He definitely had a minor crush on her, not that he ever acted on it. Cal, on the other hand, wouldn't have known Deni existed. His little brother had been like the sun even back then, with countless planets forever circling in orbit. Friends and wannabe friends trailed behind him wherever he roamed. As for the pale, heavy-set girl from the other side of the river who wore baggy clothes and stared at the ground? She floated outside Cal's galaxy. As far as Cal and his friends were concerned, Deni Rydell was nothing more than space dust.

Grant notices that Cal has yet to return any of his fiancée's glances. He just keeps staring a hole into the side of Erika's face, and it's starting to bug Grant. During their flight up from Santa Monica, Cal began peppering Erika with nosy questions through the staticky headphones, questions Grant knew Erika would never answer. When Grant twisted around in his seat and saw the exasperation on Erika's face, he said, "We're really tired, dude. How about we just let her hang, okay?" before disconnecting her headphones.

"By the way, your mother and I are flying out to Wadsworth on the thirtieth," Calvin suddenly announces, his booming voice crashing over the dinner plates.

At the mention of *Wadsworth* Grant goes cold inside. He looks at his mother at the other end of the table to see if she's going to shut his father up, say something. Why the hell is he talking about Wadsworth, tonight of all nights? Is it his father's way of reminding him what a fuck-up he is? Is it a warning?

"He just got home, Dad," Cal says, interrupting their father. "How about we not talk about the—?"

Calvin slams his drink down onto the table, sending a thin splash of amber liquid over the rim of the cut crystal. "I will not be told what I can or cannot speak about in my own house, young man."

"Sure, Pop, whatever you say." Cal has a grin on his mouth, but his cheeks are flushed from embarrassment. This is the second time in less than two hours that Grant's brother has come to his rescue. What is he playing at? He's already the favorite son. The son who was allowed to quit college so he could pursue his dream of becoming a movie star. The son who was welcomed back into the fold after that dream went south.

As for Grant, he's the son who never got the chance to be something else.

* * *

It had been expected that both boys attend Colorado School of Mines, their father's alma mater, straight out of high school. Grant didn't care where he went to college or what classes he had to take, so long as he could get away from his mother's indifference toward him. His father's conspicuous disdain.

The mining engineering degree was a bitch, but he made a few friends, felt freer than he ever had. By his junior year he actually began to enjoy studying rock mechanics and metallurgy. He suddenly understood why his father and his father's father and all the men who came before them were lured into the business of extracting minerals from the earth. By graduation, he was looking forward to being in charge of his own quarry, but first he had to prove himself to the old man. Prove that he could run every aspect of an operation from the budgeting to the blasting. He interned for a year in Redding, then worked as an assistant manager down in Willits, before his father transferred him again, this time over to Woodland. Each move meant he had to find another furnished rental, some place to crash after days spent listening to the ceaseless pounding of jaw-crushers, smelling the sour exhaust of front-loaders and trucks. After tossing out the bags from whatever drive-through had fed him that night, he'd settle onto a sagging couch that had held a thousand asses before him and he'd read some gritty novel by David Baldacci or Lee Child. Sometimes on a Friday night the few guys who didn't care that he was the boss's son would invite him along for a beer. Men who worked for a paycheck. Men whose names Grant forgot the moment he left town.

After four years of paying his dues, he was ready to be a full-blown manager. He wouldn't have minded taking over the Redding quarry, but the Truckee quarry was where he really wanted to be. He'd heard Gil Peterson, the manager there, was ready to retire, so it only made sense that Grant would get the position. Surrounded by the high Sierra peaks and filled with bars, cafés, and nightlife catering to the ski crowd, it had everything the other quarry towns lacked. Plus, it was just a stone's throw from Gold Hills. Not that he had many, but Grant imagined trying to reconnect with some of his high school friends. Going skiing in the winter or hiking in summer with them.

But that's not how it played out.

Grant was sitting at his desk going over orders in the scale shack in Woodland when his father phoned him out of the blue.

"Hello, Son."

"Dad."

"I like the numbers I'm seeing. You're moving a lot of riprap. That's good."

"Thanks."

"I bet you think it's high time I promote you."

Grant nodded to himself, then spoke. "Yeah, I do. And since Gil Peterson is—"

"I'm giving you Wadsworth."

Grant had felt the pickles and extra onions from his lunch gurgle up into his throat. He drowned the backflow with a swig of coffee before making his case. "I want Truckee, Dad. I've earned it."

Calvin stayed silent for a few beats, then spoke in his usual domineering voice, like a cop telling someone to step out of the car. "You've earned the right to stay working for me, Grant. That's what you've earned."

"Yeah, but I got my degree and with all this experience I have, you know Teichert would hire me in a heartbeat." He hadn't planned to negotiate like this. Hadn't planned to threaten to leave the company for one of C. G. Cooper & Sons' biggest competitors.

"You leave Cooper, my boy, and you leave empty-handed."

Grant could tell his father was pissed off—flames were probably shooting out of his ears right now. "What's that supposed to mean?"

"You want to be a free agent? Well, go on then. Your mother and I will cut you loose. We won't deed you any land. We'll write you out of the will. Plain and simple. Is that what you want?"

Out the window Grant watched a dump truck speed by, kicking up a cloud of dust and gravel so large the inside of the modular office building momentarily went dark. He couldn't imagine ever wanting to live anywhere near the Cooper compound, but he wanted the money. Although he had to wonder if he or his brother would see it anytime soon. Their parents were healthy. Young enough to stay alive for decades. Was the promise of a wealthy retirement worth the hell of living in yet another podunk city for the next who-knows-how-many years?

"You still there, Son?"

It wasn't meant rhetorically, but it was a question Grant often asked himself. Was he still here? Who was the man inside the flesh of his body? What did he want to do with his life? Whose laws did he wish to obey?

Grant's heart began to burn from both the half-digested burger and the resentment. He'd never had it in him to fight his father. What magical powers did he suddenly possess that would allow him to oppose him? None. He had nothing.

"Sure, Dad. I'll take Wadsworth," he'd said.

* * *

Now, as Grant watches his father stuff a chunk of meat into his mouth, their earlier conversation plays like a loop in head. He should have stuck to his guns, pushed for Truckee.

Or he should have quit and gone to work for someone else. His life would be so different if only he had.

Should have. Could have. Beneath the table he squeezes both thumbs against his forefingers as poisonous thoughts slither up from the shadows. "I control my own story," he repeats silently. Thumbs to middle fingers. "I am enough." Two thumbs to two ring fingers. "My past does not define—"

Fuck those Malibu psychologists. His past *does* define him. Once a screw-up, always a screw-up. Grant wants his father to stop talking about the memorial scholarship he's awarding on the thirtieth. He needs Erika to look at him, goddammit! Why is she sitting there listening like she gives a fuck what the man is saying? Can she not see that his cells are blistering beneath his skin?

Deni's hand is suddenly on his thigh.

Then it moves to his right fist, cupping it softly, like a mother cupping an infant's head. The warm pressure of her palm causes Grant to relax his grip. He turns his head ever so slightly and sees she is nodding at him with a smile on her face, like she knows. Like she can see inside his head, see the nightmare that doesn't end. The crushed skull. The blood. His fault. All of it, his.

"Just ignore him, Grant," she whispers, her hand still cradling his under the table. "I promise you. It will get better."

"You don't know that," he says, falling into her dark eyes.

"Trust me."

CHAPTER

5

I UNLATCH THE GATE and drive 10 mph down the long dirt road leading to Luna Rose Farm and Flowers and park next to the small house Luna grew up in. Her parents, both Berkeley dropouts, bought the six-acre property back in the early eighties and lived in a Winnebago while they built the house from the trees that grew on the land. It's funky but gorgeous; it kind of looks like a cross between Japanese Zen and hippie groovy.

As soon as I step out of the car I take in a huge breath, filling my nose with the almost suffocating scent of greenery. The air here is different, thicker somehow. Weighted down by the swirling particles spilling out from the endless rows of herbs and vegetables and flowers.

I narrow my eyes and scan around the fields until I find Luna in the distance standing like a Grecian statue in a sea of white and raspberry-colored flowers that I think are dahlias. Before I get the chance to yell, she sees me and comes over, stretching her arms out to hug me. The moment her arms wrap around me I regret not going home after work to shower first. She smells so fresh and loamy that I'm now acutely aware of the stink from Marvin's clinging to my black jeans and button-down white shirt.

"Sorry I smell gross," I say as we let go of one another.

"Don't be an idiot. You smell delicious." After she wipes some sweat off the back of her neck, she says, "I'm kind of tired. Let's go sit." She pulls me over to the carved bamboo bench beside the koi pond. We both drop down, sighing in unison. The air is stunningly quiet, save for the sound of birds and insects. A tiny splash from one of the large orangey fish.

I glance over at the rusty Winnebago parked by the hoop house. "Where are Jon and Edie?" I ask, seeing no sign of her two employees. All of Luna's seasonal employees live in the Winnebago. Or as we used to call it, "The Bag."

The first time Luna and I had a sleepover, her mother, Misha, who now runs a yoga and meditation center in Bali, didn't want to have to listen to shrieking teenagers, so she'd banished us to the old trailer. It'd been one of the best nights of my life, dancing and singing in the tiny space with my new friend Luna. My only friend, actually. One of the few people in Gold Hills who didn't care that I lived on the wrong side of the bridge. Who didn't flinch over the fact that my mother was a cashier at Prosperity Stop & Shop, or that my father was a mechanic. Who never saw me as "less than" because I didn't own an iPhone. Or a car. Or new shoes.

"Edie wanted to go visit her parents in Oregon so they just took off," Luna says, shrugging. "I was kind of surprised they stayed as long as they did, you know?" She stares off toward the grove of trees beyond the garden rows. “I mean, the flower share is pretty much done for the season and I can handle the vegetables on my own.”

I nod. One of her cats, a fat black thing named Bernie, rubs up against my shin. I lean over and give it a pat, pulling up on its soft tail. “Wait. What about the *other* plants?” I murmur nervously, as though there might be policemen looming about. For the past five years, Luna’s been growing illegal pot plants down by the creek running along the back of her property. Plenty of locals will gladly pay top dollar for Luna’s organic flower and vegetable shares, but that money barely covers the cost of running the farm. Ounce per ounce, marijuana nets way more than zucchini and zinnias.

“There’s no way you can harvest it all on your own,” I say. A couple years ago, before starting my job at Marvin’s, I’d signed on to be one of Luna’s trimmers. The pay was good, but it was mind-numbingly hard work. Using spring-loaded trimming scissors, I had to cut away all the leaves from the buds to make them look pretty. It sounded simple enough, but by the end of that first day spent leaning over a tray of dried weed, snipping, snipping, snipping, I was done. Maybe if I’d gotten stoned nonstop like the other trimmers did I would have gotten into the work, but I hated it. My back hurt. My hand hurt. The skunky smell nauseated me.

I lasted all of three days.

“Don’t worry,” she replies. “I’ve got the same crew from last year coming. They should be here end of the month. I’ll harvest then.”

"Okay, cool," I say.

"By the way, why are you even here?" she says, smirking. "You're never here."

I reach down and pull the cat onto my lap, instantly triggering the memory of Jean picking up Nugget right after I yelled at her. I shudder and slide the cat back onto the ground. "I had dinner with the in-laws last week."

Luna slaps her cheeks and squeals, "Oh. My. God! How fun!"

"Yeah, so much fun." Bernie waddles over to the pond to watch the fish, his tail swishing dramatically, like a maestro's baton. "I've, um, actually got something I have to tell you," I say hesitantly. "It's about the wedding."

She turns to look at me, her eyes wide with anticipation. "You're calling it off!"

I push her shoulder. "I *might* be changing the date, but no, I'm not calling it off!"

She shoves me back. "Well, then, you're still an idiot."

"I am not an idiot," I say, crossing my arms across my chest and leaning back. "I love him. I'm marrying him. Period. End of story."

Luna crosses her own arms, leans back against the bench, and lets out a dramatically exasperated sigh. "He's a douche, but sure, knock yourself out."

"Knocking, thank you very much."

We sit there like that in comfortable silence for a few beats, although I know she's not going to let it rest. I know she is going to keep trying to talk me out of marrying Cal up until the moment the minister says, "I now pronounce you . . ."

I also know that Luna wants only the best for me, and, in her opinion, Cal Cooper is not the best.

* * *

Luna and I became friends back when we were juniors in high school.

Back when she was Cal Cooper's girlfriend.

I'd taken the bus into Gold Hills on a Saturday afternoon to look for a birthday card for my mother. Prosperity stores only carried the same Hallmark crap you saw in every CVS on the planet and I wanted something special. Something hand painted. Something original.

When I'd opened the door to Yours Truly Paper & Gifts and saw Luna Rose standing in the birthday card aisle, her long blonde hair trailing down her back, her long lithe fingers sliding card after card from their slots, I retreated.

I was afraid of Luna. Intimidated by her popularity and beauty. I was also fiercely jealous of her. Not only was she dating the boy I was madly in love with; I'd heard she lived in a gorgeous mansion on a hundred acres. Also, she was a *Gold*.

Kids from both Prosperity and Gold Hills went to Monroe High, where the 2,000 students had a social scene straight out of *West Side Story*, only instead of the Jets and the Sharks, we were the Golds and the Spurs. The Golds traveled the hallways as if they were prides of lions, the stench of entitlement shimmering off their skin as they passed by. We Spurs were mostly loners—the kids who received free or reduced lunches, who ate the tasteless hamburger noodle mush while at the tables by the sunny windows, the Golds unpacked their homemade sandwiches and baby carrots from fancy lunch bags. Like most kids from Prosperity, I kept my distance from Gold Hills people.

I'd stood outside the store with my hands in my jeans pockets, waiting for Luna to leave. I waited two minutes. Three, before I finally decided my mother was more important than my fears, so I went in and stood next to her, trying to act casual, trying not to bend the pretty cards as I yanked them free.

I was so nervous I dropped the card I was holding onto the floor. Before I could react, she bent over to pick it up, then began to study it. On the front was a watercolor painted by a local artist named Shanna. No surname. Just Shanna. It was a sunrise over low undulating hills, muted splashes of orange and red melting over different shades of green. The words inside the card said, "No matter how much I say I love you, I will always love you more than that. Happy Birthday. Happy Every Day."

"How'd I not see this one?" Luna said to herself. "It's so beautiful."

It was beautiful. Perfect in every way. "It is," I said, glancing at the empty slot. There was only the one and I wanted it.

She didn't hand it back to me even though I was the one who'd found it. I swallowed and tasted something foul and bitter on my tongue. Heat started to pulse through my torso and into my arms and in that moment I felt removed from myself, panicked that another Deni who was not me might do something horrible.

I quickly wound my arms across my chest, clutching my upper back tightly as if I were cinched in a straitjacket.

Luna looked from the card to me. Either she didn't notice or she didn't care about my weird bodily contortion because she just grinned and asked, "Whose birthday is it?"

"My mother's."

"No way. I'm looking for a card for my mother too." Her arms flew up all excitedly like she thought it was the weirdest coincidence in the world. "What day?"

I unfastened my arms and let them drop, but kept an eye on them, worried that one of them might still lash out and grab the card before I could stop it. "April 29."

"Are you kidding me?" She jumped up and down and squealed like a toddler. "That's *my* mother's birthday!"

I didn't quite know what to make of the scene. Over by the counter I saw an older lady leaning past the cash register, a slightly concerned look on her face, while Luna, still giddy over our small cosmic connection, was saying, "This is so cool. I mean that we both loved the same card and our mothers have the same birthday, and oh—shit." She glanced from the card in her hand to the shelf where it used to be. "There's only one." And before I could suggest we ask the concerned lady if there were more in the back, Luna thrust the card to my chest and said, "You take it. I'm Luna, by the way. Do you go to Monroe?"

* * *

"Jean is hiring Hill and Dales Florists to do the wedding flowers. But don't worry—I'm going to insist you make my bouquet," I finally say, breaking the silence. And then I tense, expecting Luna to get as mad as I got at Jean's kitchen table last week.

But all she does is shrug and utter a small, "Whatever."

I spent my entire shift at the restaurant as well as the long drive up here worrying because I was about to devastate my best friend. It was bad enough that Luna wasn't coming to the wedding. I'd kept my promise and kept apart the two most important people in my world. I thought that would change once Cal proposed in August, but it didn't. Luna still wanted nothing to do with him or his family. Offering to provide the flower arrangements, she said, would be her wedding present to me.

"I just thought . . . I don't know, like I pictured having really low-key arrangements, like wildflowers and bark spilling out of mason jars. Knowing Jean and her awful taste, the whole wedding will probably be decked out in pink carnations."

Luna stands up and goes over to the pond, squatting down next to Bernie. "Deni," she says to the fish rather than to me, "you're marrying the man you are supposedly madly in love with. I don't think the flowers are really going to matter." She sounds sort of sad, but I can't see her face so I have no idea what she's actually feeling. Luna is notoriously easy to read. If you're looking at her, that is.

I know she thinks Cal's a dick, but there's a part of me that wonders if maybe Luna is still in love with him. When he asked me out back in January, the first thing I did was drive straight up here to tell her; to find out what she thought I should do. I made it clear that if for even a millisecond she wouldn't be cool with my dating her former boyfriend I would immediately text him and cancel. Our friendship, I insisted, was way more important to me than any lifelong crush.

I remembered how I'd watched her facial expressions run the gamut of emotions, as if she were an actress at an audition. After a few minutes of silence I'd pushed her to tell me what she was thinking.

"It's your life, Deni. I want you to be happy," she'd said finally. "If you think Cal Cooper can give you what you're looking for, go for it. But. I don't want to hear about it. Like, I want you to keep us as separate parts of your life. Can you do that for me?"

Before I could really contemplate what she was asking me to do, or question my ability to keep the promise, I'd answered her. "Of course I can," I said quickly.

* * *

Outside the card store that Saturday, Luna had insisted I find her in the cafeteria on Monday and sit with her. I'd gone home feeling as if my entire world had shifted. Like I'd finally crossed the river.

Monday's second-period English class had felt as if it were four hours long. My legs shook with impatience as I stared at the clock, wishing for 11:30 to come quicker. When the bell finally rang, I had to force myself to slow down as I made my way down the hall. I didn't want to look desperate. Inside the large, loud cafeteria I looked around for Luna and saw her sitting at a table by the window with three other kids I didn't know. Regrettably, Cal Cooper was not among them. I wandered over and tapped her on the shoulder.

"Hi," I'd said, raising my hand in an awkward wave. The other kids looked from me to Luna with quizzical frowns.

"OMG, Deni!" she yelled before jumping up and actually hugging me. Luna Rose had hugged me. I could have died and gone to heaven right then and there.

But then she did a strange thing: she didn't introduce me to the other kids. Instead, she'd grabbed her lunch bag and said, "See you guys later," before leading me over to a table on the other side of the room. One smack dab in the middle of where the Spurs normally sat. I wasn't sure why she didn't want me to meet her friends, but I was so enamored by the idea that I was sitting across from her, I didn't care. Not wanting to spoil the moment by going over to the lunch line I'd said I wasn't hungry when she asked why I wasn't eating. I'd been content to watch her eat her cheese and rice crackers while beneath the metal table my empty stomach rumbled.

It wasn't until our second time sitting together in Spurs territory that she'd finally confessed what the deal was. "I know they're jerks, Deni," she'd said, stuffing some popcorn into her mouth, "but they just don't want you to sit with us."

I sat back, stunned. "Why are you friends with people who act like that?" Luna was so warm and welcoming. I didn't get it.

She'd blushed a little before leaning forward and talking in a low voice. "They're Cal's friends and he kind of said . . . well, he thinks . . ." She didn't continue, but I'd heard enough. At Monroe High School, Cal Cooper was king, and he decided who was in and who was out. As his designated queen, Luna needed to obey.

I probably should have gotten pissed off; should have deleted my crush on Cal the King right then and there. But

I didn't. I'd accepted the long-held belief that Prosperity kids weren't cool. It made total sense to me that Cal wouldn't want us tarnishing his exclusive circle. Suddenly I was even more determined to prove to him that I was different. That I belonged.

"But you and I, we can hang out at my house after school sometimes, okay?" she exclaimed, wanting to make sure I knew she wasn't going to diss me too. "In fact, we should totally have a sleepover next weekend!"

"I'd love to," I said, feeling like I'd just been given an invitation to a whole new world. My friendship with Luna would be my way in. Once he'd met me, Cal would know I wasn't a loser.

But that never happened. Over the next few weeks, Luna and I hung out a lot but always at her house. We'd walk down to the creek on her property or drink tea and listen to music in the Bag. She loved to talk about Cal, about his crazy big house, about him learning to fly a plane, about the way he touched her. When she told me about the first time they had sex in his ginormous room when no one was home, I hid my jealousy as if I were a killer concealing a knife in my front pocket.

And then, just as I knew I was close, when I could almost taste the moment Luna would insist I join their friend group, Cal made the unintended mistake of introducing Luna to his parents. How could he have known that *Rose* was a name not easily forgotten or forgiven in the Cooper household?

The next day Cal told Luna he didn't want to go out with her anymore.

Instead of becoming one of the Golds, I became the friend who held Luna while she screamed out her pain like a fox whose leg was crushed in a trap. I became the friend who spun Luna around whenever Cal walked by her in the school hallways so that she didn't ever have to see his face.

And now I'm the friend who is marrying him.

* * *

"But you know how much I hate the color pink," I say to Luna's back. Bernie has wandered away and now just Luna is observing the fish. "And as far as carnations are concerned, I don't even think they're actual flowers. They look like they're made of plastic."

Luna stands slowly and tosses a pebble into the water. We both watch the tiny ripples spread out one after the other, each wave trying its best to catch up the one that came before. "You've got to let it go, Deni." She wipes her hands on her dress and stares at me. "You're marrying Cal Cooper, the love of your life," she says. "It won't matter if the centerpieces are filled with dead fish."

CHAPTER

6

It's Sunday morning and I'm topping off a customer's coffee when Cal opens the door. Even after all these years, my heart still pushes up against my chest and my mouth goes dry the moment I see his face. I smile at him and he winks back at me. I don't get why he's standing there when it's obvious there are plenty of open tables, and it's not as if Marvin's has a hostess seating people. I'm about to say, "Take the two-top by the window," but then Erika and Grant are there behind him.

I almost want them to sit in Maya's section. I have no interest in talking to Erika, let alone serving her, but of course they take table 6. I place the coffeepot back on the warmer, grab three menus and wander over. "Good morning," I chirp as I toss the menus down onto the table instead of handing one to each of them.

Normally I'd give Cal a kiss hello, but for some reason I don't want to. It's as if Erika's presence taints our morning ritual. She's wearing a tight white tank top underneath a pair of light gray Free People overalls. I know they're Free People because I've been saving up to buy myself a pair. The color is almost a perfect match to the highlights in her pixie haircut. Her lipstick is a shade of pink so bright it makes her pale skin look almost translucent. Before I allow myself to get too worked up about her I remind myself that I'm the one who snagged the better brother.

"Hey, beautiful." Cal gets up, puts his hand on my lower back and kisses my cheek. Every single time that mouth of his touches my skin, I expect to wake up and find it has all been a dream. I am marrying Cal Cooper.

"Hi, Deni," Grant says cordially enough. He looks tired. Weary. And slightly unsettled. Maybe it's because the last time he tried to eat a meal at Marvin's, Sue Marvin had to call the cops to drag his doped-up ass away. His parents bailed him out of jail that day, but then a week after that, he got busted for possession with intent to sell. Allegedly, the Coopers made a deal with the city attorney, and Grant got carted off to rehab in Malibu instead of having to serve time.

Two months after that, on a cold and foggy January morning, Cal Cooper had walked into Marvin's to grab a coffee and an egg sandwich to go and I'd casually asked him how Grant was doing. He'd stared at me, puzzled. Then he said, "How do you know my brother?"

I'd almost laughed at the absurdity of his question but kept my face blank. "Um, we all went to Monroe together?" I replied, my body pulsing with nervousness. Other than passing him in the hallways in high school, I'd never before been that close to Cal Cooper.

"Really? What's your name?" he'd asked, his eyes traveling over my body in a way that would have made me feel icky if it'd been anyone else doing it.

"Deni Rydell."

Again his eyes traversed me from head to toe. He was thinking, trying to place me. A few seconds ticked by before he snapped back to the present, as if he'd only just remembered where he was. "You were that, um, girl from Prosperity who hung around with Luna, right?"

The girl from Prosperity. The mousy chick who wasn't good enough to be friends with. I didn't need him to remind me of who I used to be. I only wanted him to see me for who I was now. "Yup. 'Twas me indeed," I'd said, grinning.

"Well, it's nice to see you *again*, Deni Rydell," he'd said, holding out his free hand. "I'm Cal Cooper."

Cal Cooper Jr. had no idea I'd been keeping track of him since high school. It wasn't as if I were a creepy stalker or anything, but I just wanted to know what he was up to. I knew he dropped out of Colorado School of Mines after two years and moved to Los Angeles to try to become a movie star because I followed him on Instagram, along with about 3,000 other people. He didn't post much, at least not until he started getting some work. First he appeared in a deodorant ad in *Teen Vogue*. A year later he landed a tiny role in a super lame Hallmark movie, *Ryan's Cause*. By then he had over 40,000 followers and I stopped checking his posts every day because seeing him with his arm around a different pretty girl each time I looked hurt too much.

He went quiet for a while, and I thought maybe something horrible had happened, like he'd gotten married, but then suddenly he was back on campus in Colorado, finishing his degree. I figured Jean and Calvin must have said, "Enough is enough" and made him drop his quest for fame, because it wasn't as if he didn't already have the fortune waiting for him back home.

After college he moved down to the San Jose area. From his posts it was obvious he was working in his father's quarries, though by then most of his Instagram followers had abandoned him. Pictures of him wearing a hard hat weren't, I'd supposed, what hot girls were searching for.

Last December he moved back home to take over the Truckee quarry. On January thirteenth, he walked into my life.

"What can I get for you?" I ask Erika now. I don't meet her eyes but keep mine fixed on my order pad. I haven't seen her or Grant since that awful welcome-home dinner. It'd been an ugly evening altogether, and not just because of Jean and her black binder. There was the super awkward moment when Grant introduced Erika to his parents. They were so obviously pissed off that their son had unexpectedly shown up with a stranger. They didn't even try to hide it. All through dinner they ignored her. We all did. Well, other than Grant, who kept his eyes trained on Erika as if she were a mirage about to fade away. And Cal, who stole what he thought were secret glances at her every chance he got.

By the time Sue's apple custard pie got devoured—it was by far the best part of the tasteless meal—I was feeling like a can of shaken soda ready to explode. First there was Jean's suggestion that we postpone the wedding. Then Calvin's constant outbursts at both his sons. Watching Cal stare at Erika was the final straw, so while he walked me to my car I'd unloaded on him.

"Why did you keep staring at Erika all night?" I asked, stopping in my tracks with my arms crossed, not sure I even wanted to hear his reason.

Cal had given me one of his adorable pouty smiles as if I were a child asking a silly question. "I thought I recognized her and was trying to figure out how I knew her. That's all."

I wasn't sure I totally believed him, but there was a more important issue to discuss. "Just so you know, your mother wants to move the wedding to December," I said, my voice shaking. "She's decided she wants a *winter* wedding."

"That sounds great," he'd said, pulling me into his arms. "The sooner we get hitched, the sooner I can make love to you in our own bed."

I'd pushed him away, my body hot with anger. "No, you idiot. Not this December. *Next* December."

He'd merely scratched his head, as dumbfounded as I was by Jean's change of plans. "Let me talk to her," he'd said, once again pulling me close and kissing me, promising he'd take care of everything.

* * *

"A poached egg and wheat toast and coffee," Erika says, handing me the menu. I turn toward Grant, who looks a little uncertain, like a kid standing alone on a crowded playground. He's gripping the menu in his left hand and staring at it as if it's written in another language.

When he starts nervously rubbing his left shoulder, Cal leans over and pulls Grant's hand away from his body. "Dude. Order already. It's not rocket science."

Grant lets out a loud breath. "Sorry. Um."

"How about a cheddar cheese and mushroom omelet with a side of bacon?" I suggest. I have five other tables waiting for their meals, and I've already heard the bell ding enough times to know a few people will be getting cold eggs. "Sound good?"

Grant says, "Sure." I take his menu and start to walk away when Cal grabs my arm.

"Hey, what about me? Don't you want to know what I want?" he asks playfully.

I whip around, smiling deviously. "I always know what you want," I say, pulling my arm free.

CHAPTER

7

Grant is in bed, staring up at the ceiling. He can't hear anything from this wing of the house and wonders if his parents have left yet. It's the thirtieth. The day they're supposed to fly out to the Wadsworth site where they will unveil a plaque memorializing Craig Hinkley and announce the creation of the Craig Hinkley Memorial Scholarship fund.

Craig. Grant doesn't want to think about him, doesn't want to see those dead eyes, but it's as if his brain is stuck on repeat, those same shocking images flashing again and again. He tries doing the box breath technique he learned at Malibu: He breathes in for four counts. Holds for four. Breathes out for four. Holds for four. Breathes in for—he's sweating. His shoulder burns.

"Goddammit!" he shouts, throwing off the quilt. He sits up, grabs his phone and texts Erika. Like everyone who has ever stayed overnight at the Cooper compound, Erika has been banished to the large guest suite above the four-car garage. It doesn't matter that the main house has six bedrooms. No one from outside the family is permitted to stay inside his mother's private domain. And no one but the guest is ever allowed in the guest room.

You awake? he asks.

Yup.

And?

She types: *Hold on, let me check.*

He waits. Then: *Their car is still here.*

Bummer.

Just once, just one fucking morning he'd like to be able to have breakfast with Erika without it feeling as if they're prisoners being watched. Dissected. Like they were in Malibu. Since returning home with Erika in tow, it's been the same tense drill every day. Cal gets up and slams the bathroom door so hard it wakes Grant, an irritating habit he's had since they were kids. Then Grant texts Erika and tells her to check on the status of the automobiles. After both Cal and Calvin head out for work—Calvin to the company's main office in downtown Gold Hills and Cal to the Truckee quarry—she texts that the coast is clear and they agree to meet in the kitchen. As desperate as they are to eat their breakfast alone, it has yet to happen. The moment Jean hears them open a cabinet door she appears from out of nowhere like a lurking school monitor. Greets them with a "Good morning," as she pours herself another cup from the long-brewed bitter drip, sits down at the table and opens the newspaper. She reads. They eat their bowls of cereal in silence.

Last night I heard your dad say they were leaving early. Go find out what's going on so I can eat. I'm hungry.

Will do.

Grant pulls on a pair of jeans and walks out into the hallway. It's a Saturday, but Cal's gone off somewhere, most likely to the gym in town. They have a perfectly adequate home gym, but knowing Cal and that ego of his, Grant's little brother wants an audience around while he's pumping iron.

As he passes through the living room Grant sees two carry-ons by the front door. Packed and ready to roll. He hears his parents in the kitchen. As much as he wants to turn around and go wait in his room, he pushes himself to step one foot after another. He reminds himself that they're vacating the house for an entire night, and with this thought he allows a smile to cross his lips. Even if Cal is still around, he'll be able to screw Erika in a bed, on the couch, in the shower. Other than going for a couple drives—after promising to be back for dinner—they haven't been allowed to be alone the last two weeks. Making love in his Subaru while parked along a dusty road is getting old.

He walks into the kitchen and pulls a mug from the cabinet. "Good morning, Grant," his mother says. He's relieved to see she's not wearing a bathrobe but rather is fully dressed in black jeans and a navy turtleneck sweater. No jewelry other than her wedding band. Very little makeup. His father is wearing a blue sports coat over a pale blue button-down shirt and faded blue jeans. The press will be at the ceremony, and Grant knows his parents will want to show the media that they are no different from the men and women who work the quarry. They are one of them. Commoners.

"So, you guys heading out soon?" he asks, hoping he sounds nonchalant and not like an itchy kid waiting at the back of a long line for the county fair's best ride.

"Just called down to the airport. Getting fueled up as we speak," his father remarks after taking a loud gulp of his coffee. He's leaning up against the stove, one leg crossed in front of the other. "Why? You got special plans once we're gone?" he asks, his words stinking of insinuation.

Grant shrugs. "What? No." He pours his coffee and when he sits down at the table Nugget barks at him from his mother's lap as if he were a stranger. In a way, he is a stranger. Ten months away can mess with a small dog's brain, but hell, he's been home for two weeks. You'd think his smell would be familiar by now.

Grant scratches Nugget under her chin until she shuts up. He can feel his mother's eyes boring into him. She turns and looks at his dad, and Grant gets the sense that a rabid opossum is about to be let out of its cage.

His father clears his throat before speaking. "We've been keeping a close eye on you, Grant."

Grant stifles a snort and keeps himself from uttering, "No shit." One of the first things he did when he threw his duffel bag on his bed two weeks ago was check his room for hidden cameras. He knows what happened in Wadsworth was horrific. He gets that his parents spent a fortune keeping him out of jail and getting him clean. But for Christ's sake, he's thirty years old! He's paid his dues. He's drug-free. He wants to scream this in their faces. "I did what you asked me to do, now let me go live my life! I am a grown man!" No, what he wants to do is hogtie them to a tree and make them hand over their hidden keys so he can unchain himself.

But he won't. He can't. He's more stuck now than ever. Even if he didn't care about the money and tried to start over, it wasn't gonna happen. What went down at Wadsworth destroyed any chance he has for getting a decent job with another mining company. Or any company, for that matter.

He clenches his teeth together tightly and waits for what's coming next.

"That program I chose was the most expensive one out there. I'm glad to know we got our money's worth," his father continues. Even in this, the man has to find a way to own it. "Your mother and I are proud of you, Son."

"Thanks," Grant utters, surprised by the words. He catches his mother's eyes. Is that an actual smile on her face?

"We think it's high time you join the real world again."

Grant sits up, a spark of hope flashing through his chest. Is it possible they finally believe in him? "I'm ready," he says brightly. He wishes Erika were here right now so she could hear the good news.

"The girl," his father utters sharply, the two words hanging in the air like birds caught in an updraft.

"Erika? What about her?" It doesn't bode well that his father just referred to Erika as if she were an object. Beneath the table Grant's right leg begins to shake. The light inside him dims.

His mother moves Nugget off her lap. Grant wonders if it's because she's worried he might lash out at her precious pooch because of something she's about to divulge. "We had someone look into her," she says. By *someone*, Grant knows his mother is referring to one of their friends on the local police force. It wasn't enough they grilled Erika every time she was in the room. Sure, she was vague with them like she'd been with him, but who cares? Why did they feel the need to dig deeper?

His mother continues. "There is no one named Erika Morris who fits her description."

Grant looks at his coffee cup, tries to appear unfazed. "So? Maybe she changed her name?" Why would she change her name? Why *did* she get so hot and bothered when he asked her about her past? Not that it matters. Grant honestly doesn't care about her past. He loves her present. Her now.

His father spears his thoughts with, "If she changed her name, must be because she's hiding something. It's worrisome, don't you think?"

His mother nods along to his father's words like a black bouncing ball following song lyrics. "We don't know anything about this woman, Grant," she adds. "How do we know we can trust her?"

Grant can only shrug. But he knows it's not enough of an answer so he tries, "Well, I trust her. She was totally there for me. She helped me get clean. She's helping me stay clean."

"Is it possible . . ." His mother reaches out to the fake flowers and bends one of the wire stems a little to the right as if this will make them appear more lifelike. "I am just wondering, Grant, what it is she, um, sees in you. What does she want from you?"

Grant feels that one in his solar plexus. His own mother is questioning why such an attractive woman would want to be with him. Okay, so he didn't inherit the same Hollywood handsome genes that Cal did, but he isn't a bad-looking guy. He'd lost a lot of weight while he was addicted to oxy and what he gained back is mostly muscle, thanks to the fitness routine they put him through in Malibu. "What she *wants* from me, Mom, is companionship. Erika knows me inside and out, and if you've been watching us as closely as you say you were, you'd see that. She loves me, dammit." He puts his hands on the table and makes to stand up, but his mother stops him.

"We're not finished here," she says, her voice authoritative and angry now. "Have you even for a moment considered that she is after your money? *Our* money?"

After Grant told Erika about his family fortune, he had considered this, for about a millisecond. "She had to pay the same crazy fee as you did for the program. Obviously, she isn't after my money, Mom. Jesus." And then, only because he is so riled up, so defensive, he blurts out without thinking, "What about Deni Rydell? You think she's not after our money?"

His parents exchange a look that Grant cannot decipher. He shouldn't have made Deni into the bad guy here. She obviously loves Cal. He can see it in the way she acts around him. The glow on her face that gets brighter whenever Cal is near.

"Deni will sign a prenup before the wedding," his mother says matter-of-factly. "Please do not share that information with your brother."

"Great. Okay, then if Erika and I get married, she'll do the same. Done." He grins at them.

"Listen, Son." His father puts his coffee cup in the sink and looks at his watch. "We want what's best for you. For this family. You know that." He moves over to the table and pulls out a chair but doesn't sit. Just leans over it, staring intently into Grant's face.

"What's your point, Dad?"

"The reason your mother and I are flying to Nevada today is because of you. Because of your stupidity. Because of your stupidity I had to pay out a substantial death benefit. Because of your stupidity I had to pay a hefty fine. Because of your—"

"Stop!" Grant feels like he's a seven-year-old again, getting a verbal berating for striking out in Little League. Once again Grant starts to stand up, and this time his father yells, "Sit your ass back down! I'll let you know when this conversation is over." Grant's mind grasps for a toehold. The meditations, the mantras . . . he's spiraling down into a dark hole and for the life of him he can't remember any of them, anything that will keep him from racing out of here. To keep him from jumping in his car and driving down to Prosperity. To hold him back from banging on Deez Yellen's door. From pushing past him and dropping to his knees, grabbing a straw, sticking it up his nostril, bending his head low and—whatever it takes to feel nothing. He wants to feel nothing.

He so should have just stayed in bed.

His father must see the panic on Grant's face because now he's pulling the chair out and sitting. "Okay, let's start over," he says, sighing deeply. "I'm sorry I lost my temper, Grant." He shakes his head and almost looks contrite, but Grant is so on edge he refuses to believe anything his eyes are seeing. "I just . . . we, your mother and I, we love you, Son. We want only the best for our boys. Always have. Always will." Next to him, his mother is agreeing. Even her face has softened around the edges. Grant wants to relax, but it's like trying to walk on a sprained ankle. He's so stiff he fears another outburst from his father will crack him down the middle.

"I'm letting you take over Redding."

"What?"

"If I remember correctly, you said you enjoyed your time up there."

His mother puts her hand on his and gives him a wink. They're trying to trick him, trying to confuse him. "We know how much you wanted Truckee, but we think you'll be just as happy up there."

The Redding operation is a limestone quarry in a not-so-bad town. It'd been the first place he worked after college, and his father is correct: Grant did have some pretty good times there. Plus, Mount Shasta is just a few miles to the east. It didn't quite have the vibe of Lake Tahoe, but it was a pretty cool place to live. He and Erika could make a life there.

He's just relaxing into the idea when he sees his father glance at his watch again. They both stand up. He's about to say, "Thanks, Dad, I'll take it," when his father clears his throat and tosses off, "We don't know the girl, Grant. We don't trust her and, to be honest, we don't like her. If you want Redding, the deal is you go alone."

What the fuck? "But she's—"

They've already cleared out of the kitchen and are walking quickly toward the front door. Grant leaps up and follows behind, trying to understand what his father has just said. What kind of deal is this? What if he refuses? What then? Grant has more questions. So many questions. But before he can say another word, his father is taking hold of both suitcases and striding out to the large brick landing. After clumsily bouncing the cases down the wide cement steps, he stops next to where Grant's mother waits, the dog in her arms.

Grant has his hands out in front of him, palms up as if in supplication. He wants to know why they don't like her. Why they are so cruel. Why he shouldn't go inside, grab the Winchester from the safe and blow their brains out before they make it to their car.

Grant watches them walk off down the driveway toward the parking area and just as they are about to disappear around the corner of the house, his father stops and yells over, "I'll expect your answer when we're back tomorrow. Don't do anything stupid while we're gone."

Grant can't move. Can't comprehend what his father just said. It's a deal with the devil is what it is. Take the job, leave the girl. Keep the girl, have nothing.

He watches the Cadillac Escalade head toward Cooper Hill Road, and the moment it's out of sight he snaps out of his fluster and runs across the driveway in his bare feet, passing the garage and rushing up the outside staircase, taking them two at a time. He is almost out of breath when he throws open the door to the guest suite.

"Erika!" he calls out when he doesn't see her. He listens for the shower. Nothing. The room looks no different than a premium room at a Holiday Inn. Queen bed with a beige quilted headboard, bookended by generic wall lights and built-in wooden night tables. There's a brown sofa bed in the corner fronted by a square MDF coffee table with metal legs. A large television jutting out from black metal mounting looms above a long wooden desk. No art. No personality. If he didn't know any better he could be in Cincinnati.

He goes back down to the driveway, and it's only then that he notices his car is missing. Back inside the house, he finds his phone in his room and checks his texts.

Got tired of waiting. Gonna grab breakfast and maybe some shopping. Back later. ♡

He calls her, but it goes straight to voicemail. He texts her. Tells her to call him. Waits.

Thirty minutes and three bowls of Rice Krispies later he still hasn't heard from her. He needs her here with him. Needs to talk through this situation with her. She'll figure it out. She'll know what their next move should be.

Two hours later and the house is glaringly empty. Erika hasn't replied to a single text. He's pissed off. Impatient. Unsure and far too aware of his solitude. It's the first time, he realizes with a growing sense of unease, that he hasn't been utterly and completely alone in almost a year. From the moment he started detox last November, until the moment his parents drove away, there has been a steady stream of humans surrounding him. People caring for him. People watching him. People listening to him. All of them within earshot. All of them within reach.

Now there is no one.

Grant goes out to the backyard, yanks off his T-shirt and lays down on one of the lounge chairs. Other than the hum of the pool filter, it's eerily quiet. He checks his phone again and decides to call Cal to find out what his plans are for tonight. Grant will ask him to please stay gone so he and Erika can finally spend a night together. Alone.

The call goes to voicemail.

Grant stands up. He unzips his jeans and kicks them off. He steps onto the top step of the pool and feels a sting under his right foot. Balancing his left hand against the concrete, he lifts the foot up and sees a small gash beneath his big toe. He must have scraped it on a rock when he went running across the asphalt. No big deal. He sits down and swishes his legs in the water, transfixed by the eddying ripples.

A movement in the forest out beyond the sweeping lawn catches his eye. Grant stares, waiting for whatever it is to move again. Must be a deer. It has to be a deer. Rustling now. He gets out of the pool, puts his shirt back on and pulls his jeans over his wet calves, keeping his focus on the trees. A cool breeze rustles by, and the tall pines bend, then straighten.

He calls Erika again.

Texts her. *Where are you?*

He goes back inside and slides the door closed. He tries to lock it, but the hook won't catch on the faceplate. He slides it to the left again and jams it against the plate harder this time, but again it doesn't catch. "You fucking piece of shit!" he howls as he begins to slam the door against the frame over and over until he hears something crack.

“Fuck me,” he says, running his hand over his face.

He tries again. This time the hook latches.

He picks up his cereal bowl from the kitchen table and downs the rest of milk, warm now that it’s been sitting out for hours. After he wipes his fist across his mouth, he walks through the living room, down the hall to his room. He needs a shower. He throws his phone onto the bed and is just unzipping his jeans when a thought strikes.

What if she *doesn’t* come back?

Doubt digs into Grant’s belly like a sharp splinter. He’s known the woman for—he counts in his head—eight months. But what does he really know about her?

Not much. He knows she came to the Center an alcoholic also addicted to coke.

He has no idea where she was born. If she has any siblings. What she did for work.

How could he have been such an fool? His parents are right to be suspicious; she must be after something. Why else would such a hot chick want him? He’s a recovering junkie. A guy who digs up earth for a living. A man whose friend died because of his negligence.

God, he’d kill for a hit of O right now.

Reflexively, he jams his forefinger against his thumb, squeezing them together, lashing out for the soothing words, trying to pin them into his brain. “I am in control,” he whispers. No, that’s not right. “I control my own story.” Yeah, this is his story. His life. So why the hell is everyone around him still manipulating him? He moves quickly now, striding to the front door and walks outside, his paranoia gaining rapidly on him with every step. He’ll go through Erika's stuff, see if he can find a clue, something, anything.

He crosses the driveway, walking more gingerly this time, his eyes on the ground, avoiding any large pieces of gravel. When he reaches the other side of the garage he sprints up the stairs. He's picturing her large black suitcase. Remembering when he asked her if that was all she had and her saying it was all she needed to start her new life. At the time it had seemed so romantic since her "new life" was going to be with him.

He turns the knob, opens the door, and stops dead. Erika is sitting on the edge of the bed wrapped in a brown bath towel. Her hair is wet and the air in the room is heavy with humidity. The scent of something floral but chemical-smelling lingers like dust particles caught in a ray of sun.

"Hi there," she says sweetly.

Grant releases the tense grip he has on his body. Takes in her naked legs. Breathes in the thick air. "Where's the car?"

"In the garage. I took it to the car wash and I don't want it to get dirty from the rain. What have you been up to?"

That there is no rain in the forecast is of no consequence to Grant in this moment. He is once again caught up by her beauty. "Not much. I've just been waiting," he replies.

"Well, Grant. You don't have to do that anymore." Erika stands up and lets the towel drop to the carpet. "I'm here now."

CHAPTER

8

GRANT WAKES CONFUSED. The ceiling over his bed is unfamiliar, as is the cloying smell in his nostrils. Where is he?

Next to him something moves. Smiling now that he knows exactly where he is and what he's been up to, he turns on his side, reaches under the sheet and finds Erika's bare ass. He traces a finger lightly along the crack, up her spine to her neck. When his hand reaches her hair he winds the fine strands around his finger, fiddling with it until she finally stirs awake.

"Hi there," she murmurs, turning over to face him.

"Hi."

"Man, I was out like a light. Did you nap?"

"I did," he says, although he feels anything but rested. His left shoulder aches and his lower back feels sore. It's because of the sex. The sort of sex he's only seen on porn sites. Nothing he's ever done. Erika had been more aggressive than ever before, kept demanding that he fuck her harder. From behind. Slamming her up against the wall. He gave it his best shot, but she kept at him, urging him to be more physical, more forceful. At one point she threw him on his back and rode him, going so far as to bite him on the neck while he was pumping away inside her.

He stares into her face, a thousand questions rolling around in his head. He wades through them, deciding which one, if any, should take precedent. Though he wants answers, he's hesitant. If he asks her the wrong thing, probes the wrong place, he will scare her off. "You're beautiful" is all he manages to come up with.

Erika sits up and plucks her phone off the table. "You're not so bad yourself," she utters, but her attention is now on her screen.

Sighing, he rolls onto his back and gazes out the window. Based on the way the sunlight is refracted against the vivid blue he's guessing it must be early afternoon. He continues to stare, contemplating the hues, thinking how the light at dusk, that low burnished glare that hovers just before the dark of a sunset, sometimes unnerves him. Why is that, he wonders? Why is it that that particular time of day has always been when he most desperately craved another line, another pill, another psychological state?

A cloud comes into view and the sky darkens. Is he completely off with the time? He knows, of course, that he can simply ask Erika what time it is, but he wants to see if he is correct. It's silly, sure, but he's suddenly convinced that if he guesses correctly, if he wins this game, he will gain back his power. He will have control over his destiny.

His thoughts quickly track along the day's path: breakfast with his parents, the argument. Them leaving—he thinks it was around 8:30. Maybe 9:00. Then, the waiting. Rice Krispies. The deer in the woods, or whatever it was that spooked him into getting out of the pool. He curls his toes, remembering the cut on his right foot. The pool. More waiting. Coming over here.

The sex. Okay, so his second erection took him an embarrassingly long time to achieve, but that's not the point of this game, is it? Altogether, he figures the whole thing lasted about half an hour.

Then, the cat nap. Twenty minutes?

He has it. "The time right now is 12:53!" he crows with proud certainty. "Am I right?"

Erika glances at the top of her screen. Frowns. "Nope. Actually, it's time for you to get a watch," she replies without even glancing at him.

He snags her wrist and attempts to flip the phone in his direction so he can see the time for himself, but she fights him, tightening her arm so it's impossible for him to see the screen. "Stop it!" she yells, pushing him away. She clambers out of bed, an angry look on her face. "Jesus. What's your problem, Grant? You want to know what time it is? It's 1:07, okay?"

Grant watches her stomp into the bathroom. Hears the sink turn on and the sound of her brushing her teeth.

"I don't have a problem, Erika. I just wanted to know what time it was," he says to himself, stunned by her outburst and her blatant need to hide whatever she was looking at on her phone.

So much for having control over his destiny. He sighs, gets out of bed and puts on his clothes. Just as he's about to head back to the house, Erika comes out of the bathroom. "Wait up," she demands. Grant does as instructed, leaning against the door while she pulls a pair of blue sweatpants and a black hoodie from her suitcase, the same suitcase he'd planned to ransack for answers. He thinks it's kind of weird that she's been staying here for two weeks and still hasn't unpacked but does not comment on it.

She walks over to him and kisses him on his cheek. "Can we go raid the fridge, please? I'm famished."

* * *

The message light on the telephone in the kitchen is blinking. Grant isn't sure if he should check it or not. It's not as if the message will be for him. He ignores it and joins Erika in the pantry where she is standing, hand on hip, contemplating her choices. "Your parents have, like, the whitest taste in food," she says. "I mean, Campbell's Soup? Really?"

"We can go into town and grab something if you want."

She shakes her head. "Nah, I'm fine with cheese and crackers. There's also some frozen pizza we can heat up." She backs out of the pantry with a box of Ritz in her hands.

None of this sounds good to Grant. He goes to the refrigerator and opens it. When he sees that there's a full carton of eggs, a package of bacon and a couple of dried-out carrots, he considers throwing together a frittata. Part of the routine at the sober house included taking turns cooking dinner for the other residents. Up until then, Grant had no experience cooking. It wasn't as if his mother ever baked cookies with him or asked him to help in the kitchen. Fortunately for the men who lived at Reflections, one of the guys had been a superstar chef in his pre-sober life. By the time Grant moved out, he knew how to make a mean stir fry and a pretty decent frittata.

"Did you eat eggs this morning?" he asks, knowing if she did, a frittata probably wasn't the best idea.

"Did I eat eggs?" she asks as if his question makes no sense. Then her face registers the meaning. "No. I just got a bagel to go at Marvin's."

"Where did you go after Marvin's?" he asks, rushing through the proverbial door she has just held open for him. "I mean, you were gone a long time."

"Nowhere special. Just wandered around all the little shops and stuff. And then the car wash." She walks past him to the door. He's about to tell her how he had to wrestle it to get it locked when she easily clicks the button up, slides it smoothly aside and goes outside. She flops down on a lounge chair, retrieves a handful of crackers and stuffs them into her mouth.

She's clearly done explaining herself, and Grant is starting to feel impatient. No, he isn't *starting* to feel impatient. He needs answers now. In less than twenty-four hours his father will be back here, expecting Grant's decision. If he accepts his father's offer to run the Redding quarry, he will have to do so without Erika.

Six hours ago, he would have said his answer was a foregone conclusion. Sure, the job's one he's been wanting for years, but no way was he going to dump this woman just so he could stay in his parents' good graces.

But six hours ago this woman was still Erika Morris. Someone he thought he could trust.

Now, she'd become more of a mystery than a sure thing.

He needs to man up, go out there right now and confront her. Make her come clean. Until he knows who she is, who she was, he's not entirely sure he's willing to throw away a tempting job opportunity—and a hefty inheritance—for her.

The landline rings. Grant waits for the answering machine to pick up so he can see who it is. It clicks on after four rings. "You've reached the Cooper residence. Please keep your message short and to the point."

Grant rolls his eyes at his mother's cold voice. The beep sounds.

"Hello, Cooper residence. This is Geri. I have no idea if Cal or Grant . . . if either of you are home or will hear this," she says, her oldish voice crackling through the line. "I tried calling everyone's cellphones but no one is answering which is why I'm calling the home phone . . ."

Geri Johnson is his father's executive assistant. She's been working for the family for as long as Grant can remember. When did she call him? Grant realizes he has no idea where his phone is, but instead of moving off to find it he continues listening.

"And, well, I'm not sure what's going on, but John McNeil, you know, the manager at Wadsworth . . ." She pauses to clear her throat, Grant assumes, because she's worried that mentioning *Wadsworth* might hurt his feelings when he hears this. "He just called and said your parents still haven't shown up for the memorial, and it was supposed to start at one o'clock. I called them and they didn't answer, and then I called Washington Regional. I thought . . . I thought maybe they decided to drive over instead, but no, it turns out they flew and I'm starting to . . . it's just a little strange, don't you think? I'm more than a little concerned, given that your father is never late . . ."

With every word her voice goes higher and breathier as if it's climbing a set of steep stairs and quickly running out of steam. Grant can tell how anxious Geri is, and if he gave a shit about the memorial he'd pick up the phone and tell her to relax; there could be a thousand reasons why they're a little late. But he doesn't. He lets jittery Geri rattle on. She implores Grant or Cal to call her the moment either of them hears anything and then says she feels bad for all those poor people having to stand around waiting on such a cold day, and by the time she hangs up Grant is on his way to his room, which is the last place he remembers seeing his phone.

CHAPTER

9

Marvin's was so busy today that it is not until I stop moving that I notice how much my feet hurt. From the moment we opened this morning until ten minutes ago, when Sue hung the CLOSED sign on the door, I've been going nonstop. The only people left are the young well-dressed couple at table 3. I've already cleared their plates and dropped the check, but they're still chatting away, oblivious to the emptiness around them. I've never seen them before, and I'm guessing they're tourists. On weekends tons of people drive up from the Bay Area, eager to spend the day strolling the wood-planked sidewalks along Main Street, filling their cameras and reusable shopping bags with Gold Hill's history and charm. Sometimes a misdirected soul will make the mistake of stopping in Prosperity on the way up here, but once they see there's nothing Instagramable there, they quickly speed north.

I know it's time for me to clock out, but since I've already cleaned and set the tables and as long as the couple is still hanging, I start filling the salt and pepper shakers. When the restaurant phone rings, I let it go to voicemail since we're closed. The ringing must have made the couple realize they were the only people here because suddenly the guy looks around, throws some money onto the table, and they both stand up. "That was great," he says when they reach the door. I'm about to say, "Thanks for stopping by," but they're already gone.

The phone rings again, and this time Sue comes out of the kitchen to answer it. "Marvin's," she says impatiently. "Deni? Yup. She sure is. Just a sec." Sue holds out the phone to me. "No idea who it is." As I take the phone from her, I see her glance to her right before scooping some toast crumbs off table 4 into the palm of her hand. She raises her eyebrow at me before walking back into the kitchen.

"Hello?" I say, wondering who on earth could be calling me at work.

"Deni. It's Grant. I called your cell, but you didn't answer." He sounds perturbed.

I start to explain that Sue doesn't allow us to use our phones when we're working, but he bluntly interrupts me. "I don't care. I need to talk to Cal. Now. Do you know where he is?"

"No, I do not know where he is. I assume you called him?" I say half sarcastically.

Grant actually growls, so loudly that I move the phone away from my ear. "Goddammit, Deni! He wasn't here when I woke up this morning and—"

"He probably went to the gym like he always does on Saturdays."

"Yeah, but *then* where did he go? I can't get ahold of him and . . . I need him, Deni. I don't know what I'm supposed to do . . ." His voice trails off, and I think I hear him whimper. His unease is only now starting to hit me.

"What the hell is going on, Grant?" I say this so loudly I see Sue and our dishwasher Ben look up from what they're doing behind the counter. I give them a small smile and turn away.

"My parents never landed in Nevada."

"What? What do you mean?"

"I *mean* they supposedly took off this morning, but they never showed up for that stupid memorial. It was supposed to start at one o'clock. And Geri—you know Geri Johnson? She works for my father? Anyway, she keeps calling here and leaving these hysterical messages, and now she's kind of starting to freak me out too."

I look at the clock by the coffee station. It's 3:20. A thousand narratives begin to splash around my mind, sloshing against one another like wild waves in a choppy sea. "What if they changed their minds about going to the memorial and went somewhere else?" I suggest, realizing too late how lame this sounds.

Either he didn't hear me or he determines my theory is too ridiculous to acknowledge because he just skates over it and demands, "Just find my brother and tell him to call me."

"I will, but, Grant, you should call Geri back and see what she knows. Who she's spoken to." I am trying to sound as calm as possible. There's no reason, at this point, to panic. Or to panic Grant. I'm no expert, but I'm pretty certain the last kind of state a recovering addict should be in is a distressed one. "And then one of you should probably call the police." I have no idea if this is protocol, but it feels like a logical step to take. "I'm sure that's what Cal would tell you to do," I add, thinking that giving Grant a clear task might focus him, ease him out of his frenzied state. "Why don't you start with Geri while I go find out where Cal is."

I'm guessing he went to the quarry after the gym. He sometimes goes up there on weekends if I have to work. He likes to wander around the enormous pit when the machinery is shut down and the place is quiet. When I asked him why he would want to spend a day off at a place he works forty-plus hours a week, he initially had trouble explaining his reasoning. He tried, "Don't you sometimes eat at Marvin's on your days off?" to which I'd replied, "Only because I can't make a decent Hollandaise sauce. The rocks you see on Tuesday are the same rocks you see on Saturday."

He'd laughed, of course, but then asked me to fly up there with him the following weekend. I think I held my breath during the entire twenty-minute flight over the Sierras, it was so beautiful. We both wore headphones, and Cal talked me through everything he was doing as if he was teaching me how to fly. I loved every minute and—not that it was possible—I think I fell even more in love with him while watching him steer the small plane through the endless blue sky.

After he toured me around his office and pointed out which piece of equipment did what, we hiked up to one of the higher benches that had yet to be blasted and took in the huge expanse of . . . *beige*. Honestly, all I saw were mounds of dirt and sand and rocks, some large and conical-shaped, some just misshapen heaps. I was about to say, "Um, what's the big deal here, Cal?" when he quietly laid it out.

"What we're doing here is we're peeling back the layers of the earth, you know? Exposing what took millions of years to produce. Just look at it, Deni. You probably just see a bunch of brown rock. I see a billion different colors and shapes." He'd stood up and stared at the pit below us, as if transfixed by a magical kingdom. "Rocks are what built civilization."

I'd looked again at the silent barren landscape, through his eyes this time. I still didn't get his awe, but I respected his devotion to his job. This coming from a woman who spent her days pushing sides of hash browns.

"I'll call you the minute I hear anything and you do the same, okay?" I say to Grant.

He lets out a relieved sigh. "Okay, yeah. Sounds good. Thanks, Deni."

Giving him something to do was definitely a good idea. Then I think about Erika and wonder why she didn't suggest calling the police. I question if she's being any help at all. I walk into the kitchen and give Sue and Ben the thumbnail version of what the call was about.

Sue puts her hand to her chest. "Yikes," she says. Ben, a pale tatted-up dude who plays bass in a local rock band and who hasn't said more than twenty words to me since he started working here, blinks and then goes back to washing dishes.

I see a chunk of onion on the floor by Sue's feet and pick it up, tossing it into the trash bucket before heading into the storeroom to fetch my phone from my sweatshirt pocket. I pull it out and when I unlock it I see that there are two missed calls, three texts from Grant and a text from Cal, which I immediately click on.

D. don't be mad but wanted to be a nice brother and give G and E 💑 *some alone time. Also a good son* 😇*.* ✈ *to memorial* ☠ *with the folks. Back tomorrow afternoon. Don't miss me too much* 😉 *will call when I land* ♡ *C.*

I feel my brain trying to slam itself shut before the meaning of the words can cross over. All I see are words and emojis.

I read it again.

And then I begin to scream.

* * *

Fernley, NV (AP)—Three people were killed after a single-engine plane crashed into rough mountainous terrain about six miles southwest of Nixon, Nevada.

On the morning of September 30, the Piper PA28 Cherokee departed from Washington Regional Airport outside of Prosperity, CA, and was headed to Silver Springs Airport, Lyon County, Nevada, when the crash happened, according to local officials and the Federal Aviation Administration.

The victims, identified as Calvin Cooper, 69, Jeannette Cooper, 66, and Calvin Cooper Jr., 28, were residents of Gold

Hills, CA. Calvin Cooper was the President and CEO of C.G. Cooper & Sons Aggregates, a privately held company.

According to company spokesperson Geri Johnson, the family was on its way to a memorial service for 35-year-old Craig Hinkley. Hinkley, a worker at Wadsworth Quarry, was struck and killed by fly rock during a quarry blast in June 2021. Cooper's other son, Grant Cooper, who was not a passenger on the downed flight, had been the quarry manager at the time of the accident.

After the family was reported missing, a search and rescue operation was mobilized. Nearly three hours later, a search plane located the aircraft, which was completely destroyed. The crash site was only reachable by helicopters and all-terrain vehicles.

Due to dangerous conditions and steep terrain at the accident site there was no on-site examination of the wreckage. The official cause of the crash will be investigated by the Federal Aviation Administration and the National Transportation Safety Board.

CHAPTER

10

I AM SEATED ON a pew inside the United Methodist Church of Gold Hills. My father keeps reaching over and patting my knee like he's got some weird tic. Whenever I feel his touch, my heart jumps in my chest as if I hadn't been expecting it. As if he hadn't just tried to console me twenty seconds ago. Every sensation, every sound, even a small change of light, rattles me. I feel naked. Exposed. Like a slit-open frog in a high school lab, it's as though my body consists only of parts. This is a heart. It is on fire. These are the hands. They are balled into fists. Down here are two thighs, sweating against the hard wooden bench beneath them. And up here is the brain, a raw, pink hunk of fury.

It is only when the pastor finishes his sermon and begins to speak about the dearly departed that I coerce the disparate parts into reuniting. I literally pull myself together.

All of me needs to be here. For Cal.

I do my best to stay present, but when the pastor says, "The Coopers were the type of people who kept their good deeds and generosity out of the spotlight," I shut down.

I take a deep breath and focus on the backs of the heads of the people in the front row, where I should be sitting. Apparently, those in charge of this service deemed me, a mere fiancée, unworthy of a spot in the VIP section. The roped-off "Family Only" section had been reserved for Grant and Erika, and some miscellaneous Cooper relations, all of whom are nameless faces. Faces I'd planned to meet at my wedding. Faces that have yet to offer me a morsel of condolence.

I guess I can't blame them. Why should they even know I exist? Jean hadn't picked out the invitations yet. The wedding was nothing more than a list-filled black binder. Still, it would have been nice if Grant had introduced me to a cousin or two.

Grant. I can just make out the left side of his face with its downturned mouth. His ashen skin. I reach forward and touch his shoulder, just to let him know I am behind him, sharing his grief. Without turning around he lays his hand gently on top of mine, as gently as I laid my hand on his during his homecoming dinner weeks ago. Removing my hand, I sit back and when I look up, Erika is staring at me through narrowed eyes. "What?" I mouth, having no idea what her problem is.

I'd been with them when we got news of the crash. After I read Cal's text at Marvin's, I'd sped up the hill, barged into the house without so much as a knock and found Erika sitting in Calvin's spot on the couch in the living room with the television tuned to some cooking channel. I stopped in my tracks and stared, wondering how Grant's girlfriend could be so lackadaisical when the possibility of disaster loomed, only to remind myself that this woman probably had zero concern for the fate of the Cooper family.

I turned and ran into the kitchen. Grant was in there pacing, repeatedly checking his phone. When he saw me, he walked up to me and hugged me tight to his chest. He smelled pungent, of sweat and something sexual. It wasn't a pleasant smell. "Deni. Oh, my God."

I'd pulled away and asked who he'd heard from, what was being done, what he knew. After offering me little more than "I don't know" and "No idea," he looked past me toward the living room. I assumed he was going to say something about Erika, maybe about her being such an unsupportive bitch, but he said, "Where's Cal? Isn't he with you?"

"You don't know?" I figured by now some official somewhere would have seen a flight plan logging three passengers. "Cal wanted to give you guys some time alone so he went with them," I whispered through the pain. And then I rushed into the guest bathroom and vomited.

During the next hour Erika stayed fixed to the television while Grant and I waited in the kitchen. For a little while we tried to make small talk, reminiscing about the few people we both knew from high school, but mostly we just sat in silence. I nervously plucked the polyester petals off the fake flowers while Grant played games on his phone. When we finally received word that Search and Rescue had located the site of the crash and found no survivors, we'd held one another and wept. Hearing our cries brought Erika running into the kitchen. She unhooked Grant from my arms and cradled him against her chest, cooing, "I'm so sorry, I'm so sorry," over and over.

Without either of them noticing, I slipped out of the house, closing the door quietly behind me. I walked down the steps and stood alone in the darkness, wiping the tears off my face with the back of my arm. Somewhere off in the distance an owl hooted. I breathed in the stillness. I felt the wind as it brushed by the dampness on my skin.

I got in my car and just sat there, trying to process, trying to make some sense of what this meant. I knew that when that plane crashed, my future had crashed right alongside it. I'd not only lost my beloved Cal. I'd lost everything.

* * *

I allow my gaze to finally alight on the caskets, which until now I've tried to avoid. All three are adorned with bulging multicolored flower arrangements that topple over the edges. I assume Jean's friend Bev provided the garish mix. If I'd had any say in planning this funeral I would have chosen simple flowers, something like black-eyed Susans, maybe with some white tulips thrown in.

But I had no say. No one, not even Grant, thought to include me in the program. No one asked me if I wanted to speak—not that I would have. I have no interest in sharing what I loved about Cal with a roomful of strangers. But the least they could have done is let me choose what kind of flowers I want covering the broken body of my love.

Flowers make me think of Luna, who I just now realize I haven't heard back from. I called her from the Coopers' driveway that night and again the next morning. Both calls went to voicemail. She had to have seen the front page of the newspaper. I'm sure she's sitting somewhere behind me right now. But why she didn't call me? She might not have any affection for the Coopers, but at one point she loved Cal. And I'm pretty certain she loves me.

When the pastor begins speaking about Cal, I shake off thoughts of Luna and sit up straighter. He tells us what a brave and intelligent young man Calvin Cooper Jr. was. What a devoted son and brother he was. He mentions nothing about Cal's movie-star past, his love of fast cars and moonscapes. And then, just as he's about to conclude his worthless tribute, he throws me a bone: "Also, as many of you know, Cal was engaged to be married to Deni Rydell next winter." There's movement when he says this, people shifting, turning their attention toward me. I keep my face forward, but I can feel strangers' eyes on me, their sympathetic glances landing on me like spitballs. Grant turns around, and it's his eyes I allow myself to lean into. I am about to mouth, "Hello," but Erika nudges him and he quickly spins his head back around.

"I'd recently spoken with Jean about officiating," the pastor continues, "and I know it would have been a beautiful celebration, worthy of the family's fine taste and joyful spirits."

And then, before I crumple beneath both the sadness and the acrimony that are threatening to fracture me all over again, he asks us to stand so we can all sing "Amazing

Grace." My father, sensing that my body is now an open wound, helps me to my feet. As the participants join in, I glance around for the first time since taking my seat. The place is jam-packed. People standing three deep at the back. There's a large group of burly men all dressed in unpressed buttoned-down shirts and jeans. They must be guys who work in the quarries. I notice a very pretty woman in her twenties and wonder if she, or any of the people I don't recognize are friends from Cal's time in Los Angeles. The mayor is here, as are a few uniformed police officers. I look around for Luna, knowing she will be easy to spot. I expect her long blonde hair to be a beacon amid the sea of strangers dressed in dark colors. But she is not here.

Where is Luna?

CHAPTER

11

THE SCENT OF death is thick in the air—copper, rot, and something sickly sweet beneath it all. Even with the mint, my stomach clenches.

I fix on her throat. The gash is short but deep. Not ear to ear. Almost like whoever slit her open wanted out of here as quickly as possible. They didn't linger. Didn't need to feel the sick glow of satisfaction as the life ebbed out of her eyes. My gut tells me this was not a crime of passion. It wasn't someone she knew. It was someone desperate enough to kill for some easy cash.

I swallow down the nausea and stand up to survey the scene. The sun is too hot for early October, and the hairs that escaped my hastily tied bun stick to my neck. Over in the dirt next to the stolen marijuana plants is a large steel lopper, big and sharp enough to cut through thick stems. Not the murder weapon, but obviously what the thief or thieves used. The plants may be gone, but the phantom funk of pot, sticky and sweet, sneaks up into my nose hairs, mixing with the stench of the rotting corpse. I scan the wasted rows, counting twelve decapitated stalks sticking up out of the ground like skeletal fingers. That's double the number allowed in this town. A pretty small illegal grow. Street value, given today's not-so-hot cannabis market, we're probably looking at around $35K. Worth slitting a woman's throat over? A piece of shit meth or oxy addict might think so.

I see Tom Horner, my partner, collecting statements from the young couple who found the body: a white dude with dreadlocks and a girl with a batik turban on her head. She's got something swaddled in a sling against her chest. From here, I can't tell if it's a baby or an animal. They're both stoned. Stoned and scared. She's crying. I already know they know nothing. I already know they're itinerant trimmigrants, seasonal employees who show up at harvest time to cut the leaves off the hairy buds. Hard work but good money, if you can stand the smell.

I stroll over to catch the residue of the conversation. "Detective Robyn Torres," I say, extending my hand to the male. He nods and shakes it. His skin is soft and that puts me off. I glance at the female who's got her head buried in the fur of what looks like a white dog with a flat face.

Horner says, "Howard and Lacey are up from Tucson."

"Trimmers?" I ask.

They both nod. "We were here last year and we, you know, connected," the male squeaks out as if his lungs are only half inflated. "So she asked us to come early this year to help with the drying and said we'd, you know, hang out." He steals a peek at the body and stifles a whimper.

"How about we continue this conversation up there?" I say, pointing my chin up the hill toward the farm. Tom nods. He should have moved them away from the crime scene first thing, but Tom can't help himself sometimes. He's like a kid who can't stand missing out.

We trudge up the hill, pass through the woods and make our way across rows of flowers and vegetables, most of which I couldn't put a name to even if you put a gun to my head. As we near the house I see the medical examiner coming down the gravel drive followed by another vehicle. Brian Pearse from Washington County's Special Investigations Unit gets out of his car and intercepts the M.E. before she has the chance to shut her door.

I hustle over. "Hey, Vera," I say, interrupting the conversation before it takes root. Vera Lamberti and I grew up on the same street in Prosperity and ran track together at Monroe High. I was as surprised as the next guy when I learned she moved back to the area after getting her degree and became, of all things, a medical examiner. We've run into each other enough through work channels that our long-ago friendship based on shared sweat and crossing finishing lines began to turn into the real deal. After her husband left her for one of his patients (he's a dentist), it was my door she knocked on at eleven one night last year. I'd just brushed my teeth and when I heard the pounding I reflexively touched my hip. I assumed anyone showing up unannounced on a Tuesday night was looking to cause trouble.

I live alone in the house I grew up in. It wasn't my intention to return home when I got out of the police academy, but the job opening had been laid out before me like a virgin on an altar. While I did my time as a street cop, I hunkered down in a tiny studio with a Murphy bed above a fancy boutique in Gold Hills. I'd always dreamed of someday moving up from Prosperity to Gold Hills, and there I was, finally living that dream, even if it barely measured 400 square feet.

Once I made detective, I figured it was time to stop living in a one-room apartment so small I couldn't invite more than one person over for a drink after a shift. When my parents suddenly got a bug up their butts and decided they wanted to move to Missouri where my aunt lives, I became their de facto house sitter. Free rent meant I could afford the good stuff.

Which is exactly what I brought out after I opened the door and saw Vera's red eyes and slumped shoulders that Tuesday night.

"Hello, Detective Torres," Vera says now, trying not to smirk. We drank ourselves silly last night while binging on *Unforgotten*, the British crime series starring Nicola Walker. I have a major crush on Nicola Walker and I'd be happy watching her shine shoes. When she's thinking really hard about solving a murder case she does this adorable thing where she scrunches up her nose like she can almost smell the lies around her.

"Show me what you got here, Torres." Pearse shoots the words at me before I have the chance to be polite and say hello to my friend. Since this case involves illegal cultivation and theft of marijuana, he's got every right to be here dipping his stick in. It has all the signs of a pot robbery gone south. I'm betting it will be an easy solve. *My* easy solve.

* * *

Three hours later, the crime scene is a wrap. Photos and video shot. Evidence tagged and packaged. Fingerprints taken. Footwear impressions made. The body gone. I get in my vehicle and start heading back to town, but the hysterical woman yelling at the officer we have posted to keep the public away stops me. I pull into the small parking lot next to the Luna Rose Farm and Flowers' farmstand and get out.

I walk over to the two of them. "Hi there," I say, gently moving Officer Rood aside so I can face her. "I'm Detective Robyn Torres. Is there a problem here?" I want her to talk first. Tell me who she is and what her relationship to the victim is without my asking.

Her face is a smeared mess of black and red from both her mascara and her distress. She's wearing black pants and a black sweater, an absurdly unsuitable outfit, given the day's weather. "I don't understand what's happening. Where is Luna? What is going on?" She looks from me to Rood and adds, "He won't let me in. And he won't tell me anything."

"Can you please tell me your name?" I pull out my notebook because at this point I have so many thoughts bumping up against one another that I am not sure I trust my short-term memory to catch what comes my way.

"Deni Rydell. Oh, my God, what the fuck is going on?" She is clearly at the end of her rope and I owe it to her to let out a little slack before she hangs herself with it.

"How about we get you out of the sun, Deni, okay?" I nod to Rood and start walking back toward the small three-sided wooden hut with a green corrugated metal roof. Nailed onto the side is a brightly painted sign that says CSA PICKUP. Deni follows me inside and we each take a seat on opposite ends of the empty wooden shelf that runs along the wall. It's at least ten degrees cooler in here, but as soon as Deni sits she pulls off her sweater. Underneath it she's wearing a white button-down blouse, its underarms stained a pale yellow. After she unbuttons it down to her cleavage she wipes her hands across her face. "She wasn't at the funeral. I knew something had to be wrong."

"What funeral was that, Deni?"

"This isn't about me," she says sternly. "What's going on with Luna? Please, please just tell me."

What I'm about to say to this woman is pretty much my least favorite part of the job. Breaking bad news to the loved one of a murder victim is no easy feat, and not just because of the emotional fallout. I assume everyone and anyone is a suspect, Deni included. Which means I need to tread lightly. Carefully. Catch her reaction. Probe past the expected behaviors. "I'm sorry, but your friend is dead, Deni. She was murdered."

"What? No, she wasn't. She wasn't. Not Luna. Oh, my God, no, no, no." She gets up and walks out of the hut and leans over, putting her hands on her knees like she's about to throw up. She hovers over the ground for a few seconds, then straightens, looks in the direction of the farm, then over to the gate where Rood is, then utters a barely audible, "Oh, Luna, why?" before coming back into the hut and sitting back down. "Tell me what happened," she demands.

This is a typical response, if there's actually such a thing. Initial shock followed by denial followed by confusion followed by anger followed by insistence. She's collected now and wants answers.

As do I.

Once I hand over the bare minimum of facts and allow another convulsive outburst of emotion to wax and wane, I begin gently pressing Deni for some background. Given that she attests to being Luna's closest friend, I've got to believe I'm barking up the relevant tree. "You were aware she was growing marijuana on her property?"

She nods. "Yeah, the farmstand wasn't enough to live on. I mean, it kind of was, but this way she was able to buy equipment and, you know, be more financially secure. But it wasn't like she was a big-time dealer. It was only, what, like a dozen plants?"

"Still an illegal grow," I state, before shifting around on the hard plank so the half of my ass that isn't asleep bears my weight. "Other than the trimmers Howard and Lacey—"

"I know them. They were here last year. Do you think they killed her?"

I almost smile. If only it were so easy. "I doubt it very much," I reply before forging on. "Other than those two, you, and whoever she sells the harvest to, anyone else know about the grow?"

"No one," she replies emphatically. "She was super careful about keeping the operation hidden. Like *super* careful.

It's her mother's property, and she knew she'd get in trouble if she ever got caught."

"But people come up here to buy her flowers and produce." I circle my forefinger around in front of me, indicating the obvious. "She didn't let them explore the farm?"

Deni's eyes fill up a little, as though she's reminiscing, picturing families with young kids running wild through her friend's fields. "Yes and no. She had an Open Farm day once a season where she'd invite her customers, or actually anyone who wanted to see the farm, to come up and explore. But she was really conscious of keeping people restricted to just the farm. She'd string a rope barrier at the far end of the rows with a 'No Trespassing' sign. I'm pretty sure no one ever went down to the creek." She shakes her head. "But maybe someone did? I mean, how hard could it have been to sneak down there, right?"

"Right," I agree, because someone saw the plants. "Do you know who her dealer is?"

"Dealer." She chuckles. "You're making Luna sound like this shady underworld drug runner. She wasn't. She was—I mean, come on, it was only twelve plants! Why would someone kill her for so little?" As soon as the words "kill her" hit the air, Deni's skin goes ashen and her eyes close. "Why would anyone want to kill Luna? She was so beautiful."

I let her sit with her pain for a minute. A bright bluebird zips by, and I watch it alight on a branch across the road. A second later a dull-plumed female joins him.

"Anyway," she continues, pulling my attention back, "I have no idea but I'm pretty sure her *dealer* was this dude from San Francisco who she gave all of it to every year."

Not a likely suspect, but I'll get Tom to follow that trail. "Family? You say her parents own the place?"

"Just her mom. Her dad died a long time ago. Her name is Misha. Misha Rose. Are you going to call her because I sure don't want to have to be the one to tell her."

"Yes, we'll notify Luna's mother. Do you have her contact information?"

"No clue. She's in Bali at some meditation place. Been there for years." She lets loose a short whimper. "God, she's going to be heartbroken."

I make a note to hunt Luna's mother down in Bali. "Whose funeral did you attend today?"

"What? Oh. Yeah." I've shaken her out of Luna's world and shoved her back into her own reality. "It was for my fiancé and his parents. They died in a plane crash," she says flatly, almost angrily, as if she preferred I stick with this particular death, please.

I realize she's talking about the Cooper crash that happened last Saturday. I'd read about the accident in the paper. Heard the chitchat floating around the office yesterday. The Coopers and their money are—were—big deals around Gold Hills. It was impossible to grow up in this county and not notice their name staining assorted buildings and whatnot. There's the C. G. Cooper & Sons Cancer Center at Washington Regional Hospital. And the Cooper Gymnasium at Monroe High School—renovated *after* I graduated, unfortunately. The family also gifted the city one of their abandoned quarries and turned it into the twenty-acre Henry Emmerson Cooper Park, the prettiest park in the city of Gold Hills.

A couple of my fellow officers planned to attend today's funeral. Probably because the Coopers put on a yearly Police Gala. I've never gone nor had any interest in going. As far as I'm concerned, cops shouldn't have to beg to help pay for bulletproof vests or medical bills. I appreciate the family throwing a fancy shindig to raise funds for the guys and gals in blue, but not enough to warrant sitting through a dirge-filled snooze-fest for people I never met.

"Calvin Cooper Junior was your fiancé?"

"Just Cal. He went by Cal."

If my memory serves me correctly, he was the son who wasn't a drug addict.

I study the woman anew, my heart leaking a driblet of sympathy. I mean, shit, this poor thing just lost her boyfriend in a plane crash *and* her bestie to murder, all in one fell swoop.

What are the odds?

I sit up straighter. Hold on: is there a connection? I think about it for a few seconds, flick it away, tug it back again, and chew on it some more. "I'm sorry for your loss," I say because I'm supposed to. "Losses," I postscript.

She closes her eyes and makes a bold attempt to appear less rattled than she has to be. If I were her I'd be curled up in a tight little ball in some dark corner somewhere.

"Did Cal and Luna know one another?"

"What?" Her face reddens and she looks at the ground. "Why does that even matter?"

"It's just a question."

She shrugs. I can see she's fading fast. Coming out from under the adrenaline kick from the initial shock and now that it's leaving her body, she's sagging.

"Yeah. They used to date in high school, but they haven't spoken since they broke up."

"Who broke up with whom?" It was a long ago romance that most likely ended when one party got bored with the other, or some such teenage drama. I still want to know.

"Cal broke up with Luna because of something her father did and that made Luna not like him. She never got over it." She sighs and swallows hard enough I can see her Adam's apple bounce. Like she's trying to shove something nasty down her own throat. "She tried to talk me out of marrying him, but, I mean, ultimately she was happy for me." She smiles, more to herself than to me. "She was going to make my bouquet for the wedding. In fact, the last time I saw Luna it was to talk about the stupid flowers."

"When was that exactly?"

"It's not important," she says, waving her hand.

"If you want me to find out who killed your friend, Deni, everything is important."

"I don't know. I think it was the twenty-third or maybe it was the twenty-fourth. I'd come straight from work, but I can't remember if it was that Saturday or Sunday." She sighs in frustration. "I came up here because I wanted to tell her in person that my future mother-in-law wasn't going to let her do the flowers for the wedding. I thought she was going to get mad, but she was totally fine with it, like it didn't mean anything."

"Did that surprise you?"

She stares at the ground, then nudges what looks like a shriveled leaf of kale into the dirt. "A little, yeah."

"Why is that?" I have my pen poised over my notebook, but before I write another word, she stands up and utters, "I'm sorry, but I can't do this anymore."

"I still have more questions, Deni."

"I'm sure you do, ma'am, but if you haven't noticed, I've had a really fucked-up day. I'm gonna go home and sleep for a week. Find out who killed Luna, okay?"

She doesn't hear me when I say, "I will," because she's already walking toward her car on the other side of the gate.

I say nothing as I watch her go.

CHAPTER 12

"WE SHOULD GET married."

Grant doesn't bother looking up from his bowl of cereal. "Sure," he replies, as noncommittedly as he replied when Erika suggested this the first time. And the second. And the third.

Erika finishes off her coffee and goes over to the dishwasher and puts her mug on the upper rack. After Grant confessed that he was getting tired of cleaning up after her, she's been expending a little more effort. Although, in all honestly, the house has become a sty.

"I'm going to get dressed," she says, kissing him on his head. "Let's do something fun today."

"I have to go down to the office this morning. I think Geri said I'm supposed to meet with some board members? I don't remember." His eye catches on the calendar next to the fridge. It's been less than two weeks since his entire family died in that plane crash. If not for Geri Johnson's help he's pretty sure he would have drowned by now.

It was Geri who flew to Nevada to retrieve the bodies from the coroner's office and transport them back to California. It was Geri who took care of the funeral arrangements. Three days after they laid his parents and brother to rest in the Gold Hills Memorial Cemetery, it was Geri who set up a meeting with Richard Carnahan, the family attorney.

That's when Grant learned he wouldn't need to worry about the job in Redding or anywhere else for that matter. As the sole heir to his father's fortune, Grant Cooper was now spectacularly rich.

"Take the truck, okay? I want to drive the Caddy."

"Sure," he says, watching her stride out of the kitchen toward his parents' wing of the house.

The day after the crash, Erika relocated her black suitcase from the guest suite to his parents' bedroom. She expected him to move his own stuff in with her, but Grant wasn't so sure he wanted to. The room had always been off limits to him and his brother. He didn't recall ever crawling between his parents' comforting bodies when he woke from a nightmare. He never sat on the floor watching his mother get dressed up to attend one of their charity functions.

Erika had said his room smelled like *boy* and insisted he come sleep with her. He agreed to give it a try, although it had felt wrong sliding under the covers of his parents' bed. And then when she asked him to make love to her he kept seeing his father's face.

"I'm sorry, but I can't be in here," he'd said the next morning. "It's just weird."

"What if we get rid of their shit?"

"They've only been gone two days, Erika. Can't you just, I don't know, wait for the dust to settle?" He didn't expect Erika to grieve for people she didn't know, but Grant wished she'd offer a little sympathy. She acted as if nothing had happened. She'd expected him to act that way too.

"In fact, we should just gut the room," she'd replied, jumping out of bed and ignoring what he said. "I mean, dude, I can't believe how fugly it is. I'm going to take a shower."

It wasn't until she went into the bathroom that he'd glanced around the oversized room and saw for the first time that it truly was an incredibly unattractive room, one completely devoid of charm or warmth. The king bed was covered by a hideous black and brown checkered bedspread. Two oversized armchairs made of the same dark brown leather as the couches in the living room sat in two corners, facing the large arched windows, the room's best feature. The carpet was off-white and not all that soft under his bare feet. He wondered why they didn't install plush carpeting. They certainly had the money for it.

The three paintings on the walls were watercolors of nondescript mountain ranges. Generic shit you'd find at a T.J.Maxx store.

The only personal objects were the family photographs arranged in a neat line on the mantlepiece over the marble fireplace, which, from the sterile look of it, never had a fire burn inside it. He remembered the day the photos were taken. His mother had marched down the hall and ordered him and Cal to put on their nice suits, the ones they were forced to wear to funerals and weddings. Cal must have been around eight. Grant ten.

His mother was dressed in a navy-blue tight-fitting dress that came to her knees. The front had a row of large gold buttons that ran from the neck to the hem. Before she turned away Grant had asked, "Who died?"

"No one died, Grant," she'd said, sounding impatient, as if his simple question would make them late to wherever it was they were going. "We're getting our pictures taken by a professional photographer. Now, go comb your hair."

In Grant's limited memory, it had been a painful experience. The studio was small and he sweated in his wool suit jacket. The photographer made them sit on a white settee, arranging and rearranging them a hundred different ways. Parents in front, kids in back. Calvin being flanked by his sons, Jean in back with a hand on her husband's shoulder. Then Cal and Grant alone. Then his parents alone.

Grant stared at the pictures. He'd desperately yearned to feel something. He wanted to miss his family, he really did, but as he picked the frames up one by one and looked into the unsmiling faces of his father and mother and brother, his heart could find no purchase, no sense of belonging.

As he touched his finger to his mother's face, tracing the outline of her cold eyes, Grant wondered if he ever loved his parents. If they'd ever truly loved him. He was afraid of his father, sure, but for a time he was in awe of him as well. The old man took what his own father had handed him and expanded it into even more greatness. He'd expected Grant to do the same, and Grant wanted nothing more than for his father to acknowledge his accomplishments. Give him credit for good work.

That might have happened, if not for fucking up and getting a man killed. No matter that his father said he was proud of him that morning before he flew off to his death. Their relationship was broken. Even if he'd survived the crash, Grant knew in his heart it would have stayed broken.

When Erika emerged from the bathroom and caught him turning each frame around so the Cooper family was facing the wall, she said, "Stop it," as if scolding a dog who was mouthing one of her shoes.

Grant's hand had frozen in midair. Erika walked over to the fireplace and grabbed the frames one by one, stacking them so clumsily Grant could hear the crunch of breaking glass. "I say we start with these," she'd said, carrying them out of the room.

* * *

Grant turns his attention from the calendar, gets up and puts his cereal bowl in the dishwasher. He takes the sponge from the side of the sink and returns to the table to wipe the spill of milk and coffee ring Erika left behind. He rinses the sponge, dries his hands on his sweatpants, and walks through the living room toward his boy-smelling room, wincing when he notices the pile of food-crusted dishes on the coffee table. Erika's black hoodie on the floor. He stands fixed to the spot. He cannot decide if he should bring the dirty plates into the kitchen or wait until Erika comes out so he can tell her to clean up her mess.

Since the day he returned to this house he feels as if his ability to make decisions has been slowly ebbing out of him like blood from a wrist slit by someone not entirely sure they wanted to die. He tries to remember what those Malibu therapists taught him about taking control of his own life. As if by reflex he presses his thumb to his forefinger and whispers, "I control my own story." But does he? Has he ever, really, been in control?

For most of his life it his parents determined his every step. What to eat. What sports to play. Where to go to college. What to study. What job to take.

What decisions has he made?

It was his decision to allow a few of the guys to watch the quarry blast that day from what turned out to be an unsafe distance. He made that incredibly stupid decision simply because he was tired of eating takeout alone every night. Because he longed to be thought of as the cool boss.

If only he hadn't felt so rushed. If only his father hadn't been breathing down his back to clear another bench ASAP. If only he'd been out there with the team, making sure the drill holes were properly loaded with explosives. Making certain no one overloaded the stemming and then couldn't be bothered to go find some water to cool the holes off.

It'd happened before. Overloaded holes. Underloaded holes. Blasts that went awry. Blasts that didn't entirely dismantle the hill's face. Blasts that didn't detonate because someone didn't attach the wires correctly. But none of those blunders ever killed anyone.

But he didn't check. He didn't manage the blast like he was supposed to. Nor did he order everyone to put on their hard hats and go stand behind the metal shed before pressing the red button.

Nope, he'd stood out there with a half dozen men, because who doesn't love to see things get blown up? Oh, sure, he'd tried. "Hey, guys, we should clear out of—" he'd started to say, but then Craig Hinkley, his best front-loader operator and one of the funniest guys he knew, whined, "Aw, come on, Grant. We're fine."

And when the blasting whistle blew, they all froze, anticipating the rippling explosions like kids at a July Fourth picnic, their mouths forming O's of awe even before the rocks started flying.

And fly they did.

One of those rocks—a nineteen-inch chunk of earth traveling at four hundred miles an hour—crashed into Craig's face and upper chest, crushing them into a thousand bloodied and bony pieces on impact. A much smaller one slammed into Grant's left shoulder, instantly dislocating it and tearing the rotator cuff in two.

That incredibly stupid decision was soon followed by yet another. Given that Grant liked how the oxycodone his doctor prescribed for his pain made him feel, he *decided* he'd do whatever he had to do to keep his body humming with it.

Sighing, Grant begins to stack the dirty dishes, balancing them on his left forearm as if he were a waiter bringing meals to a table.

This makes him think of Deni.

Deni.

He hasn't spoken to her since the funeral. Hasn't even reached out to tell her how sorry he is about her friend's murder. Why is he so selfish? Deni rescued him that night when his father reminded everyone what a screwup Grant was. She'd grasped his hand under the table. Told him it would all be over soon. No, that's not what she said.

"What did she say?" Grant asks the silent living room.

And then he remembers. She'd promised it would get better.

What did she mean by that? What exactly would get better and how did she know?

CHAPTER

13

FIVE DAYS AFTER finding Luna Rose's body, we've still got nothing. I tip back the stained mug for the third time, knowing it's empty but still hoping there's one gulp left. There isn't. I grunt and go to stand up to get a fresh cup when my partner, Tom Horner, walks in. The look on his face signals another dead end.

Luna's iPhone was nowhere to be found and since we're still waiting for the records from AT&T, all we had to work with were the papers we found in her office and her laptop, which Colin, the IT guy, scoured for names, dates, anything worth pursuing. Luna had been careful not to leave any traces relating to the illegal side of her business, but one name kept popping up once a year for the last five years: Johnny Wonze, a mid-level pot dealer and known quantity to law enforcement in the Bay Area. I sent Tom down this morning to see if he could squeeze some information out of him.

"He's as innocent as a babe in the woods," Tom remarks when I ask him how the interview went. "He'd assumed he was going to buy her stash, same as always, but he hadn't yet heard from her this year. Alibi's tight too." Tom removes his jacket and loosens his tie. "He has no clue who any of her trimmers were, either."

I figured as much, but I'm getting tired of dead ends. My supposedly easy solve is turning into more of a brick wall. We'd rooted out the most conspicuous meth heads in both Prosperity and Gold Hills and tried to scare them into confessing. Nobody knew a thing. We talked to every CSA member who bought a share of Luna's farm products. Not a single person caused me or Tom to raise our eyebrows even a millimeter in suspicion. I had all ten of my fingers crossed when the Oregon police finally managed to track down Edie Russell and Jon Hollis, Luna's most recent farm employees, up in Eugene. We'd found their names in the records and their DNA in the Winnebago. They had motive. Easy access. An escape plan.

Contorting my fingers had proved utterly useless. They had nothing to do with the crime.

"What stone have we left unturned?" I ask Tom's back. He's hunched over the stack of investigation printouts. Every sliver of fact unearthed so far. I know what's in them—I've read through them a dozen times already. According to Vera, Luna had been dead five days. Forensics found no foreign DNA anywhere on the body. Nor, for that matter, any trace material not belonging to the victim or that could be linked to equipment on the farm. Because it'd rained between the time of death and time of discovery, the one vague footprint by the creek proved useless. We uncovered no tire tracks.

"I don't know, Torres," he says, arcing his head back to catch my eye. I lean close and now we're breathing each other's coffee-tainted air. He's got his finger pressed against one word written on the autopsy. Last time I read it my radar didn't feel the blip that would let me know it bore weight. I look at it again. This time, instead of passing through me like an X-ray, I catch a subtle change on my skin, like a breeze coming from the wrong direction.

"This," he says, "might be more relevant than we first thought."

CHAPTER

14

I CAN HEAR MY father's voice, but I can't make his words out through the staticky music roaring through my crappy dollar store earbuds. He must be asking for the seven hundredth time if I want something to eat. I click the volume up another notch and pull the quilt over my head. But he's not letting me escape this time because he yanks it down and yells loudly enough for me to make out, "The police are here!"

I spring upright and toss the earbuds onto the bed. "What?" I ask through the fog.

"They want to talk to you. Get up." He doesn't wait for me to respond before walking out of the room.

I stand up too quickly and almost faint. Taking a deep breath to steady myself, I consider changing into real clothing but get the feeling I shouldn't keep them waiting. I shuffle out to the living room where I see the policewoman from last week and another cop standing next to our black faux leather couch. They both turn to face me.

"Hello, Deni. Nice to see you again," the woman says. "This is Detective Tom Horner." I'm expecting one or both of them to reach across the couch and shake my hand, but neither offer. "Come have a seat, Deni," the woman says, gesturing to the black chair beside the television stand. I hate sitting in that chair. Like the couch, it's fake leather, but the couch at least is still in pretty good condition. The chair is cracked and peeling, and I know after I get up a piece of it will be stuck to the bottom of my pajama pants.

They sit down and I sit on the chair facing them. My father appears out of nowhere, and, since there is nowhere left to sit in the cramped room, he takes an awkward stance next to my chair. He's not sure what he's supposed to do, so he starts cracking the knuckles on his hands, which hang down at his sides. "Hey, Dad, can you get them some water?" I say, looking up and meeting his eyes.

"Yeah, sure," he says, more enthusiastically than necessary, and disappears.

I turn my attention to the two people on our couch. It's funny that the female cop looks only vaguely familiar. I mean, I know I met her, but I'm only just now seeing her as if for the first time. Like that piece of my past has been painted over.

They both look like they're in their late thirties, maybe early forties. She's bulky. Sturdy-looking. She's not pretty, but she's not unattractive either. She's got dark brown shoulder-length wavy hair devoid of any style. He's taller and thinner, with a crewcut. His eyes are remarkably blue. They are both dressed in the kind of cheap suits you see detectives wearing on television crime shows.

I'm vaguely conscious of how I must look and smell. I can barely recall anything that's happened since I talked to the female detective up at Luna's farm. I know I made it to my house where I stripped off my funeral clothes and put on my old flannel pajamas. And I know I made it to my bed, which is where I've been ever since. Other than taking small bites of the food my father leaves me or using the bathroom, I've been huddled underneath my quilt, coiled up into a writhing mass of rage and sadness ever since that horrible day. The second worst day of my entire existence.

"Deni," the female begins, "how are you doing?"

My brain is slushy, and I feel like I have the worst hangover on the planet. "I'm sorry, but can you tell me your names again?" I want to tack them to my memory board and stop thinking of them as the female and the male.

"Detective Robyn Torres and Detective Tom Horner," Torres says, pointing to herself and then her partner, which I find really funny because it's obvious who is who, but I don't laugh. I don't think I will ever laugh again.

"Well, Detective Torres, as you can probably guess, I'm not doing so great." I shift in my chair and the fabric makes a squeaky noise that any other time might have made me embarrassed, but at the moment I don't give a damn. I don't care that my pajama top is stained with food. I don't care that my hair looks like a family of squirrels is nesting in it. "My best friend was murdered on the same exact day I buried what was left of my fiancé." The moment that last word leaves my mouth I take a deep breath through my nose to keep from dry heaving.

"Actually, that's not true," Detective Horner says, abruptly leaning forward. "The M.E. thinks she was murdered on or around the thirtieth."

"The thirtieth? Then that means she wasn't found for . . ."

"Five days," Detective Torres replies, doing the math for me.

I'm shattered, thinking about my friend's body laying out there, exposed to the elements, left to rot like roadkill. I push the image away as Dad walks in carrying two glasses of water with ice and hands one to each of the detectives. After they thank him he again stands next to my chair, his hand perching like a pet bird on the top of it. "Have you caught the fuckers who did this yet?" he asks as if he's doing me a favor. As much as I know my father wants to support me through this nightmare, his very presence is making me antsy.

The detectives look at one another then back at me, not my father. "No, we have not," Horner says. "But we're not going to stop looking until we do."

"Deni." Torres stresses the D in my name like it's a bullet. Like she's about to shoot me with it. "We're trying to piece together what happened on the day Luna was murdered. According to her records, there was no CSA pickup scheduled. No deliveries were made to the property. None of the neighbors saw any unfamiliar cars on the road. As far as we can tell, you were the last person to see Luna alive. What can you tell us about that visit? You say it was . . ." She looks at her notes. "Either Saturday the twenty-third or Sunday, the twenty-fourth."

I nod so as to fill in the space while I try to recall which day it was. I usually work both weekend days—it's the busiest time at Marvin's and if I want the shifts, Sue is more than happy to offer them to me. What else had I done that day? Had I seen Cal or was he up at the quarry? Did we have plans? Before I let myself get wrapped up in missing Cal, I focus on Luna. She's the focus here. My grief is not. "I, uh, I'm really not sure if it was Saturday or Sunday. But why does it matter what day I saw her?"

"We're wondering," Horner begins, "if she mentioned that she was expecting someone or if she told you about plans she might have in the coming days."

I think through our conversation. "Let's see. We, um, we talked about the wedding. She mentioned that Edie and Jon split and when I asked her who was going to help her out with, you know"—I don't need to mention the illegal grow, do I?—"she said some people who'd helped out before were coming up." I straighten my back. "Could it have been them? Do you think maybe they killed her?"

Torres shakes her head. "Like I told you before, that's a no. They were the ones who found her."

The image of Luna being *found* rustles my inside. All I can do is nod. Okay, so not the trimmers.

"So, she said nothing at all about how she was feeling?" Torres asks.

"What do you mean?"

Horner sighs and a look passes between them that makes me feel like there are bugs crawling up my arm. I'm about to give it a quick scratch but stop with my hand midair when he asks, "Deni, did you know Luna was pregnant?"

The question shoots through the haze inside my head like an arrow through a cloud. "She was three months along," Torres adds before I can pull myself together enough to answer.

"No, I didn't," I say. I'm at a loss. I'm also hurt. Hurt that my friend didn't confide in me. Why would she not tell me?

Torres crosses one leg over another and offers me a sympathetic smile. She can tell that the news has thrown me. Wounded me. That I am the friend who wasn't let in on her friend's most intimate secret. "Any idea who the father was, Deni?"

I shake my head while simultaneously combing the depths inside it to figure out who it could have been. "There was no one in her life. I mean not anyone recently."

"What about less recently?" Horner asks.

"Yeah, last winter—I think the whole thing lasted a couple of months, if that—there was this guy Bodhi—I don't know his last name—hanging out with her on the farm. I mean, when I asked her what was going on with him she said he was 'just passing through.'" I don't tell them how relieved I'd been when I first saw her with Bodhi. I'd only just reconnected with Cal and was worried that us being together would make Luna angry or jealous. I was afraid she'd tell me it wasn't okay to go out with him. Maybe it was because she had Bodhi that she didn't care. Or maybe, like she said, she thought Cal was a jerk and she was truly over him. "I saw him up there maybe once or twice, but the next time I came up he was gone."

Horner writes something down in a notebook. Torres picks up the glass of water from the coffee table and takes a gulp. I watch her nod, like she's responding to some voice in her head. What is she not telling me? "Did you go through her phone? She must have texted the guy, right?" I ask.

"Her phone is still missing," Horner announces.

"What about her emails? Don't you have her computer?" I'm starting to panic. Who am I to tell the police how to do their job, but Jesus, how hard can it be to find out who impregnated Luna? "It can be anyone!"

"We are aware," Torres replies rather forcefully, like she wants me to know how frustrated she is. "We were hoping you knew so we wouldn't have to take DNA samples from every male she had contact with in the last four months."

"You have the baby's DNA?" I am sickened by the realization that whoever killed Luna also killed her baby.

"Of course," Horner says, standing. "We ran it through our system. So far there are no hits in CODIS."

Torres joins him, so I stand too. Are we done here? What does he mean by *no hits*? What the heck is CODIS? "Wait. Stop." I chase after them as they make their way to the front door like a kid who doesn't want her parents to leave her alone with the babysitter. "What does that mean?"

Torres turns. "It means that whoever the father is, he doesn't have a record. Never been fingerprinted. And there was no match to any DNA we found on the property."

"But . . . but . . ." I know there must be a way to find out. We have AI. The FBI. The CIA. Interpol. *Someone* smart must be able to figure this out. And then it hits me why they want to find the father. "You think maybe whoever the father is murdered her?"

Behind me, Dad cracks another knuckle.

Horner says, "We're not ruling it out."

"God, I wish I knew. I'm so sorry," I utter pathetically.

"Don't be, Deni," Torres says, putting a comforting hand on my shoulder. "If you can think of anything or anyone that might help the case, please get in touch."

"I will," I say with more force than I've managed to exert in days. Luna's murder and Cal's death have rendered me a useless zombie for too long. Now that I know about Luna's secret pregnancy, I decide it's time to act. Help find some answers. Hunkering down under my rancid quilt isn't doing anyone's memory any good. "I will," I repeat into the wind as I watch the detectives' car back out of the driveway.

CHAPTER

15

GRANT SLIPS OUT of the house and heads into the forest behind the house. It takes him close to ten minutes of scrambling down a steep, heavily treed hillside trail before he finally reaches the site. He stands next to a surveyor's stake delineating the northeast side of the property boundary and looks around. He gets why Cal and Deni chose this particular spot to build their house. For now there's not much to see, but once the trees are cleared, the eastern and western views of the rolling valleys will be magnificent. They wouldn't be looking down over Gold Hills like his parents could from their bedroom window, but maybe that wouldn't have been such a bad thing.

He squats down and sticks a pine needle in his mouth. It's a funny thing that all the time he spent running around the land, exploring its secrets, it never once occurred to Grant that he might want to settle here. Build a house. Raise a family. It'd always been his parents' place, a place he couldn't wait to leave.

But not Cal. Once he and Deni got married, Cal intended to stay permanently. Right here in this spot. Grant's little brother didn't worry about being so close to the old man. He didn't fear their father's rage because it was rarely ever directed at him. But that's only because Calvin Senior never knew the truth about his precious Junior. He had no idea what his second-born was capable of, and no matter how hard Grant tried to make his parents see through the veneer, the shine on their golden boy remained bright up until the second all three of their bodies were destroyed on impact.

Grant knows he should be grieving his brother's death, but when he remembers the hell he lived through, it's tough to feel much. Growing up, Cal had hatched some pretty good ways to stick it to Grant. He thinks back to the time when Cal made him kill a toad they found while playing in this forest. Cal had forced Grant to cover it in lighter fluid and set it on fire, threatening to tell the kids at school that Grant still wet his bed if he didn't do it. When they got home, Cal ran to their parents and told them what his big brother had just done. Their father blew a gasket, and to teach his son a lesson he made Grant ride shotgun for a whole day with the County Animal Control Officer who was in charge of scraping dead animals off the roads. The images of those oozing guts and squished brains gave Grant nightmares for months.

When they were in high school, there was this guy, Tom Natali, who, for some reason Cal decided he hated. Grant didn't know Tom all that well, and he never had any beef with him. He was a slight kid, with an effeminate way of walking and talking. He had lots of female friends, and Grant just assumed the dude was gay, not that he cared about such things. One day, just as Grant was passing Tom in the hallway, Cal came running down from the other direction and out the blue he grabbed Tom by the collar of his shirt and bashed his head into the lockers, the sound of skull hitting metal jarring enough to stop everyone in their tracks. Cal was yelling in Tom's face, "You just called my brother a *retard*. Don't you ever fucking call him that again, asshole, or next time I'll kill you!"

Naturally, Cal had come off looking like a hero sticking up for his less-popular big brother. Grant doesn't remember Tom uttering a word to him as they passed one another, let alone even looking in his direction.

Cal received two days' detention for his actions. Tom suffered a concussion, and as if that wasn't bad enough, the poor guy lost most of his friends too.

Yeah, his little brother had been a piece of shit.

Grant spits out the needle, the bitter taste lingering on his tongue, and stands up. Maybe he should build the house and move in? The plans have already been approved by the city. The permits are probably close to being ready. He certainly has the funds to get it done.

The problem with that idea is that Erika loves the big house. She thinks a remodel and some new furniture are all it will take to make it their own. But Grant isn't so sure. He glances up the hill toward his childhood home. He can't see it from here, but he can still feel it. Feel its looming presence like a giant's hand on the back of his neck.

He'd just as soon burn it to the ground.

Grant looks at his phone. He doesn't want to be late so he hustles up the slope and, once he's clear of the trees, breaks into a trot across the green expanse. By the time he makes it to the backyard he's out of breath.

He can no longer get into his own house through the sliding door off the kitchen because the construction guys have already removed it. In its place are two big sections of plywood—soon to be replaced by a set of fancy French doors. Through the plywood he can hear their voices mixed in among hammering and sawing and the low staticky hum of a radio turned to an AM news station.

Grant walks past the garage and around to the front of the house just as Deni's car circles the fountain and comes to a stop. When she steps out of the car he isn't sure if he should hug her, but she immediately hugs him.

"Hi, Grant," she says. "It's really good to see you."

"You too."

"What's with all the trucks?" she asks, nodding toward the line of pickups at the far end of the driveway.

"We're remodeling." He looks at the ground when he tells her this, having no idea how he will answer the question he knows is about to follow.

"What? But, Grant, they . . . I mean, it's only been—"

"I know." He knows it's been just a few weeks since his brother and parents died in a plane crash. He knows, objectively, that it looks bad that he's already dismantling their home, but he doesn't feel like he has much say in the matter. "It wasn't my choice," he utters.

"What do you mean? Is Erika *making* you do this?"

He shrugs. "Yeah, I guess so." He wishes he could tell Deni that it's far easier giving in to Erika's wishes than fighting against them. He'd love to have someone to confide in, share how down he's been feeling about everything. But Deni has enough going on. Who is he to burden her with his own shit? "Erika really hates the interior of the house, and she asked if she could, you know, make a few changes, and it's not like I ever thought it was nice," he says, hoping to spin some positivity into the decision. "So I said, 'Sure. Knock yourself out.'"

"It's your house, Grant. Not hers." She crosses her arms as if fending off some invisible foe. As if defending Grant from Erika.

"Well, we are technically a couple, so, I guess you could say it's hers too."

Deni shakes her head. "Whatever. It's still your house."

In an effort to change the subject, he's about to tell her that he just went down to the building site and thinks it's a really cool spot, but instantly bites back the words. Man, he really needs to focus on the present moment. Reminding Deni what she lost when that plane crashed is about the stupidest thing he could do.

"Is this why you asked me to come up today? Because you're remodeling Cal's room?"

He says nothing.

"Great. Just great. Here, I thought you were just being nice—like you thought maybe I wanted to go through some of his things because I loved him. But that wasn't it, was it? You and your girlfriend are going to gut his room, aren't you?"

Grant nods but keeps his eyes fixed on the ground.

"Fuck this. Is she here? If she's here, I'll come back another time."

The whole reason Grant asked Deni to come today was because he knew Erika was not going to be home. He doesn't understand the discord between the two women, but he doesn't actually care. It's like an ingrown hair on his face he chooses not to pick at. "No, she went down to San Francisco." After visiting the two furniture stores in Gold Hills, Erika had deemed their wares "too hick," and she said she preferred to shop where people with money and good taste shopped. She wanted him to go with her; said they'd make an adventure out of it, but Grant was quick to make up an excuse about meeting with his lawyer so he wouldn't have to tag along. He had no interest in wandering showrooms.

"She won't be back until tonight."

"Awesome," Deni says, moving past him toward the house. When she reaches the steps she turns around. "You coming with or what?"

Grant has no burning desire to ever step inside his dead brother's room again. He just wants Deni to pick through Cal's stuff and get out. "Nah, you go ahead," he says, not meeting her eyes.

Deni doesn't move. He senses her staring at him. Judging him. He feels guilty enough for letting Erika disembowel what's left of his family's memories. Least he can do is pretend to care about what was left behind. When he finally looks over at her, he can't tell if the expression on her face is anger or disappointment.

Probably both.

CHAPTER

16

THE HOUSE SMELLS like sawdust and burning metal. I'm tempted to push past the huge sheets of plastic hanging in front of the kitchen just to see what they're doing. Even though I agree that the interior of the house is as tasteless as a tract home, I'm still disturbed by Erika's aggressive insistence it be remodeled so soon after the family's death.

I follow Grant down the hallway to Cal's room and stop before I enter. Although he was a twenty-eight-year-old man, Cal's parents strictly forbade him from allowing anyone to stay the night. Even after we got engaged, they wouldn't let me sleep over or, for that matter, hang out in his bedroom with him when I came for a visit. When I'd questioned him early on in our relationship why on earth he still lived at home, he'd gotten defensive, telling me it'd be a waste of money to rent a place in Gold Hills or Tahoe, given how expensive everything is. "Besides," he'd said, "I've existed on ramen and takeout most of my adult life.

I'm over it, you know? I love my mother's cooking. I mean, you've got to admit, it's a pretty cush spot."

There was no way I was going to let him stay over at my house. The one and only time I invited him in before one of our dates I felt like a kid showing off a dead rat at show and tell. I could see the doubt and disappointment in his eyes. After that, I just waited out front.

It was only when his parents were gone from the house that I was permitted a sneak peek into my lover's personal space. Since Jean "worked" from her home office, that was rarely. I had no idea what it was that Jean did and when I questioned Cal he'd shrugged. "She's on lots of committees and shit. I guess maybe she writes letters? Fills in her calendar? Fuck if I know."

As I step into Cal's old room, my heart crumbles into tiny pieces. The first—and only—time Cal and I ever made love was in this room. On that bed.

I go over to it now and sit, running my hand across the black polyester quilt. I look around the walls, covered in blown-up photos from Cal's sparse claims to fame. There's the cover of the *Teen Vogue* issue he appeared in. And the movie poster for *Ryan's Cause*. There's also some of the headshots he used for auditions. In one of the shots he comes across as a shy, sweet boy-next-door. In another, he's an all-out sexy hunk whose bones are just crying out to be jumped.

I think I fell in love with both of those men.

"I have his phone," Grant says, snapping me out of my reverie.

"What?"

"The NTSB mailed it when they sent the preliminary crash report."

My thoughts, already flooded with memories, get snagged in a tangle of disturbing images. "His phone? How did they—?"

"They retrieved a couple of personal items that weren't completely destroyed. Cal's phone was one of them. Oh, and Nugget's collar." He shuffles his feet and laughs. "Anyway, I got the box yesterday," he says, handing me the phone.

I take it from him. The screen is so cracked it looks like it's been overlaid with a spider web. "Does it work?" I ask quickly. I want to see if Cal texted me before he died. If maybe he had a few seconds before the crash to say that he loved me but never got a chance to hit the blue arrow.

"I don't see why not. But, hey, Deni. Can you maybe deal with that later? I mean, just in case, you know. I mean, you should take whatever." He begins to pace, nervously. I watch him go over to the closet and open it. "You probably want some of his clothes, yeah? And what about those?" He points to the shelf lined with gold-plated soccer and baseball trophies. "I mean, we're just gonna toss them."

I wince slightly at his words. Grant and Erika are going to *toss them*. They plan to get rid of Cal's past, present, and future to make way for their new lives. I want to scream at Grant for his coldheartedness, but I don't know how to gather my emotions into a string of words that will make sense. "I know you guys weren't close, Grant, but this is pretty harsh, don't you think?"

"What's harsh, Deni? Throwing out some stupid trophies. Letting you take his shirts?"

I shake my head. "No, I don't mean that. I'm just saying, maybe there's something here you want to keep, like for old time's sake? Something of Cal's that, I don't know—will keep his memory alive."

When Grant chuckles at my words, I realize that I don't really know the real Grant Cooper. In high school I saw him as a quiet but ultimately nice person who had no choice but to languish in the shadows cast by his popular younger brother. Sometimes I found it hard to believe the two of them were even related. The randomness of genetics is an amazing thing. They were only two years apart but you would've thought they were no more part of the same family tree than a pine and a hawthorn.

Even when Cal insisted Luna keep me and other Spurs out of his friend group, Grant, at least, tried to be sympathetic to those of us who loitered in the corners. When he passed me in the hallways or noticed me in the cafeteria, he'd always raise his chin an inch or two in my direction, acknowledging my existence. Once he waved and asked me how I was doing. I'd said, "Great" but was so stunned that one of the Cooper boys was actually talking to me, I didn't get around to asking him how he was doing.

After he graduated, I pretty much never thought about him again. Sometimes, when I was hearting one of Cal's Instagram posts, Grant's face would pop into my head and I'd wonder what he was up to. If he had found his one true love; someone who could see how big his heart was. He wasn't on social media anywhere, and Cal never once mentioned him. I assumed he was working at one of the family quarries. Or, maybe, like Cal did when he moved to Los Angeles, Grant went into another field altogether.

It was only when I saw him come out of Deez Yellen's house late one night that I knew exactly what Grant was up to. I had no idea why he was suddenly hanging out with the guy next door or why his arm was in a sling. He hadn't seen me see him, and I was too shocked to yell over to him. Then, a few weeks later I pulled into the 7-Eleven on the outskirts of Prosperity to pick up some beer for my father and saw Grant standing outside drinking a huge purple Slurpee. There were two other guys with him, and all three of them looked dirty and drunk or stoned out of their minds. I'd sat in the parking lot watching them for a while. Every time another customer went in or out of the store, the three guys would harass them verbally. I couldn't hear what they were saying, but given the fear on the customers' faces, it couldn't have been pleasant.

Not long after that Grant stumbled into Marvin's one morning while I was working. By then it was clear he'd reached the bottom of whatever hole he was trying to climb down into. He smelled awful. His eyes were all glassy, and his whole body shook like he'd just come off a crazy carnival ride. I watched him limp over to the counter, and when he tried to sit down on one of the stools, he just fell over. Sue came out and immediately called the cops.

And then poof, he was gone. I figured he was in jail, but Sue Marvin found out through her accountant, who was friends with Geri, the Coopers' office manager, that Grant had been sent off to a fancy rehabilitation center in Southern California.

While Grant was getting clean, Cal walked into Marvin's to get an egg sandwich, and soon after that he became my world. It wasn't until our third date—at Pietro's Pizza—that he told me about what happened in Wadsworth. About it being Grant's fault a man died. "He really fucked up," Cal had said after telling me the whole sad story. I could almost understand why Grant turned to drugs. It's the same reason my father turned to alcohol. Tragic deaths can force a person to do tragic things. Self-annihilation is an easy alternative to reality if reality sucks. "My parents were just going to let him rot on the street. Die there. They were so angry with him. So embarrassed. They'd even written him out of the will."

"So why'd they change their minds?"

"I changed their minds. I was working down in Sunnyvale at the time and I'd gotten a call from my old agent. She said some indie movie producer was thinking of casting me in a film he just got funding for. I called my folks to tell them the news, and, shit, I honestly didn't even know how bad it was with Grant. I mean, some of my friends told me they saw him on the street and he was in rough shape and stuff, but I wasn't really focused on him, you know? I had my own life to worry about. Anyway, I tell my dad about this film thing and that's when he tells me about what's going on with Grant. How he'd basically hit bottom and they were done with him."

"Done?"

"Yeah, he said, 'I guess now both my boys will be dead to me.'"

"What the hell?" What kind of parent says that to their kid? Of course, once I'd gotten to know the Coopers, it was easy to understand that it's the Cooper kind of parent who says such a thing.

"So I'm like, 'Dad, you need to get him clean. Get him into rehab.'"

"And?"

Cal had looked out the window of the truck. By now we were parked outside Pietro's and he still hadn't started the engine. "I knew they wanted me back here. My father was already thinking about retirement and he needed me to be in Gold Hills, learning more about running the company. I made a deal with them. Said I'd forget about the movie and move back home but only if they got Grant into rehab."

Grant's addiction to drugs was the reason Cal came back to Gold Hills. Back to me.

I watch Grant walk over to the bookshelf and pick up one of the trophies, fingering it with his thumb. I think about telling Grant the story. He should know that his little brother sacrificed his own dreams for him. But when I see him casually toss it in the trash basket next to the desk, I stay silent.

It's as if the death of his entire family has hardened him. I could be wrong; this might be the way he's grieving. Or maybe the rehabilitation place in Malibu changed him. But what most likely changed him was Erika. There is nothing warm and fuzzy about that woman. It's clear that Grant is obsessed with her. Why else would he let her purge his parents and brother from this house without putting up a fight?

"Did you not love them at all?" I ask quietly.

Grant looks over at me with such hurt in his eyes, I almost regret asking my question.

"I don't know how to answer that, Deni," he replies before walking over to the door. "I've gotta go check on the guys. Take whatever you want."

CHAPTER 17

I'M SITTING ON my bed, wearing one of Cal's flannel shirts and my pajama bottoms, staring at his cracked iPhone. I need the passcode, dammit. I thought I knew it—I'd seen him enter his birthdate a dozen times. After that didn't work, I tried my birthday, to no avail. Now I'm panicking that I'll be locked out permanently. I only get four more tries.

"Shit," I mutter under my breath. *Why did he change his passcode?*

I hear my father slam the front door and walk into the kitchen. He opens the refrigerator and the sound of one glass bottle striking another rings out. I toss the phone onto my nightstand and go out to see how he is. Ever since I lost both my fiancé and best friend to violent deaths, Dad's been a lot kinder. He's been like the old Joe Rydell, the loving father who held my hand when we crossed the street. Who explained how airplanes fly and showed me how to use his tools, laughing when the drill turned on and I screamed in horror from the sudden vibration. The Joe Rydell who worshipped my mother. Who danced with her in the tiny living room whenever "their song" played on the radio.

"Hey, Dad," I say, walking into the kitchen. He's downed half a Bud and is leaning his elbows on the counter, staring at something out the window over the large white farm sink. He turns around and politely stifles a burp before asking me how my day was. It's not an empty question. He notices me these days. Every morning since I've returned to work at Marvin's, there's been a piece of buttered toast and a cup of coffee waiting for me. There's still a space between us, taken up by a sadness too big to burst through, but he's clearly making an effort to keep me propped up.

I tell him about going to Grant's. About Erika remodeling the house.

"She's moving in fast and furious," he states, shaking his head. "I didn't like her. At the funeral, I mean. There's something crooked about her."

I open the cabinet next to the fridge and take out a bag of Goldfish. "I know. She's got Grant wrapped around her finger," I say through a mouthful of salty cheesy bits. "It's like the accident never happened. He's already forgotten his family and now he's moving on."

At that moment I suddenly remember something Grant said. "Hey, are preliminary crash reports made public?" I ask.

"Of course. The NTSB releases them as soon as they're written." Dad gets a worried look on his face. "Hold on,

Deni. You don't need to go poking around in that," he says. "It's not gonna bring him back."

"I know it's not going to bring Cal back. I just want to know *why* it happened."

He takes another swig. Swallows. "Stupidity is why it happened."

I pause, my hand halfway into the Goldfish bag. "You read the report?"

"Of course." He shrugs and heads into the living room. "They departed from Washington Regional. Management was notified the moment it posted."

I follow after him. "Then why didn't you tell me?" I have my hands on my hips as I watch him throw himself onto the couch and reach for the remote. "No. Don't turn it on," I demand as I plant myself in front of the TV. I catch him turning his head ever so slightly to the right. Since he's half blind on his left side I know it's his subtle way of blocking me out.

"Fine! If you won't tell me I'll just go read it on my own," I grumble as I storm off toward my room, stopping when he yells, "Come back here now!"

I walk back and lower myself down onto the crappy chair across from the couch. A shard of material pokes at my pajama pants so I wiggle in the seat until I find a smooth surface, then turn my attention on my father, who is now focused on me with both his eyes.

"Listen. Um. Deni," he says so hesitantly I think for a moment he's going to change his mind. "You don't need to be seeing the details of the crash. There's just a bunch of technical stuff about weather and broken fuselage. And . . . some other things." He wipes his hand across his mouth. "Anyway. It won't do you or your heart any good to have those pictures in your head. Understand?"

What *other things* is he talking about? Do they describe what the bodies looked like? I definitely don't want to read about that. Not yet. Maybe not ever.

"Plus, just so we're clear, it's not a final report. They're still investigating the crash."

"Okay."

He downs the remainder of the bottle and leans forward onto his dirty black pants, smeared with grease stains. Shakes his head. "They report says the probable cause is 'Continued VFR flight into IMC.'"

I stare at him. "And that means . . . ?"

He sighs. "VFR means the pilot isn't instrument rated—he uses only visual cues."

"And IMC?"

"Instrument meteorological conditions," he states matter-of-factly. When he again sees the blank look on my face he continues. "Okay, so, to put it plain and simple: from what I can tell from the prelim is the pilot failed to get an updated weather report and flew into some bad weather. I'm guessing they hit ice, tried to descend, but he lost control of the aircraft and, well, that's pretty much it." He sits back, looking as defeated as I feel.

Failure to get an updated weather report? "That means it's Calvin's fault! He crashed the plane because of bad weather?" Rage burns through my chest. What, was Calvin Cooper too lazy, too *entitled*, to bother checking the goddamn forecast? I cover my face with my hands and scream up toward the ceiling, "That fucking asshole. I can't believe this. I can't believe he killed Cal."

Dad clears his throat. I can almost feel his good eye staring at me, but I don't lower my head. "What?" I say.

"Calvin Senior wasn't flying the plane, sweetheart. Cal was."

CHAPTER

18

I PULL UP BY the house and get out of the car. The air no longer smells fresh, dense with greenery and life. The early morning wind that rustles by smells rotten, like a bucket of compost that's been left out in the sun.

I stare out at the fields where I last saw Luna surrounded by flowers. I close my eyes and will the past to return, for time to fold in on itself. My friend is alive. We are laughing together on the bench. Discussing what flowers will adorn my wedding bouquet.

At the sound of my name being said, my vision fades into vapor. I turn around and see Luna's mother Misha, her arms outstretched. I walk into them and let her envelop me. The smell of her, a mix of musk and lavender and something citrusy, is overwhelmingly familiar and calming. We stand quietly together like that for a long time. When she finally releases me, she repeats my name. "Deni," she says softly. "I'm so happy to see you."

Her daughter's throat was slit by some crazed asshole and she's happy to see me?

I'd expected her to break down in hysterics in front of me. Instead, her tanned face is peaceful. Almost joyful. "I'm happy to see you too," I utter clumsily.

"Come in."

I step inside and wait while she walks into the kitchen, returning a moment later holding two glasses of water with lemon slices floating in them. "Thank you," I say, as my glass and I follow her into the living room where the smell of long-burned incense and freshly dug soil linger, like a memory. Over the years, whenever I'd hang out at Luna's house these magical scents would follow me home on my clothing. Even after tossing my shirts and pants onto the floor of my room, the dark earthy smells would continue to perfume the air like an invisible diffuser. Sometimes I'd wear the same clothes I'd worn to Luna's to school the next day, even if they were dirty, just so I could keep smelling that smell. I'd imagine that people passing me in the hallways or sitting near me in a classroom would somehow see me differently. Like they would think that I, too, lived an enchanted life in a house filled with beautiful art and cozy furniture.

The walls of the living room are painted in soft muted earthy tones of tans and rusts. Overgrown houseplants soften every corner. The leaves of a huge ivy tumble down over the shelves of a teak bookcase, obstructing the small framed photograph of me and Luna taken on the day of our high school graduation. I have the same photograph on my bookshelf. We'd decorated our mortarboards with silly stickers and dried flowers and had huge matching grins. I am at once sad and grateful that the green tangles hide my dead friend's smile.

I sit down on the large beige cotton sofa, trying to keep from sinking into the softness of it. I don't deserve to be comfortable, I think, as I watch Misha lower herself into a cross-legged position on the Indian rug in one fluid motion. She sips her water like a kitten.

"I'm so sorry," I say. *Why are you not writhing in agony over the death of your only child?*

"Thank you," she replies. "It was too early for her to leave us."

"Um. She . . ." I cannot get anything else past my lips.

"She was loved, is what she was," Misha says through a deep sigh. "Did you see the farmstand?"

I nod. It was impossible to miss the massive piles of notes and bouquets. After I'd driven through the gate, I'd stopped and stared out the passenger window at the makeshift memorial and almost got out, just to see if maybe I could find a clue in all those notes. Had the murderer, I wondered, left something, just for the sick thrill of it?

"She was more than just loved," I say as I look into my glass. I can't meet her eyes. I'm suddenly annoyed with Luna's mother for being gone for so long. For missing out on seeing the thriving business her daughter created. Misha left Gold Hills because she said she wanted to discover more of her spiritual self. Sure, but she also left her child.

"I know, Deni."

"Then, why aren't you—" I cannot find the right words to finish my question. I'm not even sure what I want to ask.

Everyone deals with loss in their own ways. Look at Grant. He's redecorating his house. My father drinks himself numb every night. And me? How am I dealing with the loss of the two most important people in my life? If I were to be perfectly honest with myself, I'd say I'm not dealing. I'm just acting. Moving forward, like a dark-hearted shark through a deep, dark abyss. Going about my days, distracting myself with work and errands. Making feeble promises to the universe that I will somehow AVENGE MY FRIEND.

The other day Sue Marvin took me aside before my shift began and asked if I was seeing a grief counselor. I'd just stared at her, blankly.

"You know when Bob passed, I was so lost, Deni," she said gently. "I had no idea what to say to people when they asked me how I was doing. Like I'd forgotten how to speak English. What got me through the pain," she continued, "was GHGG—the Gold Hills Grief Group. We meet at seven thirty the first Tuesday of every month at the high school."

"Okay, good to know," I said, quickly whipping around and heading into the storeroom where I tossed my pack and switched off my phone. I knew where she was heading, and I had no interest in sharing my sorrow with a bunch of widows and widowers. It felt to me like I was being invited to a haunted potluck where everyone brings a dish no one else wants to touch.

I've been focusing all my extra energy on Luna instead of Cal. Thinking about what I lost when that plane went down is, for now, too scary, too strenuous for my heart or brain to handle. At some point I'll have to face up to the realization that I am not ever going to be rich. I am not ever going to live in a gorgeous house surrounded by acres of silence. I will most likely spend the rest of my days serving eggs over easy and having to listen to the sounds of rumbling old engines bursting through my windows.

God, I am so tired. I take a drink of water and place my glass on a side table. I want to get the ceremony over with already and go home. I want to crawl back under my covers and pretend nothing has changed. I'm about to suggest we get started when Misha gets up and sits next to me.

"Darling Deni. I know you're having a tough time. But you must be willing to embrace impermanence." I am not entirely following her, but I don't take my eyes from hers. I latch on to their intensity as though they are a lifeline. She takes my hand in hers and begins to massage it "We are all going to die, Deni. It was their time. There is nothing you or I can do to change that."

I push off the sofa and stand in the middle of the room just as Bernie struts in and flops onto his back. I pick him up and hold him close. "I'm sorry, Misha, but I don't think I want to *embrace* death. Cal died because he was too stupid to check the weather before he flew his plane into ice. Luna died because—because she was trying to grow something beautiful out of this place and some drugged-out douchebags decided her life *and* her baby's life weren't worth—" I stop speaking when I see Misha's face. "Did you know she was pregnant?"

"I did, yes. The police told me when they interviewed me." She's nervously fingering the silver charm that hangs off her necklace. "And they mentioned that no one knows who the father is, not even you."

"No. I don't. Luna didn't . . . I mean she never . . ." I drop Bernie and sit down on the couch again, keeping a larger space between us this time. "She honestly didn't say anything to you either?"

Misha shakes her head.

"Did you go through her stuff?" I picture Luna's bedroom, the walls still painted the same bright lavender they were when we first met. Lavender was her favorite color. After Misha left for Bali five years ago I thought Luna would move into her mother's large bedroom with its own bathroom, but she preferred to stay in the room she'd slept in since she was born.

"The police did a thorough search of the entire property," Misha says, grimacing. "In fact, the house was pretty wrecked. I had to sage every room."

I nod sympathetically although I can't pretend to imagine what it'd feel like to know there were strangers going through my personal belongings, let alone my dead daughter's private stuff. All those latex-wrapped fingers rifling around all that remained of a beautiful life.

"What about her phone?" I ask suddenly. "There must be something. Texts? Calls?"

"I'm guessing the detectives didn't find anything questionable," Misha replies, frowning, "because all they told me was that they did retrieve the records."

"I don't get it. You'd think she'd be over the moon about being pregnant, or, I don't know, maybe she was confused? Maybe whoever the guy was didn't want it and she was . . .

jeez, I just don't understand." I'm thinking so hard, shuffling through so many crazy possibilities that my head begins to hurt. "I mean, three months is too late for an abortion so we know she wanted it, right? And if that's true, then why would she not have told us?" My face burns with confusion.

"I'm not sure we'll ever know the answer to that, Deni. Well," Misha says as she abruptly stands up. "I think it's time to send Luna and her baby on their way."

* * *

Misha and I walk along the farm path running between the rows of dead plants in silence. She's holding what's left of Luna in both hands. I'm surprised by how big the box is—given how slight my friend was. I had no idea ashes could take up so much room.

Once the neglected fields peter out, we pass through a grove of scraggly oaks. Misha, who is dressed all in white, slows her steps on the uneven ground, careful not to drop her daughter. Soon the trees thin and we are in a grassy clearing that slopes down toward the sunny rectangular patch of land where Luna grew her illegal plants. Coyote Creek, a fast-moving tributary of the Osborne River, lies just beyond.

I'm so fixated on the dirt and leaves stuck to the bottom of Misha's long skirt in front of me and the pulsing drum of the creek in the distance that at first I don't even notice the shredded pieces of yellow police tape flapping loosely from a stake. But as soon as I do, I stop. "I can't go down there," I whisper while Misha continues down the hill, passing right by the spot where Luna's life came to a sudden and violent end. I stare at the ground next to the tape, imagining there's an indent where her body lay before it was found. My brain tricks me into seeing blood mixed in with the dark soil. There—her head was right there! She died there!

"Deni," Misha says, forcing my eyes away. "Join me, please."

This is so surreal, to be in a place that is at once familiar and, at the same time, so hostile. I'm totally creeped out and, as much as I loved Luna, I can't wait for this . . . whatever *this* is to be over.

Misha places the box of ashes down on the bank of the creek, looks up and starts singing something toward the sky. I can hardly hear her because the creek is really loud, but I'm pretty sure whatever she's saying is in another language.

She then lowers herself down into a cross-legged position and begins to chant. I have no idea if I'm supposed to join her on the ground or just stand where I am and listen. I don't understand why she couldn't have had a normal funeral. Then, at least, there could have been other people around. When she called me two days ago to ask me to scatter Luna's ashes with her I'd assumed there'd be an actual service first, and I wanted to know when and where it would be, but she said she had no intention of freeing her daughter's spirit among strangers.

"Just the two people who loved her the most will bear witness to her soul being set free," she'd said. "I hope you can come."

So, here I am, standing around like a dork, listening to Misha chant and sway. There's no way I'm going to chant along with her, so I begin to wander down along the bank, watching the water gurgle and jump over the rocks and branches jutting up from the creek bed. I come to a bend and follow it around, almost tripping on a huge tree root bulging up from the ground. The further I stroll the softer Misha's "oms" become, and I am suddenly worried that Misha might be getting close to the ash-tossing part. As much as I don't want to touch the burned-up bones of my friend, I feel obliged to at least be there when Luna's spirit flies away.

I start to head back, and this time I slow as I come to the tree root and notice something odd protruding from beneath it. I reach down and pull out a fat leafy branch of what is clearly a marijuana plant. The once-shiny green leaves and oily buds are now totally dried out and crusty, but it is definitely pot. The end of the branch has been cleanly cut. With a very sharp edge. I look up and scan the area for more branches, and holy shit, there, on the other side of the creek, I see the top half of another large shoot of marijuana trapped under a boulder, swaying and moving with the rush of the current. Without thinking, I wade into the rushing water.

CHAPTER 19

TOM AND I are just walking into the station when Elise, the lobby receptionist, who's got a phone pressed to her ear, holds up her hand, indicating she needs us to wait. I grunt my annoyance. We've just spent an hour chasing a lead left on the tip line by someone who saw a suspicious red truck with a camper shell parked at the Prosperity Inn. The caller said the windows were blacked out, and, from his last count, at least ten people had gone in and out of room number 14.

It sounded promising enough, given the timing. It's been more than three weeks since Luna's plants were poached. Knowing that it'd take about two weeks to dry out the weed, plus another week to trim and package it for resale, Tom and I figured Luna's weed would be hitting the streets just about now.

Of course, that's assuming the people who did the robbing and killing are locals.

I'd pulled into the Prosperity Inn lot, parking between two barely discernable white lines and cut the engine. Before settling in, Tom and I took a quick look around. Over by the concrete stairs a trash can overflowed with fast-food wrappers. Half the numbers on the doors were either missing or drawn on with a black Sharpie. Calling this place an "inn" was like calling a Bud Light a microbrew. Back when I was a teenager roaming the streets of Prosperity, my friends and I skirted this part of town. We were especially careful not to go anywhere near the Prosperity Inn. Too bad some things never change.

Less than fifteen minutes after parking, we watched a beater car loaded with twentysomethings pull up in front of number 14. When they all got out of the car Tom and I exchanged a puzzled look. If it was drugs they were after it seemed pretty bizarre for all four of them to go in, but still we waited. If they were in and out in less than ten minutes, we knew we were probably witnessing something illegal.

Ten more minutes and no one appeared. "Welp, I'm guessing the guy who called it in is some bored old man with nothing better to do than stare out his window," Tom said, gazing over his left shoulder. Directly across the street from the inn were two three-story Section 8 housing units. All of them had large picture windows that faced this lot. "You want to check it out anyway?"

"Sure, why not," I said, reaching for the handle.

Seven minutes later we got back in the car. The room was occupied by the five members of Rufus, an indie band that drove down from Humboldt to perform tonight in Gold Hills. Not only was the room filled with musical instruments, there were a least half a dozen groupies and old friends from the area who'd been stopping by to say their hellos. Sure, there was definitely some weed in there, but not any weed I cared about.

All I want to do now is head back to my desk and check to see if the National DNA Index System had found any matches with Luna's fetus. Instead, Tom and I shuffle around waiting for Elise to fill us in on the holdup. But then, just when I'm about to bolt, the bathroom door to my left opens up and out walks Deni Rydell. What I notice first is that the bottom of her pants are damp. Then I see the two large branches clutched in her fist.

CHAPTER

20

GRANT IS BORED. And bored is a bad thing to be. For the past few weeks he's done nothing. Sometimes he went downtown and signed papers, either at his lawyer's office or the headquarters of C. G. Cooper & Sons Aggregates. Sometimes he trekked down to Cal and Deni's house site and wandered around while chewing on pine needles and taking in the view. Sometimes he drove through Prosperity, slowing down as he passed by Deez Yellen's house and wondering if the dude was even still alive.

And sometimes he is tasked with making ridiculous decisions. Like yesterday, when Erika pestered him to choose a paint color for the bathroom off the kitchen. He tried to take his time, to prolong the minutes he spent considering the different shades, but after about ten minutes of staring at the swatches she'd taped up to the walls, he gave up. They all looked the same to him. Was there really that much of a difference between Lulworth Blue and Kittiwake Blue? He didn't think so.

Although he didn't say as much. In fact, he's learned it's best to keep his opinions about Erika's tastes to himself. That she's turning his childhood home into an issue of *Architectural Digest* doesn't bother him. The house *was* ugly. But it was also comfortable.

These days, if he wants to watch TV in the newly decorated living room, he has to sit on an $18,000 gray velvet couch that feels like he's sitting on a padded park bench. There's no give to the cushioning and before he even sits down he must toss nine—nine!—pillows onto the floor to make room for his butt. He is not allowed to rest his feet on the glass coffee table. And he must always remember to use the granite coasters, lest he get barked at.

As annoying as the changes are, stiff furniture and blue walls are a small price to pay for having a woman in his life. Especially one who wakes him most mornings with her mouth on his dick.

Today has been no different. This morning, after a quick blow job (he really does need to learn how to hold on longer), he tried to make love to Erika, but she was up and in the shower before he could reach out for her. So he lay back in the new bed in his parents' old room and stared out the window. If only he had a job to go to, he mused. He'd have people to talk to. Things to fill his day. The last time Geri needed him to come down to the main office to sign yet another bunch of papers was more than a week ago. After he signed his name she informed him that operations at all the quarries were running status quo. He didn't care, but she'd felt the need to go through each of the sites, listing off production stats that flew by him like the wind.

When she'd finished her spiel, Grant thanked her and was just about to get up to go back home when Geri point blank asked him when he planned to step into his father's role as president and CEO and take command of the business.

The truth of the matter was that Grant wasn't certain he ever wanted to step into his father's shoes. What would it feel like to sit in the old man's whiskey-smelling office and oversee the ebb and flow? The idea of it made his stomach turn. Sure, it was one thing to manage a single quarry run by a small team of men. But did he have it in him to lead hundreds of people?

Since Grant didn't know how to answer her, he stalled her with a lie. "I'm not ready, Geri. You know how it is," he'd said, sighing heavily, as though he were carrying a load of sorrow inside him.

"I get it," Geri replied with an agreeable nod. "But we've got a vacuum that needs filling, Grant. If you're okay with it, I'm going to hire an interim CEO. Just until you get yourself back on your feet."

Grant had said of course he was fine with it.

Now, as he stretches out on the lounge chair in his backyard and watches the pool guy skim leaves and needles off the water's surface, Grant replays that conversation with Geri in his head. When he said that he didn't think he was ready to lead the company, she'd been almost too quick to agree. Maybe Geri doesn't believe he has what it takes to run the business. And what about the other managers? What do they think of him? Every one of them knows about his Wadsworth fuck-up. What kind of respect would they give him? Being Calvin Cooper's son was one thing. Being the boss of the whole outfit quite another.

Then again, C. G. Cooper & Sons Aggregates is his to do with as he please. He could sell it and tell them all to go to hell. Can he do that, or would too many generations of ghosts haunt him forever if he gave the company away?

Or, now that Cal is dead, it occurs to him that he can take over the Truckee quarry.

He's just about to ask Erika what she thinks of this idea when it hits him: there's no way he can give himself that job. The owner of the company can't be seen *managing* a rock pit. That'd be like Mark Zuckerberg selling banner ads for Facebook.

But Zuckerberg wasn't a recovering drug addict. If rehab has taught Grant anything, it's that he needs to stay busy. He needs to keep his mind from spiraling into negativity, like he's doing at this very moment.

"Hey, we should go somewhere," he says, apropos of nothing more than needing to hear himself speak.

Erika's reading a book with a dark blue cover and big yellow lettering: *THE WIDOW ON something something*—her hand is hiding the rest of the title. He can see the image of a woman silhouetted in a window, and he knows instantly it's one of those psychological suspense novels she can't get enough of—the ones filled with cheating husbands or missing children or creepy serial killers pretending to be the friendly mother or father or neighbor or teacher next door. He refers to them as "Lie and Die" books; there's always some shady character who's keeping secrets until the very end, and as far as he can tell, at least one person has to get murdered in some gruesome manner.

Erika says, "Where do you want to go?" without looking up.

Grant sees the pool sweeper glance over as if he's listening to their conversation, but then Grant follows his gaze and realizes he's staring at Erika's legs. She's got a sweatshirt on and the tiniest pair of shorts. He grabs the cotton blanket she brought outside an hour ago, when the late October morning still held its crispness close, leans over and drapes it across her exposed body parts. When she peers over at him with her eyebrows knitted in confusion, he smiles. "You looked like you were cold."

She tosses the book onto the ground and reaches out her hand. He takes it in his. "I love you," she says. "Thank you for watching out for me."

"Always."

"So," she says, sitting up and folding the blanket into a neat square. "Where do you want to go?"

He doesn't know if he actually wants to go anywhere. He just knows he needs to find something to distract him before he falls into old habits. Old thoughts. Maybe what he needs is a project. But not one that involves redecorating, that's for damn sure. "I don't know. I mean, Erika, once you're done with all this . . ." He gestures to the sounds of sawing and hammering behind them. "What do you want to do next?"

Erika laughs. "Um. Get married and live happily ever after?"

"No, I just mean, don't you want to have a job or—?" Like a cold slap in the face, it instantly occurs to Grant that he has no idea who this woman sitting in front of him is, and this realization rattles him to his core. He doesn't know anything about her life before rehab. Did she ever work? Go to college? Does she have any interests besides reading, redecorating, and shopping? Where is her family? Does she have friends?

On the beach that day when she made it clear that if he ever asked about her past she'd leave him, like the lovestruck moron that he was, he had dumbly agreed. He'd desperately wanted a girlfriend.

He looks into her face and, for the first time, he sees a stranger. How has he been so blind? Did she know he was rich when they met? Why does she want to live here in Gold Hills? Why does she keep pushing him to marry her? And what about what his parents told him just before they flew off to their deaths? What did they say? He pushes through the simmering fumes in his head to remember. They'd said they hired someone to look into her background. Who did they hire? He has no idea, but he remembers now. There was no one with that name who matched her description. Erika Morris doesn't exist.

Who the fuck is this woman?

CHAPTER

21

GOLDY'S IS QUIET tonight, relatively speaking. Vera's sitting on the stool next to mine, staring into her phone. Usually when we meet for drinks at Goldy's, Vera and I have to sit with our shoulders touching if we want to hear what the other one is saying. I actually prefer it that way, even if it means having to breathe in the residual smells of disinfectant and blood that stick to her no matter how hard she scrubs down after work.

"Busy day?" I ask across the arm-sized space between us.

She takes a sip of her brandy. "Roger Pendergast's family requested an autopsy."

"Why? Wasn't he like a hundred years old?"

Vera chuckles. "Eighty-nine. Died in his sleep."

"So why the questions?" I've seen enough autopsies to know I never want to have my body subjected to one. God willing, I'll die in a straightforward manner, like I'll get cancer or fall off a cliff: a death so obvious there will be no need to saw open my skull or investigate the contents of my stomach.

Vera ignores me so instead of repeating myself—I don't really care about old Roger Pendergast or the details of his demise—I gulp down the rest of my rye and glance around. To my right are two women I've never seen before at the other end of the bar. Both are in their fifties, but having had enough face work done, an undiscerning eye could easily mistake them for a decade younger. They're drinking white wine and laughing at something on one of their phones. There's a group of four twentysomethings hunched over one of the small wooden tables scattered around the dark bar. I recognize two of them as locals, but I don't know them by name, which both mystifies and alarms me, given that I spent five years as a patrol officer on the streets of Gold Hills before making detective. The town is odd that way; you can live here, work here, drink here, and still you aren't going to get to know the people. Unless you're investigating or arresting them, that is.

Now, if I'd been throwing back a few down at The Owl's Nest in Prosperity, chances are I'd know the names of most of the frequent drinkers there. And they'd probably know me too. When you're born and raised in a small town and your dad works for the city, your long-term memory can't help but get packed full of local faces.

* * *

I was born the second child of Gus and Anita Torres, the first being my older brother William—Billy. Dad worked for the Prosperity Public Works Department his whole adult life. There wasn't a street or sewer in that town the man didn't know like the back of his hand.

I was a squirrely kid with too much energy to sit still in classrooms but could run like the wind. All I ever wanted was to hang out with Billy and his friends, but they ignored me because I was just a "dumb girl." So when I turned eight I started dressing in "boy" clothes and demanded that people call me Rob. I figured if I could be more like my brother and his friends, they'd include me in their world, but all it did was make my parents worry that I'd fallen off the bell curve.

By high school I'd simmered down some and found my stride, literally and figuratively, by joining the Monroe High School track team. I went back to being Robyn and made a couple of friends—most of them from Prosperity since even as a team, the Gold Hills kids tended to stick together like fancy sardines in a tin. That was also when Vera and I became a lot closer. She lived five doors down from me so we took the same bus to school every morning but didn't really have much to say to one another. Once she joined the team, though, we went running on weekends and studied together after school.

By senior year, my feelings toward Vera began to grow in ways I knew I'd never share with her. I didn't mind holding onto the secret—it didn't weigh me down or stop me from living my life or cause me to break down in tears when we went off to different colleges after graduation.

* * *

And now here we are, friends once again. It's enough for me. It's enough to have Vera next to me after another day spent trying to catch a killer. A day which brought Tom and me what we hope will be a crucial piece of evidence. I had no idea why or how two branches of weed ended up in Coyote Creek next to our murder victim's farm, but a second after Tom got up to escort Deni out, I was on the phone to the supply unit supervisor. "I need two pairs of waders, two pairs of boots, a rake, and a net," I listed off while pacing in front of my desk. "We'll be down in five."

Tom had come back by the time I hung up and had an expression on his face that threw me immediately into defensive mode. I knew what he was going to say, so I said it before he got the chance. "You think I should call Brian Pearse and have him send his dive team up, right?" GHPD had been sharing info with the Washington County's Sheriff's Office Special Investigations Unit since the day we found Luna dead, but, like us, Pearse had nothing. "I'm happy to do that, but it means we're going to have to wait. Or . . ." I said, looking at my watch. "There's still plenty of daylight."

Tom had scratched his head like he was thinking about the right response. He and I were a great team. I had two years on him, but we were equals on and off the field. I watched him consider the two options, but Tom didn't like to dick around. He wanted answers as quickly as the next guy, even if it meant skipping around procedural bullshit. I knew he knew it was the right call, which was why it didn't surprise me when he said, "Marco," and started heading for the stairs to the basement.

"Polo," I replied with a grin as I followed after him.

* * *

I'm thinking about what we found in Coyote Creek when I see John Kelsey walk through the door. We're a smallish enough police force—twelve officers and two detectives—that we're obliged to ask about recently taken family trips or health issues when we run into one another outside the station. John's young and bright. I expect he'll make detective in a few years. I'm surprised to see him here. It's Wednesday, the night he and his crew of friends usually play paintball.

He sidles up next to me and orders a beer before asking me how it's going. "All good," I say, pointing at my empty glass once I catch the bartender's eye. "Why aren't you out shooting your buddies with paint?"

"My friend Charlie screwed up his knee falling off his bike so we're taking a break," he says, clinking his bottle against my glass. "Hey, I heard you and Horner went up to Greenhorn Hill to do some fishing today. Think there's something there?"

Discussing a pending murder case in public is not in anyone's best interest so I demur with a shrug and a "Hope so," but what John said has caught Vera's interest enough for her to look up from her phone and ask what's happening.

Quietly, I fill them in about the sticks Deni recovered from the creek. I tell her about Tom and me going up this afternoon and how we went exploring after a quick, bizarre convo with Luna's mother at the front door. (She really is "out there." It's strange how accepting and accommodating she is with the fact that her daughter was murdered.)

I took the north side of the creek and Tom the south. Slowly we made our way downstream along the banks, wading into the rushing water whenever something irregular caught our eye. By the time the light was doing us no favors, we'd probably covered a quarter of a mile and found another two dozen branches of waterlogged marijuana, most of them with orange-flecked, cannabinoid-rich buds still attached. We still have to wait for the lab to confirm that the DNA from the branches match the stolen plants, but my gut says they will.

While I'm relaying the upshot, John's nodding along as if he's got a vested interest, which I suppose he does. I have to keep reminding myself that Gold Hills Police Department is one big team and it's not just about me solving a case. It's the whole city's case.

Once I finish speaking, the three of us sit there in silence for a few beats. Vera takes a sip of her drink. I halve my newly filled glass. John downs most of his bottle. Then Vera sits up like someone's punched her in the back and says, "So, does this mean you're thinking the murderer didn't drive away. They, what, put the plants in bags and those bits fell out while they were escaping into the forest past the creek? I'm right, right?" She's got a shit-eating grin on her flushed face.

I laugh because I can't help myself. Vera believes she has what it takes to detect crimes, and not just ones that have been incurred on the human body. Yet, no matter how much evidence I feed her, no matter how obvious the clues are, she always gets it wrong. "I love you, Vera," I say, "but once again, you're missing the obvious." And then, before I have the chance to tell her what Tom and I already deduced, John snaps his finger and announces, "The perp just wanted to make it look like a robbery. They pitched the plants into the creek to get rid of 'em!"

"Someday, my boy," I reply in a deep manly voice, "you're going to make a fine detective."

Vera swivels around on the stool, her eyes narrowed in sheer puzzlement. "What? Why do you think that?" It's the same look and same thing she says every time we watch a Nicola Walker mystery and I guess who the killer is before Nicola does.

The ever-eager John answers before I can swallow. "Okay, so let's say you're just trying to steal one or two pot plants? You're either going to rip the plant out of the ground or pot, whichever the case may be. Or you cut as many branches off that you can and jam out of there. But in this case," he runs his palm in a circle around the smooth surface of the bar as if he's cleaning it with a rag before continuing, "we're talking, what, about a dozen plants? Big hefty ones, ready for harvest, right?" He's asking me to confirm this fact. I nod in agreement.

"That's a shitload of plant material. Chances are you're not going to take the time to cut them into bits and pieces. You're in a hurry, so you hack them off at the base, haul them up to your truck or van—it's gotta be big enough to hold them all—stuff them in and drive off. Plus, and tell me if I have this correct here, Torres, but forensics didn't find a single blade of marijuana on the farm, right?"

These are exactly the same theoretical steps Tom and I walked a few hours ago. I grin at John. "Not a one. Keep going," I urge.

"My guess is that you and Horner assumed since there were no trace leaves or sticks, the perps bagged or maybe wrapped the plants in a tarp before they dragged them to their getaway vehicle. But—and here's another blind spot—the farm road is gravel so forensics couldn't trace the tires." Again he looks at me for approval. This is good. I feel like I'm watching my own mind play out in technicolor, and I'm fascinated. I can see Vera trying to latch on to the answers, but she's not there yet. Again, I nod.

"That's the obvious way a robbery like this should go down. Chop, wrap, drag, stuff, drive. Done," John states with certainty.

We wait. I know what's coming next. Vera is still clueless.

"So, let's say there's no vehicle parked in the driveway. Instead, there's a car waiting on the other side of Coyote Creek. The closest road is . . . I think, Forest View Lane, and that's at least half a mile through dense brush. That's not doable. Didn't happen. Nope." He stops there and orders another beer whereupon Vera slaps him on the shoulder and says, "So then what *did* happen?" She's on the edge of her seat. I'm on the edge of my brain.

The bartender drops the bottle, and John waits for her to move off before he pounces.

"No one stole the plants, Vera."

"They didn't?"

This time I am the one to jump in. "No. Whoever killed Luna Rose chopped those plants into pieces and threw them into the creek. They set the scene to look like a pot robbery that turned ugly."

Vera looks from John to me and back to John. "Why? Why would someone do that?"

I slug back the rest of my drink and wink at John. "That's the million-dollar question, Vera. And I intend to answer it."

CHAPTER

22

GERI'S DESK IS more cluttered than Grant remembers it ever looking and Geri herself is a lot more harried-looking too. He wonders if the business isn't running as smoothly as she's been making it out to be, but he doesn't actually care. That's not why he's here.

While he waits for her to hang up from the call she was on when he walked in, he goes over the story again in his head.

"I'll get someone up there as soon as I can," Geri promises confidently into the phone. "The most you'll be down is a day or two. Yes. I understand. Yes. You too, Jeff." When she hangs up and lets out a big sigh, Grant feels obliged, at the very least, to appear interested in the call he's just overheard. He knits his eyebrows together into a look of concern and says, "What's up?"

"Redding's radial stacker's got some pronounced belt slippage," she says. "They need to halt operations."

“But why are you the one handling it? Where’s the manager?” It’s the job of the quarry manager to get broken machinery fixed, not his dead father’s executive assistant.

“Steve Fosse had a heart attack a few days before . . . before your brother and parents flew to Nevada.” She shifts in her chair as if nudging the memory aside. “We pulled Jeff off plant ops to fill in until, well . . . you know.” She picks up a pen, flips it up and down before writing something in a notebook.

“Until I know, what?” Grant asks, annoyed by her vagueness. Geri is usually so direct. With her hunched over the desk he can see gray roots showing through her brown hair. He had no idea she dyed her hair.

“Look, Grant,” she says, throwing the pen onto the desk. “We didn’t for a second think Steve was ever coming back. It was a pretty massive heart attack. That was why your father was giving you the Redding site.”

Grant feels a bite of guilt gnaw at his stomach, but swallows hard, hoping his saliva will drown it down. He doesn’t know how to respond so he stays silent, watching Geri watch him. “So, in addition to everything else I’m doing, I’ve got to find another manager.”

Grant looks down at his hands while considering this. His father gave him Redding, but only on the condition that he leave Erika in the dust. Now that the old man is presently turning to dust himself, Grant could move out there with his girlfriend. He’d be the quarry manager. They’d buy a new house—something without any memories lurking in the floorboards. He’d let Erika decorate it to her heart's content. He'd have a job again, people to talk to, a reason to—WTF!

You're an idiot, he thinks. *Never going to happen*.

"What is your plan, Grant?" Geri asks so suddenly and so forcefully, he rears back in his chair as if Geri has just read his ridiculous thoughts and slapped him upside his head. "C. G. Cooper and Sons has been in your family for generations. Generations! You want to sell it and pocket the cash? Is that the plan? Or maybe you just want to shut it down and put a couple hundred people out of work? Because if that's the plan, I need to know sooner rather than later."

Her anger shoots straight down into his bowels. She's never before spoken to him like this, and there's a tiny voice in his head telling him to speak up for himself. She's *his* employee now. How dare she yell at him like this?

He tries to turn up the volume on that tiny voice, but it fades so quickly he's not even certain it was ever there. "Geri, I'm still working on figuring—"

"You're still working on figuring it out. Sure. Fine." She is disgusted with his indecision. His inability to get off the proverbial pot.

He should have called her instead of coming in, but he thought it'd be easier to get what he needed in person. This was a very bad decision on his part.

"Grant. I've known you for most of your life. I think you're basically a good person who's done some stupid things." She leans down and opens a drawer, takes out a pack of cigarettes and lights one. "But I've gotta be honest with you. If you take over, I'm not so sure you won't run this company into the ground," she says, taking a drag deep enough to create an inch-long ash.

Jesus. Geri too? Is there anyone other than his girlfriend, a woman he isn't sure he even trusts, who believes in him?

Grant should just get it over with and tell Geri he doesn't *want* to run the company. He knows this as surely as he knows that the drop of sweat at the base of his back is about to drip into his ass crack. He squirms in the chair and feels the drop stick the landing. Before he can stop himself, he begins imagining what a hit of oxy might do for his brain right now. He has to get out of here. He stands up and says in a voice that sounds as if someone else is speaking, as if he's already walked out and left this other piece of flesh to wrap things up for him, "I've gotta go, Geri. If the guy you've got running things is doing okay, how about you just let him stay on a little longer? I'm in no hurry to make any major decisions."

Geri stubs out the cigarette in a half-eaten sandwich on the end of her desk. She narrows her eyes, considering him for a few seconds before nodding. "Okay. I can live with that. For now."

Grant lets out a breath and heads toward the door. Before he walks out she says to his back, "Hold up, Grant. You were the one who came to see me. Did you need something?"

It's now or never, but he knows that the bullshit story he made up about having security issues at the house isn't going to hold water. Geri's too smart for that. So much for practicing the lie all the way down here.

He turns around and straightens his shoulders, attempting to look like a man whose questions deserve answers. "My parents told me they had *someone* look into my girlfriend's background," he says, meeting her gaze head on. "Tell me who that someone is."

CHAPTER

23

Ever since my mother died, I've made a habit of keeping my focus fixed to the shelves running along the aisles whenever I shop at the Prosperity Stop & Shop. That way I can avoid accidentally making eye contact with any of her former coworkers. Otherwise, whenever someone recognizes me as Bonnie's kid I get trapped in some awkward conversation, like the one I'm presently having with Heather.

This is probably the tenth time Heather has cornered me in the store to tell me how much she misses having Mom next to her on checkout. While she repeats a story she's told me many times—the one about the cookies Mom used to secretly toss into people's bags during Christmas—I'm regretting that I didn't just suck it up and go food shopping at the stupidly overpriced VIP Grocers in Gold Hills after I left work today.

I didn't go to VIP because those few extra dollars I would have had to spend are dollars I don't have. My father's fifteen-an-hour paychecks plus my waitressing job are barely keeping us afloat. Of course my economic situation was supposed to have changed dramatically once I married Cal and became an heiress to a fortune. Now that Cal is dead I'm left with nothing but his locked iPhone and a two-carat diamond engagement ring, which I will probably have to sell. The dreams I had for my future are fading so quickly I sometimes feel I imagined what I thought my tomorrows would look like. Had Cal really been in love with me? Were we truly going to live in a brand-new mega-house in the middle of a forest? Was I finally going to find some peace and quiet? These are things I will never know for certain. What should have been mine now belongs to that bitch Erika. How she hustled her way into Grant's life is a riddle. I get that Grant was in a vulnerable place when he met her, but she doesn't belong here. She doesn't deserve to inherit the Cooper dynasty.

Heather is ignoring the grimace on my face. She has no idea how annoying she is, and I am counting the seconds until she remembers she has to get back to work when I see Detective Torres making her way down the aisle toward us. It's only after she grabs a box of Kraft Mac & Cheese and throws it into her basket that she notices me. "Hi, Detective Torres," I say, cutting Heather off.

Heather whips around to see who I'm talking to and then quickly removes her phone from her pocket and blurts, "Hey, Robyn," before announcing that she has to run. "Take care, Deni," she says, hustling away.

Detective Torres watches her go then glances into my cart. "You having a party?" she asks when she sees the multiple six packs of Budweiser.

I flush. "They're for my father."

"Ah."

It feels weird to be standing next to the detective out of context, in such an normal place. The only thing we've ever talked about is Luna's murder and now she's asking me about beer. It's also weird to see her not wearing her Detective Suit. She's got on a pair of tight-fitting blue jeans and a Columbia Fleece jacket over a T-shirt with writing that I can't read beyond the letter O. "I'm glad you showed up," I say. I want to ask her if she's found out anything more about the pot branches I brought into the police station the other day, but I have no idea if it's okay to talk about a murder investigation in a public place.

"What do you mean?"

After I tell her about my constant run-ins with my mother's former coworkers she nods. "Yeah, I get it. I grew up here too."

"You did?"

"Yup. It's the reason I usually do my shopping late at night, but since they've cut back on the store's hours, I'm in the same boat. Lots of people in this town know me. Heather and I—we go way back. Please don't ask me about it." Her expression is impossible to read, but I immediately start picturing Heather, a forty-something woman who I remember my mom worrying about for a reason I've long forgotten, as a criminal. Was she a drug addict? Did she write bad checks?

Detective Torres interrupts my mental list of possible crimes with a snap of her finger. "Your mother is Bonnie?

Long silver hair and always wore a pearl necklace." She looks around with a startled look as if seeing the store for the first time. "Now I know why I recognized the photograph in your house."

We have one small framed photograph of the three of us on the bookcase in the living room. I'm kind of impressed she remembers. "Yup, that's her. That's my mom."

"I remember hearing about her passing. I'm really sorry, Deni."

I shrug. What can I say that I haven't already said a thousand times to people who tell me they're sorry? "Did anything ever happen with those branches?" I ask, wanting to change the subject, even if it's to one that's quite possibly not okay to discuss.

"Nope. Still waiting for the lab results." She leans close to me, and I'm expecting her to whisper some important information relating to Luna's case, so I pay close attention. "Your mother once caught me shoplifting," she whispers.

My head springs back in surprise. "No way!"

"Yup." She laughs. "I was fifteen. Stole a bottle of Bailey's. Shoved it under my coat and was one step away from walking out the front door when your mother grabbed my hood. I'll never forget how scared I was."

"What happened?"

Detective Torres grins. "She put her arm around me and walked me back to the shelf where I nabbed it. She didn't say a word. Just stood there waiting for me to do something. I knew I was busted so I took it out from under my coat and placed it back on the shelf. As soon as I did she walked back to her register. I still to this day have no idea how she even saw me do it."

"Yeah, that sounds like Mom. She had eyes in the back of her head."

"And you know what? I never stole another thing again."

We wait while a young couple with a screaming toddler walk past us with their cart. The kid is trying to climb out of the seat and the father is pushing him down as the mother keeps rolling along, oblivious to the drama taking place right in front of her. Once they've passed, Detective Torres walks back to grab her cart. "I promise I'll keep you updated, Deni. We Spurs need to stick together, right?" She wheels by me, but before she gets to the end of the aisle I take a chance. "Detective Torres. There's one more thing." She turns to look at me. "I read about this thing you guys use. MDFT?"

"The mobile device forensic tool? Yeah, what about it?"

"Um. Well, the FAA recovered Cal's—my fiancé's—phone from the plane crash and I don't know his passcode. I'm down to one more try. Is there any way, maybe you could . . . I mean . . ."

The moment she frowns, I know it's hopeless. "Sorry, Deni. We'd need a probable cause to search his phone. Unless your fiancé was a suspect in an investigation, there's nothing I can do."

So much for us Spurs sticking together. "Okay. I figured it wouldn't hurt to try. Have a good night." I give her a wan smile and flip my cart in the direction I'd started down before Heather accosted me. Just as I lean down to grab a box of generic crackers from the bottom shelf, I hear the detective's voice from twenty feet away. "If all else fails, try his pet's name."

CHAPTER

24

I F HE'D BOTHERED to make an effort, to go through a mental list of people who *owed* his father, Grant might have guessed that it was Deputy Sheriff Ted Campbell who was the "someone" his parents asked to look into Erika's background. If he had, he could have skipped that unnerving meeting with Geri yesterday. He could have avoided getting himself so worked up over the way she spoke to him that he'd actually considered speeding down to his former dealer's house in Prosperity and banging on the door.

Way back when Cal forced Grant to light that innocent toad on fire, Ted Campbell was the County Animal Control Officer who'd been tasked with meting out Grant's punishment. Grant remembers being deathly afraid of the man. He was a big guy with deep-set blue eyes that showed no emotion. He smoked like a fiend. They'd spent five hours driving around Washington County, shoveling up squished skunks, opossums, a few cats, and one poor dog. Mostly, though, they hoisted mangled deer carcasses, heavy as lead, onto the truck bed. Campbell had said less than a hundred words to Grant the whole day. When he got home he would have stayed in the shower all night if not for his mother demanding he join them for dinner. Even after two full scrubbings, the stink of death and smoke didn't fade for days. Nor did the images of maggots crawling over those furry faces leave his brain for months.

The next time Grant ran into Campbell was years later, when he'd pulled him over for going 95 mph up Highway 20. Grant had been surprised to see the man, now a deputy sheriff, peering down at him through his open window with those same empty blue eyes, puffier now and ringed with wrinkles. Grant almost wanted to remark, "Congrats on the promotion. I bet pulling people over is way better than scraping up guts," but thought better of it.

When Campbell saw that it was Grant, he'd sniggered as he hitched up his gun belt. "Lucky for you I still owe your father. Don't let me catch you going this fast again," he said, handing Grant back his license.

After Geri gave Grant the name of his parents' contact, Grant immediately called the sheriff's office and asked to speak to Deputy Sheriff Campbell. The moment the operator patched him through to his cruiser, Grant's mouth went dry. Did he really want to pursue this paranoia of his? He managed to say, "This is Grant Cooper. My parents were investigating someone named Erika—" before Campbell cut him off and said he'd call him back from his personal cell.

Now, as Grant waits by his car in the parking lot behind the county government building, his heart is beating too fast. He begins to do his finger exercises, but he feels like he's being watched so he switches to breathing in to the count of four, holding for seven, breathing out for a count of eight.

In, two, three, four.

Hold, two, three, four, five, six, seven.

Out, two, three—

"What the fuck you doing, son?"

Grant jumps. He had his eyes closed and now that they're open he sees Ted Campbell staring at him with such distaste, it's as if he's caught Grant masturbating. "What? Sorry. Just counting my breaths," Grant replies self-consciously.

Campbell slaps him on the back and laughs. "Yeah, I get it. Recovery crap, right?"

Of course Campbell knows about Grant's history, and it makes him feel dirty, exposed. He needs to get this over with and get out of here. In fact, he should bag it altogether. Yeah, this is nothing but a waste of time. Erika is great. Big whoop, she changed her name. "Hey, so I'm thinking maybe . . ." he says, not certain if he wants to finish the thought.

Campbell ignores Grant's half-sentence and the two of them remain silent in the early evening chill. Grant watches Campbell light a Marlboro. The man has not aged well. Where before, he was a solidly built bull of a man, he now seems saggy, as if someone has punctured him and the air is slowly leaking out. His hair is mostly gone too.

Campbell takes in a deep drag. "I'm sorry about your family, Grant. Has to be hard on you, losing everyone like that," he says, glancing over Grant's shoulder as if searching for them in the parking lot behind him.

"Thanks." Why is he still here? Are they ever going to get on with it or is this just a social call? "So, um, do you—"

"Your father was an asshole, Grant," Campbell says, again cutting him off, "but he was one of the most generous assholes I knew." Grant raises his chin in surprise and sees that Campbell's expression is almost playful. He takes in another drag, and as he blows the smoke out he narrows his eyes. "This girlfriend of yours. Name's Erika Morris?"

Grant nods, glad as hell they're moving on from reminiscing.

"From what I could see, there's no record of her. No history. She's nothing but a ghost."

Grant had done his own search and come up with zilch as well. He even went so far as to search Google Images from a picture he had of Erika on his phone and still there were no matches.

"But that was only a quick and dirty search, you understand," Campbell continues, "nothing your folks couldn't have done on their own."

"So why didn't they?"

He pulls on his cigarette until there's nothing left but filter, then flicks it across the pavement. "Maybe they did. Maybe they didn't, but I had to do my due diligence, right? When Calvin said to find out who the girl was, he didn't specify how deep he wanted me to go. I gave them what I had, which, at that point, was nothing."

"Hold on," Grant says, exasperated now. "That was it? You did a fucking Google search, found nothing, and from that they decided she couldn't be trusted? What the fuck?"

Campbell raises his hands as if defending a blow. "Cool your jets, boy. I *told them* that that was all I had *for now*, but if they wanted more information, I'd see what else I could come up with."

Grant was fuming inside. His father had been intent on making him choose between "the Redding job or the girl," based on—on what? Nothing. No. Fucking. Thing.

"But then, well. A few days later their plane went down, and, until you called, I figured the investigation went down with it." Campbell raises a curious eyebrow. "But now here we are again."

Grant isn't entirely comfortable admitting to this man that he wants more information on his girlfriend. He should have hired a private investigator is what he should have done. He has the money for it. Hell, he probably has enough money to hire MI6 if he wants. He could tell Campbell to forget it, say it was all a misunderstanding, and that he was just following up on what his parents were after.

Yeah, he *could* do that, but he doesn't. He's here. He might as well bite the bullet. "I want to know who she really is. I mean, I want to know why she changed her name, if that's what happened," he says. Campbell must think he's an idiot for shacking up with a woman he knows nothing about, but Grant isn't about to tell him that being loved by someone is the best thing in the world. That drinking coffee across the table from a beautiful woman every morning is his idea of heaven. "Can you find out the rest?"

"If you brought along what I asked you to, there's a chance I can get you the answers you're after, Grant," Campbell says. His expression has softened, as if he can read the shame and sadness in Grant's eyes. "Know this, though: if she's not in the system, I can't and I won't go beyond that. You'll have to take the private route."

Grant utters a quiet "I understand," before opening the car door and grabbing the mug Erika used this morning from the passenger seat. As Campbell had instructed him to do on the phone, he'd used a paper towel to pick it up and then placed it in a plastic sandwich bag.

Campbell takes the bag from Grant and stuffs it into his coat pocket without bothering to look around to see if anyone's watching this transaction. Maybe running someone's fingerprints isn't as illegal as Grant thinks. "You'll be hearing from me soon," Campbell says, striding away. "Have yourself a good evening and drive safe."

CHAPTER

25

I PRESS THE SURFACE of each number softly, barely perceptively. It's my last chance and the fear of failure thunders in my chest. 6-8-4-4-3-8 . . . and . . . I'm in! I'm in! I collapse backward, accidentally banging my head against the wall. *She was right*, I think, mentally shouting out a "Thank you!" to Detective Torres for suggesting I try N-U-G-G-E-T.

I grab a pillow and prop it behind my head and then immediately click on Cal's texts to me. I hold my breath, praying I will see one more message that was never sent. One more confirmation of his everlasting love. But the moment I recognize the emojis, I let out my breath, disappointment and sadness gushing through me. There's nothing but his last text about him wanting to give Grant and Erika some alone time.

"Shit."

I shove a second pillow against the wall behind me and begin to scroll around, looking at other people Cal texted.

I have no idea who any of them are. I click on Bill Cohen. It's all work-related stuff. The next few names are work people too. I finally find a person I know: Dad. There were a lot of exchanges between Cal and his father, but no matter how far up I scroll, the only topics they discussed had to do with quarry equipment and money. There's not a single personal note. I guess that's not so weird, given who Calvin was. I look to see if Cal and his mother ever talked by way of text and am unsurprised that her name is nowhere. Jean once told me that she found texting "an uncivilized mode of communication." *Sure, Jean, as if you were the bastion of civilized. You, with your bossy nastiness. You, with your self-serving—*

I stop inwardly cursing the woman. I hated her when she was alive. There's no point in stomping all over her dead body.

Feeling deflated and even more heartbroken, I let out an audible sigh. I don't know why I thought getting into Cal's phone would soothe me; that again seeing the intimate exchanges we had during our nine-month love affair would become a kind of keepsake. One I could tuck away like a scrapbook. It turns out that seeing our messages on his phone feels no different than seeing them on mine.

What else was I expecting to find? Maybe I wanted to see that he was talking about me to other people? In the back of my mind there was a tiny hope that I'd discover a secret—a surprise he was planning for our wedding. A present he was buying for me.

I keep searching, but there's nothing here about me. After some twenty minutes of scrolling I'm basically losing interest, but it's not as if I have anything better to do. I glance out the window and see that it's a beautifully sunny autumn day. I don't have to go into work today. I could grab one of the books that are piled on my nightstand and go to the park. I could visit Misha again. She keeps asking me to come have tea with her, but I keep finding excuses to say no. Being at that house gives me the creeps. Plus, I don't really want to have to listen to another lecture about the bardos of death and dying.

I should just go for a walk. I look down at my pale arms. When had I last spent time outdoors? When was the last time I did *anything* other than go to work, make dinner for my father, or watch bad television? Before Cal showed up in my life, that's basically all I did.

Jeez. Why on earth was Cal Cooper even attracted to someone as dull as me? What about me did he think was special? He must have thought I was special, right? Why else would he have asked me to marry him?

Before I can stop myself I am being sucked down into a rabbit hole of self-loathing and self-doubt.

I mean, who was I to him? Who did he see when he looked at me? Deni Rydell: daughter to a loving mother who died too soon, and a bitter father who drinks himself into a stupor every night. A waitress at Marvin's. A college dropout. A sometime best friend to Luna Rose, whose incinerated remains I only recently tossed into Coyote Creek.

Sometime best friend? Why did I just think that? Were we not besties? Am I not crushed by her death? It wasn't as if we spent a lot of time together since I moved back to Prosperity. Why didn't I go see her up on her farm more often? Might it have been because I've done nothing interesting in all my twenty-eight years on this planet? As opposed to what Luna has done.

Did.

I was jealous of her, wasn't I? *Admit it, Deni.* I was jealous of her beauty. Of her success. I cannot deny the obvious: when I first met Luna, I used her friendship to bolster my ego, my place in the social pecking order. Had that really changed?

Luna didn't even tell me she was pregnant or who the father was. Were we ever truly friends?

I think back to last January when Cal first walked into Marvin's and I'd asked how Grant was doing. He seemed confused as to who I was, but after he remembered that I was Luna Rose's friend in high school, he was suddenly eager to get my number. Once again it was only because of Luna's light shining in my general direction that I was deemed worthy enough.

After that, our courtship went from zero to eighty in a matter of months. A few dinner dates. A couple of walks. Lots of making out in his truck. A single night of lovemaking. Then out of nowhere, Cal was professing his love for me, proposing at the end of August. Why had he been in such a rush?

"Stop it!" I say, punching my own thigh. Cal loved me. He knew who I was inside and out. He wanted to marry me despite the fact that his parents made it crystal clear they didn't approve of me. Cal knew exactly where I came from. He knew I was good enough. We would have had a perfect life together.

Before I start bawling, I unlock the phone again and find where I left off, skimming a couple lines of texts before moving on to the next person in line. By the time I click on someone named Zach, my eyes are so glazed over I promise myself that this will be the last one before I go for a walk. I read Cal's most recent reply from September 19: *Thanks. And if you ever talk to anyone about this I will hunt you down and kill you.*

Stunned, I sit forward so quickly, the pillows behind me tumble onto the floor. Cal never talked about anyone named Zach. Who is he and why did Cal threaten him? Or maybe he was joking. Of course that's all it is. I scroll up to the start of their most recent conversation:

Cal: *Yo', you still alive?*
Zach: *Very much so, man. Glad to know you are as well. LTNS. What's hanging? Where you be?*
Cal: *Up north. Working for the old man. All's good. You ever make it to the big time? Haven't seen your name in neon yet*
Zach: *Little time, but still getting parts here and there. I had two lines in* Minx *last season. I should have texted to let you know. Sorry*
Cal: *That's great. So, hey, remember that video you took? The party?*
Zach: *Um. Yeah. Why?*
Cal: *Send it to me.*
Zach: *You told me to delete it so I deleted it*
Cal: *Once a perv always a perv. Dude, I know you still have it. Send it*
Zach: *I'm actually in the middle of something rn. If I can find it I will. btw: why?*
Cal: *Because. Just send it.*

Zach: *Found it. Here. Enjoy*
Cal: *Thanks. And if you ever talk to anyone about this I will hunt you down and kill you*

I scroll up then down. Up then down. There's no attachment. No video. Nothing. What did Zach send? If Cal thanked him, he must have then deleted it after he'd received it. Why?

It doesn't take me long to figure out who Zach is. He and Cal starting texting one another back in February of 2018, while Cal was still living down in Los Angeles. I have no idea how they met, but it's obvious that Zach was also trying to break into the Hollywood scene and become a star. Maybe they met at an audition since that's pretty much all they talked about at first. There was a lot of friendly banter asking about callbacks and wishing each other luck.

By April, the two of them seemed to be spending more social time together: there were fewer texts about auditions, but lots of texts with the names of bars and the times they planned to meet up. At the end of May, Zach texted Cal about a party:

Zach: *Got wind that Mr. B. is having one of his Beverly Hills blowout parteeees 2-nite. I snagged an invite. wanna be my plus-one?*
Cal: *As if you need ask, bro*

Then—nothing. They stopped talking altogether on May 26, 2018. That is, until this past September, when Cal asked Zach to send him a copy of some video.

I fall back, forgetting that the pillows are no longer there, and my head bangs against the headboard. "Ouch," I mutter, letting my body droop over sideways onto the bed. I let out a sigh. What now? Do I really care about some video Cal deleted off his phone? What was on it that was so important after all these years?

Before I lose my nerve I get off the bed and call Zach. He answers immediately, shouting, "What, no way. You're calling me!" I'm momentarily confused until I realize I've called him from Cal's phone, so of course he thinks it's Cal.

"Um, no. This isn't Cal," I say nervously.

"What? Who is this?"

"This is—" I hesitate. While he waits for me to finish my sentence I pace over to the window and open it, letting in a cool breeze. "This is Deni. I'm Cal's fiancée."

"Fiancée!" He laughs. "That's awesome. Congratulations."

Do I tell him? Do I wait? "You and Cal were recently texting."

"Uh-huh. Where is Cal? Why are you calling me?"

While deciding how to proceed, willing my brain to work fast, a woman's screams—I'm not sure if they're screams of agony or ecstasy—jump the fence between our house and the neighbor's, flooding our tiny backyard like a tidal wave rushing down a street.

"Who is that? What's going on?" He sounds anxious and if I don't calm him down and offer him something soon, I will lose him.

I slam the window shut. "Nothing. Just a neighbor playing with her dog. Sorry about that." I let out a casual giggle, but even I know I sound like a lunatic. "You sent Cal a video, but he deleted it and I want to know what was on it." There, it's out.

"Is Cal there? Can I speak to him, please?" Zach's voice has turned hard-edged. He's no longer in a congratulatory mood.

"Cal is dead, Zach."

He says nothing. I wait as the silence spreads from wherever Zach is through the phone and into my chest. It is deafening. It is painful. I breathe in and continue. "He died in a plane crash last month."

"Oh shit. I didn't . . . I had no—why didn't I know this? God, I'm so sorry."

I could tell him that it was in all the local papers and there was even a tiny mention of his passing in the *Hollywood Reporter*, but I don't want to make him feel bad. I feel bad enough for the two of us. "Thank you."

"I still don't get why you're calling me. Cal and I lost touch years ago. He left to go back to mining school or college or whatever he did so—"

"You sent him a video last month. From some party you went to?" I have him. I need to keep him. I need to know.

"If you don't mind me saying so, I'm confused as shit here. You're *on* his phone. What the fuck are you asking me?"

Shit. He's getting defensive. I sit down on the edge of my bed and give it my all. "The thing is, it's *not* on his phone. You sent it, but he must have deleted it. It's not here and I want to know why Cal wanted you to send it. Please, Zach," I say, my voice cracking.

"It was nothing. Honestly it was just a stupid fifty-second video I took at a party we went to in Beverly Hills. He probably deleted it because there's nothing on it."

"But then why did he—"

"I gotta go, Deni. I'm really sorry about Cal. Take care."

He hangs up.

CHAPTER

26

THE CONSTANT PACING is not helping. Grant knows that if he wants to conquer the ever-growing anxiety burning through his insides, he should do something more helpful than walking from room to room in the house.

Where is she?

He should meditate. Do some breathing exercises. Box breathing? Maybe alternate nostril breathing. He hasn't done that one in ages. Yeah, that sounds good.

He drops down on the couch and immediately stands back up. "Fuck you," he says to the diabolically unforgiving piece of furniture.

He never should have allowed Erika to give their old leather sectional to one of the construction workers. It was his couch, goddammit. Who gave her the right to just give his shit away?

He moves over to one of the large gray armchairs and squats on the edge with his feet firmly planted, just like he did a thousand times at the rehab center. Keeping his eyes closed and back straight, he closes his right nostril with his right thumb and breathes in through his left nostril, pausing for a moment before closing off his left nostril with his ring finger then breathing out through the right one.

He's just starting a second round when he's suddenly hunched over Deez's coffee table with a straw stuck up his right nostril; his left hand is blocking his left nostril so he can snort a line. The memory is so fundamentally familiar, it's almost as if he can feel the narcotic pulse through him. He decides to go with it. Pretend he's just taken a hit. Like dead weights, his hands collapse down onto his lap. His body begins to get tingly. His brain fogs over and silences the panic. "Yes," he whispers to the empty room. "Now we're talking." He snorts another line and slouches back in the chair, remembering that soft easy glow, that warm—

"Stop!" he yells out, opening his eyes. "Jesus, dude." He stands up so quickly a wave of dizziness forces him to bend over to keep from falling.

No wonder he stopped doing that breathing exercise. Way too triggering.

What he needs is some peppermint tea. Something to settle his stomach. His head. Just as he crosses the living room, the front door opens. She's back.

* * *

When Deputy Sheriff Ted Campbell called to say he was faxing some info over, Grant had waited a few minutes before even touching the sheets of paper that came through.

He'd just stood there in his mother's old office, now supposedly *his* home office, glancing around at all the changes Erika made. She'd peeled off the blue-flowered wallpaper and painted the walls a deep shade of rose. Gone were the hulking desk and high-backed leather desk chair; the fake ficus that stood gathering dust in the corner for as long as Grant could remember—replaced now by a small glass-top desk and a sleek ultramodern white desk chair that Grant sat in only once before deciding he had no need for a home office. Not yet, anyway.

At least he was able to stop her from throwing out his mother's desktop computer and fax machine. "Who knows," he'd said, when he caught Erika eyeing the outdated machines. "The computer might have some important stuff on it. And people do still send faxes."

When he'd finally turned the pages over in his hand the first thing he saw was the photograph. A mugshot of someone who could easily be mistaken for a much younger Erika. She looked waifishly thin, and the expression on her face was a mixture of fear and defiance, like someone who got caught doing the right thing but knew she was going to have to pay for it. He stared at the eyes. They were Erika's eyes, only different.

Erika's eyes no longer showed fear.

To the right of the photo were a bunch of numbers next to the words "AFIS statistical analysis." He saw "94%" and immediately skimmed to the name beneath the photograph: Katie Travers. Birthdate: May 17, 1995. Rockvale, Idaho.

The top of the second page read:

Case Information

CR08-00-02312 | State of Idaho Plaintiff, vs. KATIE TRAVERS Defendant

Court

Caster County District Court

Judicial Officer

Wallace, Brady

File Date

09/05/2012

Case Type

Criminal

Charge

Manslaughter

Case Status

Closed

* * *

"Hi, babe," Erika yells after slamming the door closed with her foot, given that both her hands are clutching shopping bags. "You have to see what I bought!" she says and bustles past him to the glass coffee table where she haphazardly dumps the bags. Grant notes that they're from Still Mountain Gifts, Gold Hill's most expensive store. He says nothing as he watches her pull a pale-yellow box out of one of the bags, open it, and slide a sleek black case onto her palm. "Check this out," she says, excitedly flipping the case open and pushing it close to his face. "It's a Montblanc!"

Grant takes in the gold-trimmed black pen nestled in a white silk indention, like a diamond ring in a jewelry box. "It's a pen," he states without emotion.

"No, it's a *Mont. Blanc.*" She repeats each syllable singularly, forcefully, as if she's only just learned how to pronounce the words, as if he didn't hear her the first time she said it. "The lady in the store said they're the best pens on the planet," she adds, not noticing his indifference. When she snaps the case closed Grant is so startled by the sound, his body involuntarily jumps. "Did that scare you?" She laughs. "Sorry."

Grant does not laugh along with her. Instead he asks her how much money it took to buy one of the best pens on the planet.

"What?"

He repeats his question. "How much did the pen cost?" Not that he cares how much she spent. He has far more important matters to discuss with her and he knows he's stalling. Putting off the confrontation he's been dreading. Once it's out there, once Erika knows what he knows . . .

"Four hundred and seventy-five dollars," she says as she places the case back in the box and tosses it into the bag. "It is going to look so good on my new desk, don't you think?" She doesn't wait for him to answer. She grabs the bags from the coffee table and begins to walk away, but Grant stops her with one word. "Katie," he says before he can change his mind.

Erika turns her head to the right and glares at him with such venom, it's as though he's just spit on her. "What did you just say?"

"I said, 'Katie.' It's your name, isn't it?"

CHAPTER

27

I'M PARKED ACROSS the street from 176 South Virgil Avenue, wolfing down a tasteless turkey and cheddar Subway sandwich. When a glob of dried bread gets caught in my throat, I reach for my water bottle on the passenger seat and mutter, "Shoot," before downing what's left of it.

I should have refilled it when ordering the sandwich, or gotten a soda too, but I wasn't thinking clearly. I was too tired from the seven-and-a-half-hour drive to do more than pee and grab some fast food. I had only one goal since pulling out of my driveway in Prosperity last night: get to Zach's apartment before he left for the day.

Not that I have any idea what the guy's schedule is or know if he's even here. Maybe he's on a movie set somewhere. Maybe he spent the night at his lover's house. For all I know he lives in New York and is renting this place to a friend.

After Zach hung up on me on Monday, I tried calling him back from Cal's phone and then my phone, but I think he must have known it was me because he never answered. He wanted nothing more to do with Cal's past or present.

But I wasn't done with Zach.

I remembered that in his most recent texts to Cal he'd mentioned his small role on the show *Minx*, which made him super easy to find online. His full name, according to IMDB, was Zach Blazi. I looked at a bunch of images of him online and, oh boy, was he hot. I was surprised he didn't have more credits to his name, but maybe he wasn't that talented.

Next, I had to find out where he lived, which was only slightly more difficult. The name Zach Blazi was not the most commonest of names, thank goodness. There were, in fact, only six people with that name in the entire state. Two of them lived in the greater Los Angeles area, one of whom was eighty years old. The other—thirty-two.

I'd found him.

176 South Virgil is a three-story multiunit stucco building with a Spanish red-tiled roof. Not fancy, but then again, the whole neighborhood seems kind of dingy to me. I'm guessing that getting hired to speak two lines in a hit show doesn't buy you a beach house in Malibu or a mansion in Beverly Hills.

Beverly Hills. A party that took place in a mansion there many years ago is the reason I am here, the reason I left my father a note explaining that I had to take a quick road trip and wouldn't be back until later today. The reason I called in sick to Marvin's.

I am obsessing over something that may turn out to be nothing, I know, but whatever it was that Cal demanded

Zach send him, only to promptly delete it, has taken hold of me. I thought I knew all there was to know about my fiancé. Okay, so maybe he didn't share all that much about his days in Los Angeles. Whenever I asked him to tell me about his short brush with fame, he'd more often than not push past my curiosity, flick it away with a vague statement like, "Those years were pretty much a blur, Deni." Yet, there he was, suddenly revisiting them. Or, well, revisiting one night in particular. Why?

I look at the clock. It's 7:52 AM. I cannot decide if it's too early to knock on apartment 202 or if I should continue to wait. I can't see any kind of parking garage below the house, but there might be one in back. I wipe some mayo off my face, throw the napkin on the floor of the car, and get out. I keep one eye on the front door as I scoot around the side of the building and see that there's nothing there. Okay, so if he has a car—and who doesn't have a car in Los Angeles?—it's probably parked on the street somewhere.

I'm just crossing back over to my car when I hear a door slam behind me. I whip around and see it's Zach exiting his building. I'd recognize those cheekbones anywhere. My heart jumps. I watch him jingle his keys for a second before stuffing them down into his pants pocket. Once he starts down the sidewalk, I rush across the street and follow behind a few paces. He stops in front of a black Nissan Sentra and is about to grab the door handle when I say, "Zach!" more loudly than I should have because his head jerks up and for a second he's confused that someone is saying his name. I smile. He lifts one of his very thick eyebrows, but he does not smile back. Maybe he thinks I'm a crazy fan stalking him—I assume all movie stars worry about such things—and I am either going to stab him or ask for an autograph.

"I'm Cal Cooper's fiancée," I say, hoping to put him at ease. "I just need to talk to you a minute."

"What the fuck?" He looks shocked. "What are you doing here?"

I walk over and stand next to his car. I need to keep him from attempting to make a quick getaway. Up close he is even more stunningly handsome than he is in his photographs. "You wouldn't answer my calls," I begin gently, "and I just, I don't know—I feel like I need to know what was on that video."

"I didn't answer because it's none of your business what Cal did before he met you," he says. "I have no clue why Cal wanted to see it again. Like I told you, it's nothing." He doesn't wait for me to respond and reaches past me to open the car door, but I push my body in front of it, blocking him. "Please, Zach. Hear me out for *one minute*."

He huffs, steps back a few feet and crosses his arms across his chest. "Fine," he says, looking around him. He doesn't want me to make a scene any more than I want to make a scene. "Cal and I were in love, Zach," I say tenderly. "We were everything to each other. We told each other everything. I knew everything about him."

I think I see one of his bushy eyebrows rise in question, but I could be imagining it, seeing as I am lying through my teeth. It's obvious to both of us that Cal kept things from me. "Whatever is on that video I know he eventually would have told me about."

"I doubt it."

My frustration is building, but I don't blink. "Please, Zach. If it was important enough for him to get back in touch with you after so long, it's something I *need* to see."

Zach's modelesque physique crumples a little; his perfect posture relaxing. He shuffles his feet while glancing down at them. "Listen. I get it. I have no idea why Cal asked me to send it again, but—trust me. You really don't want to see what's on that video. We were really fucked up that night."

Here I am, standing on a street in Los Angeles, hundreds of miles from my home, begging a stranger to hand over a moment of my dead lover's past. I am suddenly overtaken by such a total and complete sadness that before I can stop myself, I start to cry. "Zach, please. I just need to see it. Cal's gone. It won't matter to him, but it will to me. I have so little left of him. Even if it's nothing, it's something to me."

"It's Deni, right?" Zach asks quietly.

"Yeah," I nod, sniffling now.

"Listen, Deni." He moves closer to me and lowers his voice. "I've gotta be somewhere in, like, ten minutes, so I'm going to need you to move away from my car without me forcing you to." His tone is menacing, but his facial expression stays calm. "I get the feeling that you are not the kind of person who gives up very easily and that you are going to still be standing here when I come home tonight."

I nod again. I'm hoping my eyes show the threads of hope I feel wavering across my chest.

"So here's what I'm gonna do. You're going to back away. I'm going to get in my car and once I'm in, I'm going to text the video to Cal's phone. I assume you have it with you?"

I nod a third time, my pulse quickening with anticipation.

"But here's the thing. I need you to promise you will delete all my past texts off Cal's phone. I want nothing to do with this."

"Okay," I say quickly. "I promise."

"And Deni?" he says as he reaches toward the door. "I will never ever see your face or hear your voice again. Do we have a deal?"

"Deal," I say, moving aside.

CHAPTER

28

I STAND FROZEN ON the sidewalk, watching Zach drive away. As panicked as I was that he'd lied about promising to send me the video just to get me to move away from his car, I am now more afraid of opening it. Because it's here, on Cal's iPhone. Waiting for me.

After staring at the screen for what might have been four seconds or four minutes—I have no idea—I finally click on the arrow. It's barely a minute long, but the entire minute is filled with a scene straight out of a raunchy porn site. There are six, maybe seven—I don't bother to count—naked and half-naked men crowded around a young woman on the floor of what looks like a basement. Or dungeon. There is no furniture to speak of. The room is dimly lit, but I can still make out a few of the faces of the men who are taking turns thrusting their hands and penises into the woman's bodily orifices. Around her neck is a collar. Attached to the collar is a leash. One of the men who is behind her has the end of it wrapped around his wrist and has it pulled so taut the woman's neck is bent backward at a painfully awkward angle. The men are boisterous, laughing, cheering one another on as if they are friends watching a football game together. The person filming from a foot away—presumably Zach—is egging the men on, shouting, "Whoop" and "Oh yeah" so loudly I can hardly make out what the men are saying, but I hear "bitch" repeated multiple times.

When the video abruptly ends, I hold the phone out at arm's length in front of me as I walk back over to my car. Once I am beside it I angle the phone away from my body, bend over, and vomit the entirety of my Subway sandwich onto the black pavement.

* * *

During the long drive back to Prosperity I try listening to the radio but even loud music cannot stop the video from replaying over and over in my head. I cannot, no matter how hard I focus on the dull and desolate landscape flashing by on Highway 5, stop seeing the wild-eyed smile on Cal's mouth as he tugged hard on the leash while simultaneously pounding away at that poor girl from behind.

Zach warned me, told me I didn't want to see what was on the video. I can see why he wanted to protect me because now that I've seen the video, Cal Cooper Jr. is no longer the man I fell in love with. The man I'd considered to be kind—who made love to me with such gentle passion—has been obliterated. Replaced by a someone I would never have let touch me.

Over the last four hours I've tried in vain to make excuses for him, tried to rationalize his brutal behavior. He was young. Zach said they were high. Maybe he was forced to participate—warned that if he refused he'd be laughed at, or . . .

As I speed north, I make up a story. This Mr. B., the man who threw the party, was some important Hollywood figure. Cal wanted to go because he thought it'd help his career, but once he was there and saw the sick festivities taking place, it was too late to back out. He got trapped. He didn't want to participate in a gangbang, but he had no choice.

I shake my head. No. There is no excuse. Cal was not who I thought he was, and the very fact of this swells against the void inside my empty stomach. Shuddering, I move into the right lane and flip on my turn signal. I need to fuel up.

* * *

I allow the sweetness of the In-N-Out strawberry shake I bought in Santa Nella to distract me for a little while, but soon enough, without being able to stop it, the video again loops itself around my brain like a rubber band. I open all the windows, trying to deafen the images with the sound of wind rushing by at seventy-five miles per hour. It doesn't work.

A car is speeding so fast up the left lane I think it might crash into me. I hurriedly shoot over to the right lane, flipping the driver off as he flies past me. Once my heartbeat slows, I get back into the left lane and gun it.

Why did Cal want Zach to send the video again? From the tone of his text, he seemed almost desperate. Why? I want to call Zach and ask him if he knows, but I promised him he'd never again hear from me. Besides, I'm pretty sure he said he had no idea what the reason was.

I end up hitting traffic in Stockton, and it's another three hours before I turn down Wilkins Street. Since my dad's truck isn't here, I park in our driveway. I throw my backpack onto my bed and go out to the kitchen to grab something to eat. I'm suddenly starving. Inside the refrigerator I find the day-old apple custard pie Sue let me take home after work on Tuesday. There's one slice left and, after grabbing a fork, I hungrily dig in. The crust is bordering on stale but, oh man, the creamy vanilla custard is as perfect as ever. I'm three bites in when the memory hits me.

It's from one of the last times I ate an apple custard pie: the night Grant was released from rehab. I'd brought along one of Sue's pies, thinking it might make Jean Cooper appreciate me even a tiny bit more. All I ever wanted from my future mother-in-law was for her to welcome me into the family. Yet she wouldn't. Couldn't. No matter how hard I tried, it felt as if I were banging my fist against their castle walls. Why had it been so hard for Jean and Calvin to fold me into the Cooper clan? If they hadn't died, would they have ever allowed my and Cal's children to become a part of their history? What was I missing that made them refuse to believe I was good enough for their son?

"Ha!" I shout, accidentally spitting pieces of half-chewed pie across the kitchen counter. If Jean and Calvin had gotten a chance to watch that video, all hell would have broken loose. They would have been so furious, so gargantuanly embarrassed they would have—they would have done nothing. Said nothing. They would have swept it aside or covered it up. Or even more in line with the sort of privileged hypocrites that they were, they would have turned Cal's repulsive behavior into something heroic. They'd needed one of their sons to be king and, in their eyes, Grant was never going to cut it.

And now Grant is the one wearing the gold-studded crown. The son who has enough money to live the kind of quiet and easy life I so longed for. King Grant and Queen Erika, the bitch with the evil eyes and that knowing smirk she always has plastered on her mouth, as if she is in some competition with the rest of the world and she has no doubt who will win. As if—

Again I return to that night at the dining room table, and remember how pissed off I got at Cal. How every time I tried to make eye contact with him, I found him staring at Erika.

I rush back into my room and dig out Cal's phone. The reason Cal wanted to see a video of himself gleefully taking part in a sexual assault almost five years ago wasn't because he wanted to admire his own moves. It had to be because he remembered someone else who was there.

CHAPTER

29

When I was seventeen I killed my stepfather with an ice pick. Originally I was charged with manslaughter, but my super smart, very pricey lawyer argued that because of the particularly heinous mitigating factors, I should only be charged with aggravated battery with a deadly weapon. The DA agreed and the case never went to trial (although I did end up serving one year in juvenile hall, plus another year on probation). This made my deceased stepfather's (other) family particularly happy since they didn't want to tarnish the clean-cut reputation of their family business by having a big public court case. In fact, his two real grownup kids, the heirs to his tire dynasty (Travers Tires: We Keep You Rolling), almost gushed with appreciation when they found out he was dead. So much so that they gifted my mother a sizeable portion of their hefty inheritance.

Sorry. I should back up.

I was born in Rockvale, Idaho, to Mark and Kelley Halbert. Mark was a drummer in a ska punk band called Hornarchy. Kelley was an accountant for an auto parts store. In a feat that bordered on cliché, Mark took off with one of his groupies right after I was born. Kelley did her best to keep me swaddled in love and formula, but I guess it wasn't so easy being a single mom and, sure, I get it: a woman needs comfort and love. So when the wealthy widowed Ron Travers put the moves on her, she could hardly be blamed for falling for his money-scented charm.

He never formally adopted me, but my mother changed both our last names to his. To complete the picture, she'd said.

They got married when I was eight, and he started diddling me soon after. Like, offering to tuck me in and read to me and touching me where even then I knew he wasn't supposed to. I told my mother and she threatened to leave him. He promised to stop and he did for, I don't know, five, six years. By *stop*, I mean that he never actually touched me with his hands, but I could see the ever-present want in his eyes. He'd come home from the office in a surly mood and immediately head for the bar cart perched next to the fireplace. He'd pick up the sterling silver ice pick and jab it into the fancy bucket that Mom always made sure was filled. After he dropped some chipped cubes into his cut-crystal glass, he'd pour himself a few fingers. Then, once he was relaxed and knew Mom was in the kitchen getting dinner ready, he'd ask me to come sit on the couch next to him and tell him about my day. The way he looked at me while I spoke made me feel as if I were a lost fawn in a clearing. Like he could see I was vulnerable and he was preparing to strike.

Once puberty hit me and I started growing into a pretty young thing, he became more aggressive. He came into my room one night long after I'd turned out the lights and he got into bed with me. I heard him whisper that he was glad I was his daughter and he was proud of me. I kept my eyes closed, pretending to be asleep even though his breath was hot on my face. I figured that was all there was to it, but when he cupped his hand over one of my growing breasts I sat up and screamed, "Mom! He's feeling me up!" Mom rushed into the room, her face half-smeared with some yellow moisturizer.

"I didn't touch her, Kel," he'd insisted. "I was just telling her I loved her and was giving her a goodnight hug. I swear."

Mom's face morphed into a mix of confusion and anger, but ultimately she took my side and told him to get the hell out. Go, Mom.

But then . . . Ol' Richie Rich said it was his house and if anyone was going anywhere, it was us. Mom started to cry. She hadn't worked since the day he swept her off her desk chair. But since they were married I didn't understand her worry. Didn't divorced women get alimony (not that Mark ever sent us a dime)?

Not if they were forced to sign a prenup, they don't.

Dumb Mom.

Now the man had both the doe and her fawn in his sights.

He swore up and down on the heads of Peter and Amelia (his actual children) that he'd never touch me again. And so we all went on living and eating and working and going to school as if that bedroom scene had never happened.

I fell in love with a boy named Luke. I let him put his hands on my growing breasts, but, I don't know, it felt dirty somehow. Like as Luke would touch me, I'd see Ron's face in front of my eyes. The man had most definitely contaminated my view of sex, and I started hating him even more because I could sense that a wound had been inflicted on my burgeoning personhood. I couldn't put it into words exactly, but there was this persistent fear, like a stink, following my young body around.

Then one night, when I was seventeen, I was sitting at the dining room table leafing through *The Complete Book of Colleges*, when Ron came home looking particularly irritated. I'd heard him and Mom discussing some union strike at his company so I figured it was that, but when, out of the corner of my eye, I saw the way he was stabbing at the ice, my body started to freeze up. As I got up from the table, he said, "Come over here, Katie."

"I'm going to help Mom with dinner," I replied, heading toward the kitchen.

"I said, Come. Over. Here. Now," he said slowly, his eyes staring into the ice bucket.

I walked toward him but kept some space between us. He threw the ice pick onto the cart, reached out and grabbed my wrist. Squeezing it tight, he said, "Did you speak to Amelia last night?" Amelia was Ron's twenty-nine-year-old daughter who lived in upstate New York. I'd only met her and her brother Peter once, at my mom and Ron's wedding. They didn't ever visit us. They didn't come for holidays. At the time I didn't think it was weird we never saw them because they were already grown up when Ron married my mother. Plus, they both lived in other states. But what I did think was weird was that Amelia called me one night out of the blue.

"I know you don't know me from Adam, Katie," she said after identifying herself as Ron's daughter, "but I'm calling because, well, I've just returned from Peru. I did an ayahuasca retreat."

I had no clue what she was talking about, but her tone was so serious there was no way I was going to interrupt her.

". . . and while I was there, I saw things. Remembered things I've been keeping hidden away. And well, I feel like I owe it to you, to warn you, I mean." She'd sounded so completely confident and well-spoken that I'd immediately sat up in my desk chair and paid close attention. I could tell that what was coming was going to be important. What I didn't know was that her admissions about what her father had done to her throughout her own childhood would trigger something savage in me, a cruel darkness so unfamiliar I felt as if I'd been possessed.

Ron asking me if I'd spoken to his daughter was a rhetorical question since right after Amelia called me, she'd called her father and told him about all the sick stuff she suddenly remembered him doing to her when she was a kid. She also mentioned that she'd just told *me* everything too. I knew this because while Ron was holding tight to my wrist he said, "Whatever she told you about me is a lie. I never touched her."

I tried to pull out of his grip, but instead of releasing me he clenched his left hand on the back of my neck and pulled my face right up close to his, like he intended to kiss me. "I'd never try anything with my own flesh and blood," he hissed. I could smell whiskey on his breath, which confused me since he hadn't yet poured a drink from the cart. "But you—you're nothing to me. I own you." And with that he yanked my mouth onto his with such force I thought for sure he'd broken one of my incisors. The moment he let go of my neck and stuffed his hand between my legs I reached out blindly for something, anything to hit him with. My hand found the ice pick, and before I could stop myself, I plunged it through his left eye. I guess it reached all the way to his brain because, well, he died.

CHAPTER

30

WHAT A SHIT show. I should be focusing all my energy and efforts on solving Luna Rose's murder, but now the Chief wants me and Tom to lend a hand to Cord Philips, the NTSB investigator who's looking into the Cooper plane crash. The NTSB has no regulatory or enforcement authority, so if they suspect any level of criminality in a transportation accident, they're required to get local law enforcement involved. They handed it off to the Washington County Sheriff's Office, but since the county is so short-staffed at the moment, they asked if we'd take over. My Chief doesn't know how to say no, especially since Tom and I have come up with fuck-all on our murder case.

It's not a big deal, but it's an annoying time suck. I've spent the last hour reading through the NTSB notes and their probable cause analysis and, although I must defer to the expertise of the experts, what they're saying doesn't hold much water.

Snorting at my own inside pun, I stand up from my desk, accidentally bumping my coffee cup, which topples over onto the reports. "Fuck!" I holler. Anyone who's within earshot is so engrossed in their own paperwork and phone calls that no one even looks over to see where the expletive came from.

When I come back from the break room with a roll of paper towels, Tom is standing next to my desk with his arms folded.

"What?"

"Joseph Rydell is here."

"Does he seem nervous?" I ask, unspooling most of the roll. I try to blot the spillage gently, but I can see some of the papers have already disintegrated beneath the hot sludge. I'll need to make a copy of Tom's packet if I want to continue reading, although now that Joe's here, I'm going to have to lean on Tom during the interview.

"More confused than nervous." He watches me push the wet papers around for a few seconds before he puts a hand on my arm. "Can you maybe finish this later, Torres?"

"Sure." I toss the towels onto the desk.

GHPD has one room specially designed for both interviewing and interrogating individuals, whichever the case may be. It's soundproof, decked out in state-of-the-art inquisition technology, and totally void of comfort. When I first walk in, Joe's got his face in his hands. The moment he hears us enter he looks up, startled, like a rabbit caught chewing leaves in a garden. Last time I saw the man he was handing me a glass of ice water in his living room. He'd looked pretty startled back then too.

"Do I need a lawyer?" he asks before Tom and I take a seat.

"Thanks for coming in, Mr. Rydell," I begin. "Can I call you Joe?"

He nods.

"Good. Thanks." I lean back in the metal seat, trying to look as casual and disinterested as can be. I prefer not to have to wait for a lawyer to come. "Listen, Joe. You're not under arrest. We just need you to answer some questions. Clear up some confusions. You are free to leave at any time." I make a point of not mentioning anything about lawyers. Best not to let that word linger.

My last statement is enough to loosen the worry lines from around his eyes. I glance at Tom who grins. He hates waiting as much as I do. "A couple weeks ago you talked with Cord Philips from the NTSB, is that right?"

Joe nods again. It's obvious he's come straight over from work since he's still got on his uniform: thick oil-stained black work pants and a short-sleeved blue work shirt. I'm betting he wants to get home and down a few of those beers I saw in his daughter's shopping cart last week. I wish I could have helped the woman break into her dead fiancé's phone, but I'm too much of a do-it-by-the-book kind of cop. Usually.

"Yeah, he asked me about fueling the plane that morning."

Tom beats me to the next question: "And were you, in fact, the person who fueled the plane?"

Joe looks put out. "Yeah, why?"

"And you filled the two tanks with—" Tom has the luxury of having the NTSB report in front of him, whereas I have nothing but empty space—"Avgas. Is this correct?"

"What's going on?" Joe leans forward as if it's only just now hitting him how serious this might be, even though, personally, I am still indeterminate. We're only here to see if we can uncover motive. The actual crime has yet to be established. It's an ass-backward way to go about things, if you ask me, but no one is asking me so I move on.

"And you didn't notice any condensation around the cap," I say because I remember reading something relevant about this in the notes before the Great Coffee Spill.

"Why are you asking me the same question Philips asked me? We already went through this. Like I told *him*, no, I did not." He slams his hand down. His previous nervousness is now haloed by anger. "And before you ask me, no, I have no idea if Cooper sumped the fuel before taking off." He sits back again and crosses his arms in front of his chest, clearly annoyed.

"What does that mean, 'sumped'?" I ask. Philips briefed us, but I want to hear it again.

"Drain. Sump. Same thing. After a plane gets fueled the pilot's supposed to drain a little fuel into a cup to, you know, see if it's the right fuel. Check for water or other kinds of contaminants, that sort of thing." He shakes his head and looks down. "Now that I think about it, I don't think I ever saw either Cal or his father sump." His eyes suddenly face forward. "Are you suggesting that the fuel was wrong because if you are, I'm telling you now I have never once, not *once*, misfueled a plane in my life!"

"Noted," Tom says. "But they did find water in the fuel tank. And the—" again Tom flicks through the pages—"the gascolator."

"Are you kidding?" Joe looks surprised.

"No, Joe. The NTSB report shows that the fuel was 'non-conforming,'" I say, slightly giddy that I at least remembered that part.

"Joe, is it true you worked on Calvin Cooper's Piper a few months ago without his permission?" Tom says, moving on to what could potentially be damning.

"Ah, shit. I knew this is why you called me in. Why Philips was digging around." He nods. "Yeah. I did."

I jump in this time. "Why would you do that?"

He sighs. "Couple of months ago I overheard Calvin saying to one of the boys in the shop that his plane was flying crooked and had a heavy right wing so I said maybe his ailerons were mis-rigged. But he didn't care. Told me to mind my own business." Joe's eyes move away from mine when he says this.

"Is that really how the conversation went? Because it's not how some of your coworkers remember it." I've rattled him, but I want him there, in that place where he either finds it in himself to tell the truth or he pulls back so much I know he's lying.

"Okay, yeah, so maybe Calvin lost his temper a bit. Important guy like that has better things to worry about than some service tech telling him what's wrong with his plane." He shrugs. I wait for him to fill in the rest, but since he doesn't, I do.

"He referred to you as a janitor and said that he wished you and your—quote 'waitress daughter' unquote—would stay the fuck out of his life. Isn't that what he said, Joe?"

"I guess. Something like that." He is trying to come off as if Calvin Cooper's derisive outburst didn't make a dent, but I don't buy it.

"But you still went ahead and did something to his plane," Tom says.

Joe's mouth stays shut. There's no sound in the room beyond Tom's pen tapping the report. Finally, Joe opens up and says, "Deni told me she and Cal were planning a trip up to, um, Seattle, together. Flying, I mean." I watch his right-hand twist around his left like he's cleaning it with a dirty rag. I also notice, for the first time, that his left eye is kind of cloudy and then I remember: he got axed from his job at Southwest after an accident that left him almost completely blind in that eye. He'd been drunk on the job.

"And you were worried about her safety?" Tom asks as if he's a drinking buddy sitting on the next stool over.

"Yeah, I was, so one morning I snuck into the hangar and adjusted the jackscrew on the left flap. Nothing major, but I never heard him complain again," Joe answers. There's a tiny rise in the corner of his mouth.

"Someone saw you come out of the hangar?"

"Yup. My boss, Manny. I told him what I did, and he made me write out a service report to have on record. He's a good guy, Manny. Hired me when no one else would. I think he made sure Calvin never got wind of that report."

"The NTSB got wind of it, Joe."

"Okay."

As I watch Tom gather the papers together in front of him so they're in a neat pile, something gnaws at my gut. "Did Deni and Cal ever take that trip?"

"Trip?"

"To Seattle. Deni and Cal were going to fly to Seattle?"

He shifts his eyes back and forth, pretending to think about it. "No, they didn't," he replies. "Must have gotten too busy."

CHAPTER

31

GRANT WAITS TO be sure Erika has finished speaking before he stands up from the chair and sits down beside her on the couch. He pulls her left hand to his lips and kisses the knuckles. "I'm sorry you had to go through that." He is so unbelievably relieved, so goddamned overjoyed by the story he's just heard. It all makes so much sense now! The reason she didn't want him to ask her about her past. Her rationalization for changing her name. If he'd killed someone when he was a kid and wanted to start over, he would have done the same. What name would he have chosen, he wonders? He's always hated the name Grant and would, if given the opportunity, maybe change it to something cool, like Justin or Lucas. Wait. Didn't Erika say she had a boyfriend whose name was Luke? He doesn't want to ask her to repeat that part of the tale because he can see from the way her body is slumped against the back of the stern couch that she is depleted.

He feels so energized by Erika's—should he start calling her Katie now?—tragic past that he wants to fuck her. He wants to fuck her. then jump in the freezing cold pool and do a hundred laps, then eat an entire sausage pizza from Mountain Mike's, then—dammit, he wishes his parents could be here right now. How great it would have been to prove to Calvin and Jean that Erika isn't with him because of the money. That she has no evil or selfish intentions. That she loves him fair and square.

"You hungry?" he asks because he has no idea what else to say. Actually, he has a lot to say—rather, questions to ask, like what happened after she left juvenile hall and why doesn't she ever mention her mother and how did she end up a coke addict and alcoholic, but she's already given so much of herself that he is smart enough to move those questions to the back burner for the time being.

"You're not mad?" she asks, pouting like a little girl who's just busted her mother's favorite vase. If he'd broken his mother's favorite vase she would have been angry enough to shove Grant's soft skin into the sharp slivers, but Grant feels no grudge toward Erika whatsoever. Break a vase. Off a stepfather. What difference does it make? He's over the moon that his hot girlfriend is also a murderer. How fucking sexy is that? She killed the person who wronged her. Grant's lost count of how many times he daydreamed about killing his father.

"Hell no! You're a rock star," he says, which elicits a huge smile from Erika. "If I'd known you back then I would have helped you off the fucker."

"You?" She laughs. "There's no way you would have had the nerve. You barely have the courage to ask the workers to clean up after themselves."

Is she actually laughing at him? Is not his timidity completely irrelevant at the moment? Hey, he killed someone too. She knows about that, so why is she calling him a pussy?

"Huh. Okay." He stands up. He no longer has any itch to fuck her or to go swimming. He doesn't even have any interest in changing his name.

"I'm gonna go get some fresh air," he declares, walking out of the room.

* * *

By the time he reaches Cal and Deni's homesite Grant is feeling a whole lot better. Once he's on level ground he squats and leans back against a tree. Picks up a pine needle and sticks it in his mouth. Takes in the view. The sun is low on the horizon, its rays streaking like laser beams through the dense forest, splashing the ground around him.

It's quiet here. More quiet than at his parents' place, although he doesn't understand why that is. Why does it feel so much more peaceful on this stretch of land than up the hill? Why does his childhood home feel as if it's always filled with noise? He ponders this for a while and settles on the idea that it must be his memories that are making the racket. Sure, Erika/Katie whitewashed most of the surfaces of the place, but the remembrances have remained just as vivid. The yelling. The constricting loneliness. Being afraid of his father. Wanting and getting no affection from his mother. Remodel or not, all those unhappy times remain like grooves etched into an old table.

He spits out the needle and pushes himself up. Breathes the air deep into his lungs. He likes this spot. So much so that before he's made it back to the house, before he finds Erika sprawled naked across the bed in his parents' old room, he has decided that he has the perfect project: he's going to build Cal and Deni's dream house.

CHAPTER 32

I'M IN MY room, about to click on the video again, when I hear the door slam. I walk out into the living room expecting to see my father making his way into the kitchen, but he's just standing by the front door. "What's wrong, Dad?" I ask when I see the look on his face. "Where have you been?"

"I was up at the Gold Hills police station," he says flatly. "They asked me to come in to answer some questions."

"Why? What's going on?"

"I'm not a hundred percent sure, but I get the feeling the NTSB thinks someone sabotaged the plane."

"Whose plane?"

"The Coopers' plane."

"I'm confused. You said Cal crashed because he flew into bad weather. What's that got to do with *sabotage*? And, what's it got to do with you?"

"They found out that I worked on the Piper a few months ago. Maybe they think I killed the Coopers."

"WHAT?"

Ignoring my outburst, he removes his coat, hangs it on the hook and goes over to the couch. "Jesus, I've had a hell of a day," he says tiredly. "Do me a favor and get me a beer."

Just as he's reaching for the remote I rush to position myself between him and the television, and like I've done a hundred thousand times before when I wanted his attention, I begin waving my arms around. "You cannot just leave it there! Tell me."

He sighs. "Look, I'm only going by what I picked up from the interview, but the fuel might have been contaminated or . . . or they're thinking maybe someone messed with the engine," he tells me more calmly than I expect.

I sit down on the couch and he pivots around so he can still see me with his good eye. Sometimes I forget to place myself on his right side, but I'm too anxious to be thinking about that right now. "Why would you even touch their plane?" I know my father misses working on airplanes almost as much as he misses my mother, but working on Calvin Cooper's plane? "Did Calvin ask you to fix it?"

"No." He grins. "But that plane is so old it needed—sorry—*was* old," he corrects himself. I flash on the scene of a mangled plane, burnt metal parts and crushed bodies strewn across the mountainside.

"It just needed a little correction is all," he says, jerking my attention away from the mental images. "How about that beer?"

I don't like how casual he's sounding about this. "Daddy, are you in trouble? Do we need to hire a lawyer?" Not that we can afford one. We barely have enough money to pay the mortgage every month. So much for my plans to finish my college degree. If we do end up needing a lawyer, I'll have to beg Sue to let me work more hours. Or take another job. My father has already lost one good job—and a good eye to boot—so if there's a chance he's about to get fired from his current position, we're screwed. "Dad. The cops called you in for questioning. I don't understand why you're not taking this more seriously."

"I am taking it seriously." He closes his eyes and lets his head fall back. "I guess I'm just fed up with all of it. I didn't mess with the plane, but"—he releases a rumbly sigh—"I honestly don't care if I go to jail."

"You're not going to jail, Dad!" He opens his eyes when he hears the panic in my voice. "We'll get you a lawyer. We'll figure this out. I promise." I hate the thought that my father is ready to write off his life, but I see now that ever since my mother passed and he lost his mechanic job at Southwest, he's been doing exactly that. He hates having to fuel planes, carry luggage, and clean toilets at a measly regional airport. The only things waiting for him after a long day of work are beer and television. The man has no friends. And ever since I started dating Cal, it's not as if I've been around to keep him company. When was the last time we ate a meal together, my father and I? Went to the movies?

With one fell swoop I take the pulse of our lives and what I feel is sadness. Loss. It's as if the house is filled with a gray fug of surrender. Before Cal, I had my job. Luna. Not much else, come to think of it. Both Dad and I went about our lives on autopilot. Get up. Go to work. Come home. Eat. Sleep. Repeat. On occasion I'd drive up to Luna's farm.

But then Cal appeared like an apparition out of a fantasy book. He let me imagine a life that only existed in fictional worlds. Being with Cal meant I was going to have a lot of money. I would be able to move my father into some fancy retirement community where he could make friends. Maybe learn to play golf. I'd live in a big house surrounded by trees. I would finally have the peace and quiet I so desperately wanted. Once I married Cal Cooper Jr., I would get to live the perfect life with the perfect man.

With that thought, I remember the video. I stand up and head into the kitchen to grab my father a beer. "I gotta go check on something, Dad," I say, handing it to him. He's already got the TV on and is clicking through the channels.

"Thanks," he replies and before I turn to leave he tells me to hold up a second.

"What?" I ask impatiently.

"Hey, um, I need you to do me a favor." He's still clicking away, and I stand there, tapping my foot, waiting.

"If the cops ask if you and Cal were planning to fly up to Seattle last August, tell them you were, okay?"

"Sure, Dad," I reply, having no clue what he's talking about, not that I care. I have more pressing matters to attend to.

C H A P T E R

33

I'M SOME FIFTY yards in front of Vera when the competitive edge in me quits, and I slow down to a fast walk. I can hear Vera's heavy breathing behind me long before she catches up. When she finally does, I stop moving. "You need to rest a little, old lady?" I ask her, smiling widely. In the olden days, Vera outran me most every time we raced together.

"Ha ha." She continues on down the trail, grinning at me over her shoulder. I stay perfectly still as I watch her pump her arms with every stride. For a sunny Saturday in late autumn, the park is relatively quiet today. When I knocked on Vera's door an hour ago—coffee in hand—and announced that we were going on a run, she readily agreed. We haven't been spending enough time together, and since we're both the sort of humans who get too lost in our jobs, she even seemed grateful.

A bluebird sweeps by me and lands on a nearby oak. I can see by the bright blue of its head and wing edges that it's a male. He chirps and I look around. I don't see any other bluebirds in the vicinity. Who is he speaking to? Or is he simply wanting, like males in all species, to be heard by the universe?

I am about to start running again when the memory of watching a different bluebird zaps my brain. It was when I was sitting with Deni Rydell in Luna's farm shed the day Luna's body was discovered. Why did I suddenly flash on that? I resume walking instead of jogging because I know walking won't interfere with the firings between my synapses. When I run, I become an unthinking machine, nothing more than muscle, bone, and breath. Now, though, I want to think.

I've gone maybe a quarter mile when I spot Vera leaning against a tree. I offer her my water bottle and she downs some. "I am in such bad shape," she says, handing it back to me. "When did I become such a sloth?"

"When you started cutting up dead bodies?" I reply wryly. Vera is definitely more plump than when she first arrived back in Prosperity, and I am willing to take partial blame for that. It's on me that most of the times we do manage to hang out, it's to either drink too much alcohol or eat too many carbs while watching television. I let the guilt linger for half a second, then take a sip of some water and push the cap closed. I never would have brought along a water bottle for a three-mile run on flat ground, but I had an inkling Vera would need it.

"Let's walk for a little," I say, gently shoving her forward. "I want to do some out-loud thinking."

Since my best friend is the M.E., she's sworn to secrecy. She already knows who all the major players are in my investigations, so the prelims are unnecessary and I decide to lead with a bombshell. "Deni Rydell came into the station yesterday with an old video she found on Cal's phone. It shows her dead fiancé taking part in a gangbang. With Grant's girlfriend Erika." Without skipping a stride, I wait for that to sink in.

It takes less than four seconds before it does. "Yo! Hold up!" Vera grabs my arm and brings me to a stop. "What?"

I pull her along with me while bringing her up to speed about the NTSB investigator suspecting sabotage but not yet having enough clear-cut evidence. I tell her about Tom and me questioning Deni's father Joe. Then about the most recent occurrence: Deni showing up less than twenty-four hours later with what she believes is proof that if the plane *was* sabotaged, it was Grant who did it.

"How does she figure?" Vera asks.

"She said that Cal told her repeatedly about the tension up at the house, that there was no love lost between his parents and Erika. They didn't want her in Grant's life. Full stop. A couple days before the three of them flew to Nevada, Cal confided in Deni that he had something that would make the parents totally freak out. He said he was still deciding whether or not to show them because he was sure they'd force Grant to kick Erika to the curb. But when she asked him what it was, he refused to tell her."

"It was the video," Vera says, hooking her eyebrows together. She's paying such close attention to the story I make sure to face forward; I don't want her tripping on a tree root.

"Yeah. NTSB found Cal's phone after the crash and sent it to Grant, who was nice enough to hand it off to

Deni," I continue. "She found the video on his phone. Says it must be what Cal was threatening his brother with. It actually makes perfect sense, except why—"

"So, she thinks that if Cal showed them the video they'd make Grant dump the girlfriend?" Vera stops and puts her hands on her hips. "Why? Because she had sex with their other son? That's not enough of a reason."

"Do you not remember the kind of people the Coopers were, Vera? Reputation was *everything* to them. It was bad enough Grant met Erika in rehab. If it ever came out that their son's sweetheart used to be a prostitute . . . ?"

"Who says she was a sex worker?"

Sharing case facts with Vera is as fun as eating a chocolate-coated ice cream bar on the river in summer. Tom is great to bounce ideas off of, sure, but sometimes it's Vera's cluelessness that leads me out of the cave of the unexplained and into the light of certainty. "Based on what I saw, she most definitely wasn't enjoying herself. I have no doubt she was only in it for the money." It's unfortunate that, having watched it twice, I will never be able to unsee that video.

Vera's gait speeds up, but, thankfully, she staring at the ground. She's thinking. "But Grant wasn't going to let that happen," she says, coming to a stop again. With all this starting and stopping I'm starting to feel a little vertigo like I always did when I rode in my Uncle Phil's car. The man tapped his brakes every eight seconds for fear he was either going over the speed limit or he'd hit some imaginary kid who planned to run out into the street the moment the car approached.

"Right." I don't want to feed her my question yet; I'm hoping she finds the loophole herself. We walk on silently. The wind is nonexistent. The only sounds are the birdsong, the faint voices of other walkers on the forest trails, and the low hum of the Osborne River a few miles away. I drink in a breath and wait.

After another few minutes go by, Vera tilts her head toward me. "Why?" she says.

"Why what?" She caught it. I know she did.

"Why did Cal need to threaten Grant? What did he want from him?"

Exactly.

"I'm not sure." I stop to tie my left shoe. "I asked Deni that very question and I didn't love her answer. She said that there'd always been a nasty rivalry between the two of them." Boys will be boys, yeah, but was Cal enough of a sonofabitch to hold this over his brother's head? I'm not sure. The more relevant question: Was Cal's threat against Erika enough to make Grant want to kill his entire family? Again, I'm not sure.

"So, what's your next move, Detective Torres?"

"Get you to finish this run without dying," I say, taking off down the trail, "then go find Grant Cooper."

CHAPTER 34

WHILE HE'S WAITING, Grant snaps off a chunk of Styrofoam from the cup in front of him and then breaks it into tiny pieces. Why are they making him sit here like this? He takes another sip of the rancid coffee, and this sip is as bad as the first. He spends the next minute chastising himself for being stupid enough to think the coffee would somehow get better with age, and the minute after that, bashing his thumbs against his other fingers while chanting his memorized mantras. He is just getting to a second round of "I choose to be happy today," when—finally—two detectives walk into the room, sit down across from him, and introduce themselves.

When the female one—Detective Torres—phoned him this morning and asked him to come in for a quick chat, he'd asked what it was about and she'd said the plane crash. Though he heard his father's voice commanding him to protect himself, he hadn't bothered calling the family lawyer. He doesn't know anything more about the plane crash than the friendly receptionist who greeted him from behind the bulletproof glass does.

He'll be fine.

"Now that we've gotten the formalities out of the way," Detective Torres says, pulling her hand from his, "we've got a couple questions if you don't mind."

She's so nice that Grant relaxes a little. He likes looking at her. She has some familiar quality about her. She's older than he is, but he feels like maybe he knows her. For a second he tenses. Did she ever arrest him during his oxy days? If so, she's hiding it from him. In fact, she seems like she's really glad he's here.

"Absolutely," he says, dumping the white bits into the broken cup and sliding it to the end of the table. "Ask me anything."

The partner, Tom-something—Grant was so busy looking at Torres he missed the guy's surname—says, "Do you have your pilot's license?"

"Nope."

"But you've flown your family's Piper. Is that correct?"

"I mean, yeah, I took a couple flight lessons in it."

"Why didn't you get your license?" Torres asks.

"No reason. Just wasn't into it." He shrugs to show them it doesn't matter whether or not he completed his training. Fact is, he would have loved to have been able to fly off for a weekend with his friends like Cal did. He aced ground school, but once he hit the cockpit, things veered way off course. His father insisted on being his flight instructor, which was about as good an idea as tying your dog to the back of your motorcycle so it could get in a good run. Every single time he made even a small mistake or used an incorrect term, the asshole would make Grant aware of how much of a moron he was.

Grant never got past the lesson on descending. He'd had enough.

"You knew the plane, though?"

"*Knew* it? What do you mean?"

"How to fuel it, how to check the engine, that sort of stuff," Tom clarifies.

"Of course." Why are they asking him such basic questions? "You can't get into the cockpit until you know all that."

"Okay, great. Thanks," Torres says, as if his answer just made her day. Thinking they're done, Grant scoots his butt back in the chair and starts to stand up. "Whoa, Nelly!" Torres shouts while putting out her hand. "Just a couple more minutes, Grant, okay?"

He sits back and eyes them cautiously. Torres pulls her iPhone out of her suit jacket pocket and for a moment Grant thinks she's texting someone—that is, until she skates it across the table and says, "Hit Play for me, would you?"

On the screen is a frozen video overlaid with an arrow. He touches it and watches what looks to be a porn video. Ten seconds in, he looks up, utterly confused. "Why are you making me watch this? What does it have to do with the plane crash?"

"You're probably tired of seeing it, right?" Tom says with a knowing smirk.

Grant looks from him back to the frozen screen. "I've never seen this before," he says, catching a look pass between them that he is certain borders on confusion. He starts to hand it back, but Torres tells him to start over and watch the whole thing through to the end. She asks nicely enough, but her tone makes it clear to Grant that he has no choice but to hit Play again. This time he focuses in on the face of the guy holding the leash and that's when it hits him. "That's Cal!" he shouts, almost pleased with himself for getting something right for once. This is why they wanted him to watch this thing. Wait. Why are they making him watch Cal fuck some chick?

When the video ends, he slides it back across the table and wipes his hands across the top of his jeans as if he's just touched something sticky. "Yeah. So? My brother liked rough group sex. What's your point?"

Torres has her eyebrow raised. "You recognize anyone else in that video?" She makes as if she's going to slide it back and Grant holds his hands up like he's a goalie blocking a penalty kick.

"No! Please don't make me watch it again." It was gross enough the first time. "And to answer your question, no, I didn't." Then something dawns on him. "Where'd you find this?"

Torres exchanges another unreadable look with Tom before resting her elbows on the dingy table and leaning forward. She hooks her eyes on his. "It was on Cal's phone, Grant. Did he ever show it to you?"

"No. Why would he?"

"Thanks for your time, Grant," she says, leaning back with a small shake of her head. "You're free to go."

CHAPTER

35

"WELL, FUCK ME," I say, the moment Tom returns to the interview room.

He leans up against the wall behind Grant's vacated chair and crosses his arms. "I would, but I kind of get the sense you're not partial to my particular anatomy."

I ignore his juvenile quip. "So, what have we got here? Deni finds a video on Cal's phone. She storms into the station with this grandiose theory that Cal was threatening to expose his brother's girlfriend's past, and that was enough to motivate Grant to sabotage his family's plane."

"Hold up. Isn't it possible the girl in the video is *not* the girlfriend?"

I had considered this, but Deni was adamant that even though her hair is different now, there's no mistaking her for the Erika Morris she met on more than a few occasions. "Maybe subconsciously Grant didn't *want* to recognize her?" I throw out just to see how it sounds. To see if what my gut is saying makes as much sense when I let it speak. "Sometimes we see what we want to see."

"You and I need to set up a meet and greet with this young woman. Pronto. Make sure she's the girlfriend."

I grin. "Yup. I've got Colin running Erika through the system as we speak."

Tom pushes off from the wall and grabs the back of the chair. "Assuming she is the same person, why didn't you point her out to Grant?"

I almost did, but something told me to hold on to that piece of evidence because it might come in handy down the road. "Why didn't you?"

Tom frowns. "Once I knew for a fact that he'd never seen the video, I—uh, I suppose I feel kind of bad for the guy."

I nod my agreement. Whether or not he had anything to do with it, Grant Cooper just lost his entire family. The man has to be doing some serious mourning.

On the other hand, he has also recently inherited a great deal of money, I think cynically. With or without Cal threatening him, that's motive enough to want his family dead.

This murder investigation of ours is jumbling my brain. It's trying to make connections where there might, in fact, be none.

"Wait, hold up," I say when Tom starts toward the door. "I want to get down a visual. You can tack it up to the board when I'm done." I rip an empty page out of my notebook. Draw a line down the middle of it. I header the left side LUNA and the right PLANE CRASH. Then I list off who's remotely involved in each case.

LUNA	**PLANE CRASH**
Luna Rose	*Cal Cooper*
Unborn Fetus	*Calvin and Jean Cooper*
Unknown Father	*Grant Cooper*
Misha Rose	*Erika Morris*
Deni Rydell	*Deni Rydell*
	Joe Rydell

I then turn the paper so it's facing my partner. Something in this picture seems so mightily suspect, I can feel it wind down my entire spinal column.

Tom flips the chair around and straddles it before fingering the sheet. "Okay. What's your point?"

"The connection between both cases is Deni Rydell. Her fiancé and pregnant bestie die at the same time. Literally." A familiar sensation blows across my brain like a tornado picking up speed as well as everything in its wake. I noticed it the day I first met Deni. I am keenly aware of it now. "What are the odds?"

"A million to one," Tom pronounces.

"Yup," I say, more frustrated now than I was ten seconds ago.

"You think *she* had something to do with the plane crash? Why would she want to kill her own fiancé?" It's as if Tom's reading my mind as quickly as my thoughts are rushing through my head.

"She wouldn't," I say, "but I can see why her father *might*. He hated Calvin. And he had the know-how."

"Nah. I don't buy it," Tom replies skeptically. "The guy seemed pretty decent, if you ask me. Besides, once his daughter married Cal, she was going to be rich as shit, and you could be sure he was going to reap some of those benefits."

I nod again. "Fair enough." Joe Rydell didn't come off as a killer, that was for sure. "Regardless of his innocence, I believe Deni showed us that video to deflect us from her father."

"That's good reasoning."

Deni doesn't want us thinking her father killed the Coopers. She wants us to think Grant did it. Why? Does she have some vendetta against him? Does she know something else that she's not telling us? I can't get the connection out of me. It's like a tick digging into my skin.

"But as long as we're looking into him," Tom says, drawing continuous circles around Grant Cooper's name on the paper, "What if we drill down a little deeper?"

"What do you mean?"

"We have Grant's DNA on record from his priors."

I sit up higher in the chair. "Yeah, so?"

He gives me a huge grin and makes for the door but stops before opening it. "Just for the hell of it, I'm gonna run it through the system again."

CHAPTER

36

I'M JUST PLACING a plate of eggs Benedict with a side of grits in front of the customer seated at table 4 when I see Misha Rose walk into Marvin's. I smile and give her a small wave, but my hand stops midair when I see the strange look on her face. Something is definitely up. "Hi, Misha," I say as I wipe my hands on my apron. There's probably nothing on them, but the woman is so immaculate I don't want to chance leaving any grease on her if she decides to hug me. "It's so nice to see you."

Misha is dressed in a long beige wool skirt and black cashmere sweater. She leans forward and gives me a peck on my cheek, but our bodies remain apart, thank goodness. I have never much loved being hugged by people. Cal and I were well matched in that way; he wasn't a hugger either. At the thought of him ever touching me I stiffen and quickly wash the image of him from my mind. "We don't have any tables available, but there's a seat at the counter if you want."

"I called you and left a message. Three times, in fact," she says in a low and uncharacteristically stern voice.

"Pick up! Table 6," Sue calls out behind me.

"My phone's off while I'm at work. Sorry." I give Misha a quizzical look before steering her toward the counter. "Have a seat. I'll be back in a few."

The place is mobbed, and it's a while before I get a chance to walk behind the counter so I'm facing Misha. In front of her is a mug of jasmine tea and an untouched order of wheat toast. I don't think I can recall Luna's mother ever coming into Marvin's. It's not the sort of place that serves tempeh or matcha, her preferred kind of food. "Okay," I say, smiling. "Sorry about that. What's up? How are you doing?"

"I was going through Luna's clothes this morning—I'm going to donate them—and I found this," she says, setting a small black flip phone on the counter, "in the pocket of an old pair of jeans." She picks up the mug of tea and wraps her hands around it.

It's obviously a burner phone. Detective Torres had already informed Misha that there was nothing of interest and nothing related to any of her marijuana dealings on Luna's iPhone. Now I know why. "It makes total sense she'd have one," I say. Misha wasn't entirely happy that Luna grew pot on the land, but she was so wrapped up in her life so far away in Bali she didn't have much sway in the matter. "For the pot business," I add.

Misha takes a sip of the tea and shakes her head. "No. It wasn't for the business."

Behind Misha I see Laila, one of the new waitresses, bump up against the back of a customer's chair and almost drop her entire order on the floor. That would have been a disaster.

"Then what did she use it for?" I ask, looking back at the phone.

"To text someone named J."

"Jay?"

Misha glances to her right, then back at me. "Not the name *Jay*," she says, suddenly lowering her voice to a whisper. I am momentarily confused, but then I recognize that the person sitting beside Misha is Cathy Reamer, a local reporter at the *Gold Hills Ledger*. She's wolfing down a pile of scrambled eggs and pretending not to eavesdrop. "The *initial* J. Do you know who that is?"

Who did Luna know with that initial? "Her dealer in San Fran—his name is Johnny something," I say, keeping my own voice low. "It has to be him," I state with utter certainty. Who else could it be?

"You're not hearing me, Deni," she says with an annoyed tinge to her voice. "It was the father of her child."

I take a step back as if a cold slap of wind has just hit me in my chest. "What? How do you know? Show me." If this J person was the father of Luna's baby, it was quite possible he was the person who murdered her.

I watch her press the power button, but nothing happens. "Oh no. It's dead."

Is she serious? I'm about to lose my mind here.

Misha says, "I was hoping—" when Sue Marvin suddenly hip checks me with a plate in each of her hands. "Hey, kiddo, you've got three tables that need refills. And two that need their orders taken."

"Oh, sorry!" I turn to Misha. "Can you leave the phone with me so I can look through it later? I'll find a charger."

Misha thinks about it for too long. Does she not see that I have to get back to work? "I wanted you to take a quick peek before I brought it to the police." She stands up and puts the phone in her tiny beaded purse. "I thought you'd know who it was."

"But if I read the texts maybe I *will* recognize the person—please, Misha. Let me have it. I promise I'll bring it to Detective Torres right after I look." Once the police have it, I'll have no access and who knows what they'll be able to find. "I was her best friend, Misha. If anyone can figure it out, it's me!" My pleading sounds pathetic.

"Deni! Now!" Sue hollers.

Reluctantly, Misha pulls the phone out of her purse and deposits it in my hand. "You have until five to bring it to the police."

CHAPTER 37

After introducing ourselves and flashing our badges, Tom and I wait while Erika decides whether or not to allow us in. We're standing on an enormous concrete and brick landing leading into a colossally large house. After driving around the circular entrance and pulling to a stop, Tom had whistled his astonishment.

"Who would ever have thought digging up rocks could buy you a place like this," he'd remarked as we got out of the car and stared at the glass-covered turrets bookending the two corners of the structure. "I'm in the wrong line of work," he threw out as an afterthought.

"No, you're exactly where you should be, O partner, my partner." I wasn't sure he got the Walt Whitman reference, but it made me smile, remembering the poem. I read it in high school at a time when I was still searching for myself within myself. I'd thought it was a stupid bunch of words about mourning a dead president, but our teacher was steadfast in her quest to make us see the metaphors and meanings the piece contained. I fought it for as long as possible, but then one night, after reading it aloud for the fifth time, I finally understood what she was attempting to inculcate: that there's no sadness without happiness. No victory can arise without the understanding of defeat. How can we know our own true self without first dissolving our preconceived notions?

I slice into Erika's hesitation and ask, "Is Grant home?"

"Do you have a warrant? I don't have to let you in, you know," she finally utters.

Tom snorts and I almost kick him. "No, we don't have a warrant," I reply calmly. "We just want to ask you a couple questions and then we'll get out of your hair."

"About?"

She's a tough one, this woman. Pretty too. Far prettier than she looked in that video where she was getting it from all sides. Gone are the stringy hair and fearful eyes, replaced by salon-colored roots and defiance, respectively. "Luna Rose."

"Who?"

Tom quietly knocks his knuckle against the door jamb in frustration. "The local woman who was murdered in September? It was in all the papers?" He's as incredulous as I am. Is she that good of a liar or is she truly ignorant? At this point I cannot say for sure since Colin's preliminary search has uncovered nil regarding one Erika Morris.

"I have no idea what you're talking about, but, yeah, sure," she says, checking behind her as if she's making sure the coast is clear. "Come in." We follow her through the expansive entryway into a living room that could easily be featured in a glossy design magazine. There's an enormous gray couch that looks as if it's just had the shrink wrap removed ten minutes ago. There's not an indent, divot, or wrinkle anywhere on the fabric. In front of it sits a dangerously fragile-looking rectangular glass coffee table. Two modern armchairs with matching gray fabric complete the tableau. "Have a seat," Erika says, gesturing toward the chairs while she sits upright, perched at the edge of the couch like a porcelain bookend.

We settle in—if you can call it that, considering that the cushion upon which I place my ass has no give whatsoever. It's like sitting on a bleacher seat in a stadium. Tom begins by familiarizing Erika with the facts about Luna's case—those that were made public, anyway. I watch her as she listens, her neutral facial expression giving away nothing.

"Like I said, I don't know anything about it. A few weeks after I got here my boyfriend's entire family died in a plane crash, so, I mean, all I've been doing since then is helping Grant get through it, day by day." Although she's otherwise the epitome of composure, Erika's right hand keeps fidgeting back and forth between her nose and her lap. She's either checking to see if she has a booger hanging out, or she's someone who used to—or perhaps still does—snort drugs up her nostrils. Ever since meth crash-landed here, I've seen more than my fair share of nervous nose touchers.

"I'm sure you've been a great comfort to Grant," I say, burying the sarcasm in my voice. Erika doesn't strike me as the empathetic type, but maybe I'm completely biased by the ice-queen 'tude she's got going on. Regardless, I don't want her kicking us out so I stay soft, and swiftly move on to a more relevant topic. "What can you tell us about Cal Cooper? The brother. Not the father," I clarify.

She shrugs. "Not much. I hardly ever saw him. Before the crash, before I moved in here, I mean, Grant's parents made me stay in the guest suite over the garage." She points her finger behind her in the direction of the garage area. "By the time I'd show up for breakfast in the mornings Cal was usually gone."

Tom and I nod in unison. "Had you ever met Cal before?" Tom asks as innocently as a toddler asking his mother if he can eat just one more piece of candy. She answers before his voice reaches the question mark upswing.

"Nope."

During our pre-visit triage on the drive up here, Tom and I decided it'd be best not to expose the video just yet, although at the moment I can feel it burning a small hole in my jacket pocket. "What was his relationship like with his brother?"

"Grant?" She smiles. "Fine. They hardly spent any time together. But they were your typical brothers. I think they really liked each other. Cal looked up to him, you know?"

"That's good to hear," Tom says, cheerfully. "My brother and I couldn't stand each other."

He's lying. He and his younger brother Will are best friends.

"And what about his relationship with Deni, his fiancée?" Tom continues. "Did you ever see them interact?"

She looks out toward the backyard and I follow her gaze, noticing for the first time the grassy fields that slope beyond the pool, stretching for what seems like a hundred acres toward a second-growth forest tract. The scene is postcard pretty. "I think there was some trouble in paradise, but that's not for me to say."

"Please do," I encourage.

"Well, there was this one night." She lowers her voice conspiratorially, as if someone who shouldn't be listening might be close by. "I was in my room, you know, above the garage, and they probably had no idea I was up there. Anyway, the window was open and—they were standing next to Deni's car—I could hear them arguing about a woman. It sounded like Deni just found out Cal cheated on her, and oh man, she was pissed off. She kept saying, 'I'm going to kill her. I'm going to kill that bitch' over and over, and Cal kept trying to calm her down and promising it was over and begging her to forgive him."

"Did you catch the woman's name?" Tom asks dispassionately. He's doing a bang-up job, stifling the buzz we're both feeling at the moment.

"No. But what I remember thinking was that Deni's not the meek little person she pretends to be when she's in front of the parents. She's way more—wait! Oh, my God!" Erika's eyes almost bug out of her head when she says, "Luna. I remember now. Deni said, 'I'm going to kill that bitch *Luna*!'"

CHAPTER

38

A FEW BLISTERS ARE already starting to form on his palms by the time Grant tosses the chainsaw onto the ground. After taking off the gloves, he opens and closes his hands, grimacing as he wipes the dirt and sweat off his face. There's DIY and then there's *DIY*, he thinks, knowing he is going to have to call in the professionals. At least for clearing and leveling the parcel he'll bring in an excavator. Or maybe he can give Geri a call and ask her to lend him a couple guys for a week. He owns the company, right? He's the boss. He can tell her to pull a construction team from, say, the Truckee site, and send 'em down here to do some work. No harm in asking.

Then again, he doesn't want Geri assuming he's doing anything other than grieving. She is still waiting on his decision about returning back to work. He'd be happy never stepping foot in a quarry again, but she doesn't need to know that. The money's still rolling in and yeah, there's been offers from two potential buyers, but, again, Grant is fine with letting things stay status quo.

Damn, he's hungry. And tired. What he needs is a shower and a nap. Hopefully Erika is out shopping because he doesn't have the energy for sex right now. Ever since that day when she shared her past with him, she's been a total horndog. Like, she can't get enough of his attention, and, honestly, it's kind of wearing him out. She's also been pushing him to get married and that too is starting to annoy him. Sure, he loves her. She's the hottest woman he's ever known. But is she his forever person? Does he really want to have kids with someone who's capable of driving an ice pick through the brain of another human being?

Grant wipes his sore hands across his Carhartt pants and looks back up the hill toward his parents' house. For sure, it'll be good to move out of there. The sooner he gets a crew of workers here, the sooner he can build a place of his own.

* * *

The moment Grant steps inside the house he knows he's not going to get that nap. There are voices coming from the living room. He considers heading straight for the master bedroom, but his curiosity is piqued. Erika's probably meeting with another designer or interior decorator or contractor or—who knows—maybe she wants to build a tennis court. The other day he could have sworn he heard her mention it, but sometimes when she talks about her next project he shuts down and only pretends to listen.

He walks into the living room and stops breathing. Those two cops who interrogated him a few days ago are sitting there. Before he can turn around, Torres greets him like an old friend.

"Hi, Grant. Good to see you," she says pleasantly enough.

"Hello, Detective Torres." He nods at the other one because he cannot remember his name. "Why are you here? What's going on?"

"Detective Horner and I were just asking Erika what she knew about your brother's relationship with Deni Rydell."

"They were getting married. What do you mean?"

In one very cryptic look exchanged between the two detectives, Grant believes an entire conversation has just taken place. What do they know that he does not?

"Was Cal also seeing Luna Rose on the sly?" Horner asks.

"His old high school girlfriend, Luna? No, they broke up a long time ago. Our parents made him." Cal had been so into the chick and Grant understood why: she was stunning. Long-limbed, long-haired, and kind of funny too. Not that he spent any time with her, but whenever he'd watch her—and sure, he liked to watch her—the people around her always seemed to be laughing.

Once his parents found out she was the daughter of one of their political enemies they put their foot down. No, they stomped it down. Made Cal terminate all contact with her. Grant remembers getting a pretty strong hit of satisfaction when that battle was waged and his brother lost.

"Look, Grant. I'm going to be straight with you because we're hoping you can help us out," Torres says. "Luna Rose was pregnant when she was murdered." At this, Erika lets out a small whimper, and that's when it occurs to Grant that he's still standing on the other side of the room.

"That's horrible," he concedes, moving over to the couch to be closer to his girlfriend.

"Yeah, horrible," Horner agrees. "And we're pretty certain Cal was the father."

Grant stops mid-sit. "Why would you think that?"

"Because *your* DNA, it turns out, is a 25 percent match to the fetus's DNA, Grant. And unless you have another brother stashed away somewhere, either your father or your brother is the likely sperm donor." Torres stands up after she announces this. "With your permission we'd like to take something of your brother's that has his DNA and run it to be sure."

Grant's head is swimming with the images of brightly colored sperm. Could his father have fucked Luna? No way. It has to be Cal, that slime bucket. Poor Deni; she was so in love with his brother. She thought he was—no, hold up. Deni was the one who gave the cops that video of Cal fucking some girl wearing a dog collar. Which means she already knew he was a piece of shit. Why did she show the cops that video in the first place?

Grant is suddenly disoriented if not completely confused. Nothing a good hit of oxy couldn't lay waste to. He should get up and text Deez. See if the guy's holding. He deserves a small reward for having to go through all this bullshit with his family and Erika and now he finds out his brother was even more of a scumbag than even he'd thought. He's gotta get the cops out of here first. He's got to—

Torres is speaking to him and he has no idea what she's saying. "What?" he stutters.

"We'd like you to show us Cal's bedroom, please. We can just grab a few things and then we're done here."

Beside him, Erika clears her throat. "Um, we completely gutted Cal's room. Remodeled it." She peers longingly at Grant, obviously wanting him to show some support for the quick transformation of the house. As if any of it was his idea. He gives her nothing. "It's my office now."

Another knowing look is traded between the two cops. He has no idea what's going on, but at this point he just wants them gone. "Before we gutted it Deni came over and packed up a box," Grant explains. "She has what's left of my brother's stuff."

CHAPTER

39

I COULDN'T FIND A phone cable—not that I looked very hard—so I ended up buying the same model of flip phone at Walmart. Now that Luna's phone is fully charged I power it on and am bummed when I see that there are hardly any texts.

MAY 13

J: *Did you delete everything from your other phone?*
Luna: *Yes, silly. Don't worry.*
J: *I won't. You're a smart girl.*
Luna: *Smart girl misses you.*
J: *I always miss you.*

JUNE 2

Luna: *FYI: I love you.*
J: *I know.*
Luna: *Too far and few between.*

J: *Yup.*
Luna: *Know I'll always love you.*
J: *Know I've always loved you.*

JUNE 25

Luna: *That was fun yesterday. Come back. Now.*
J: *Too busy. Soon. Promise.*
Luna: *Maybe you can call me sometime?*
J: *I'll try from work tomorrow.*

JULY 8

Luna: *Why aren't you here right now? It's never enough.*
J: *I know. Life. Work. Busy. Patience, my sweet. Please.*

JULY 17

Luna: *How you holding up?*
J: *?*
Luna: *Just wondering.*

AUGUST 5

Luna: *I have news.*
J: *Okay.*
Luna: *I'm pregnant.*
J: *Whoa.*
Luna: *You're happy?*
J: *I'm shocked. You're on the pill.*
Luna: *Epic fail.*
J: *Understatement.*

Luna: *And?*

J: *It's great. But hey, don't tell anyone yet. OK?*

Luna: *I won't.*

J: *Promise me.*

Luna: *OK*

SEPTEMBER 3

J: *You ok?*

Luna: *Glowing.*

J: *Sorry I haven't swung by. Will. Soon. Need to kiss that beautiful belly.*

Luna: *And other places too please.*

J: *Keep it between us please. Gotta figure it out.*

Luna: *I said I would!*

SEPTEMBER 22

J: *You still haven't told anyone yet, right?*

Luna: *No, silly—it's still our secret. For now. What are we going to do?*

J: *I'm working on it. Trust me.*

Luna: *You mean . . . ?*

J: *I'm gonna fix everything. Hang tight. Tell NO ONE.*

Luna: *I know. I know.*

J: *I love you. Now go play in the dirt.*

There wasn't a whole lot to go on. I wish one of them had said something detailed. I thought for sure I'd be able to pinpoint who J was, but I have nothing. I toss the phone onto the bed and growl in frustration. Luna lied to me. Why? Who is J?

My rapidly expanding black hole is interrupted by knocking at my door. I go out to open it and find my two favorite detectives staring at me. They invite themselves in and inform me, as diplomatically as they can, that my former fiancé is, in fact, the father of Luna's baby. "We are ninety-nine percent sure," Detective Torres admits, "but to get to a hundred percent we need his DNA, or, at the very least, a fingerprint."

Grant had told them that I have a box of Cal's remaining possessions, and they ask if they can look through it.

"I have a better idea," I say, walking into my room and grabbing the box from the back of my closet. "Get it out of my sight. Whatever you don't need, feel free to burn."

CHAPTER

40

I'M PEERING INTO the box we took from Deni's house and wondering what's keeping Tom. I see a few baseball trophies, a couple postcards, framed photographs. Nothing that looks as if it's retained any serious DNA residue, unless Cal Cooper was the sort of man who often kissed his own pictures, that is.

Tom opens the door to our small evidence room and rushes in. "Sorry. Got sidetracked by Colin. He said he found an alert that another user did a search on Erika Morris."

I look up from the box. "Come again? No, hold the thought," I say, tossing him a pair of gloves. "I want to see what we've got in here."

With each item I remove from the box, Tom records it in an evidence log and then bags it. Trophies. Photographs in glass frames. "Hopefully they can find a hair or some skin cells on these," I say, slipping the T-shirts into a plastic evidence bag. "Too bad Deni didn't hold on to his catcher's mitt," I mutter, before shoving aside a rolled-up poster. That's when I see it. "Why, hello there, good-looking," I say, holding up a fixed-blade Buck knife.

While Tom hustles the blade over to forensics, I shoot over to the M.E.'s office in the County Building, park and walk in. Vera's at her desk, looking at her computer screen when I knock.

"Well, if it isn't Dana Scully in the flesh. To what do I owe the pleasure?"

I grin and quickly fill the seat in front of her before she even offers. "What can you tell me about the knife that was used to kill Luna Rose?" I ask, my skin beading with impatience.

"Why didn't you just call me?"

"I did." *Plus, I wanted to see you. I never get tired of seeing you.* "You didn't answer."

"Ah. Okay, let me check my notes." I watch as she clicks on her keyboard, reads—mumbling a few words to herself while doing so—before answering. "Not serrated."

I wait for more. When she doesn't give me more, I ask, "In what manner was it used exactly?"

"You know all this already."

"Humor me."

"It's impossible to say exactly. What I can tell you—*again*—is that the incision most likely came from the front of the victim."

"Why?"

Vera sighs, but I know she's not as exasperated as she is pretending to be. I usually need things repeated, so it isn't like this is a new behavior between us. "The perp is most definitely right-handed, and if he—or she—came from behind and sliced left to right, which is what we'd expect, the left cut would be deep, then tail off toward the right. Front cuts, on the other hand, inflicted by a righty tend to be shorter and shallower. It's what I saw with Luna." She stops and takes a drink of her coffee, which I have no doubt is the same coffee she poured at seven this morning.

"Could the cut be shorter and shallower because the perp hesitated?" I'm just taking a shot in the proverbial dark.

"Absolutely, although if they were hesitant, I'd expect to see more than one incision. In this case, it was just the one slash, left to right."

"But not with a serrated blade."

"Definitely not. The blade used to slice open Luna Rose's throat had a smooth cutting edge. It wasn't necessarily very sharp, given the depth of the injury. But it was sharp enough to get the job done."

* * *

My car tires squeal as I pull into a parking spot at the station and hop out. I'm two steps from the front door when I hear my name being called. Turning around I see Luna Rose's mother, Misha, rapidly closing the distance between us.

"Detective Torres," she says breathlessly. "Why haven't you called me back! I've been wracking my memory and I finally figured out who J is!"

I've been keeping Misha posted about any and all information regarding her daughter's murder investigation and am a bit confounded by her sudden appearance at the station.

"Ms. Rose. I was just going to call you." I wasn't, actually, but I knew I'd get around to it. "There's been a new development. Why don't we go inside and—"

"I said I figured out who J is!"

She's lost me. "Jay?"

"The texts on the phone Deni dropped off?" She sees that I have no idea what she's talking about, and before she says another thing she utters a curse word I never would have expected to arise from her. "She didn't bring you Luna's phone, did she?"

"I'm not aware of any phone, Ms. Rose," I say, jonesing to get inside and see if the lab discovered anything on the knife. "Walk with me."

CHAPTER

41

Kenneth Groberg, Attorney at Law, gently removes my thumbnail from between my teeth and places my hand over the FUK U someone's etched into the wooden table. "Try not to appear nervous, Deni," he says calmly. "We want this to be quick. I'll find out what they have and you just sit still. Just make sure you answer 'no comment' to anything they ask you. Is that clear?"

When I don't respond he repeats himself, to which I reply, "No comment," in a voice so jittery I am not certain it is my own.

The two detectives walk in and start talking. I am so freaked out that I don't really hear, or at least cannot quite process their words, but I can see that Detective Torres is looking at me as if I'm a piece of garbage she found on the bottom of her shoe. She says something about recording and rights and then Groberg asks them something and I begin shaking so much I think I might throw up. Without thinking I suddenly blurt out, "How could you think

I killed my best friend? I loved Luna!" before my $100 an hour lawyer clutches me by the wrist, pulls me close and whispers, "Keep your mouth shut!" sharply into my left ear.

He asks the detectives why they're holding me. What evidence they have.

"We found a knife in that box of stuff you gave us, Deni," Torres says succinctly. I pull Kenneth close and tell him it was Cal's Buck knife—one of his favorite possessions, so of course I took it as a keepsake. He nods and asks, "What else?"

"You didn't let me finish," Torres says, narrowing her eyes. "The lab found a trace amount of blood lodged inside the sheath. It was Luna's blood, Deni. Cal's 192 Vanguard knife was used to kill Luna Rose."

"Hold on. What?" I shout. Again Kenneth puts his hand up to shush me. I don't want to be shushed. I want to defend myself. "No!" I push his hand away. "I didn't kill her. And if I did use Cal's knife, I'd have to be an idiot to keep it." I watch Detective Horner smirk. Is he insinuating that he does think I'm an idiot? "And another thing. Who brought you those pot branches? I did. Why would I bring you evidence of the crime if *I* committed it?"

I sit back, as exhausted as if I'd just pleaded for my life, which, I guess I did.

Torres speaks right through my pronouncement as if it were nothing more than smoke. "We have an eyewitness who overheard you and Cal arguing and you threatening to kill Luna."

I am sure my face is on fire with shock over this. I glance at my lawyer, then back at the detectives. "Who? Who heard us? We never argued about her because I didn't know he was cheating on me! Whoever it was was lying. They're lying!" Tears shoot across my eyes before I can stop them. Who would say such a thing?

"Why did you keep the burner phone, Deni? You told Ms. Rose you'd bring it to us right after you looked at the texts."

That stupid phone. I should have gotten rid of it. I promised Misha I'd drop it off, but I had no idea who this J was and figured the police wouldn't be able to either. By the time the two detectives and a uniformed cop showed up at my house with a search warrant, it was too late. I wonder what else they found.

"I forgot?" I know it's the lamest answer on the planet, but she's trying to make me admit to something I cannot.

"Can you tell us Cal's middle name, Deni?" Horner asks, which throws me off.

"James. Why?"

"According to Luna's mother, while Luna and Cal were dating in high school, she often referred to him as J. Is this correct?"

"I can't recall," I say, mimicking something I must have heard on a cop show. I honestly forgot that Luna used to call him that. Back then I was so jealous that they were together I most likely squeezed it out of my memory like a big old whitehead.

"So, here's how this is going to play out, Deni." Torres speaks so calmly that for a split second I think she's going to let me go. "You are being charged with the crime of murder. Based on the evidence we have gathered, we believe there is probable cause to arrest you for this offense. You will be taken into custody and held pending further proceedings. You have the right to request bail, but until then, you will be held in jail. You will be given the opportunity to appear before a judge for an arraignment where you can enter a plea."

As soon as she stops talking a uniformed cop comes into the room and starts toward me. Kenneth leans over and mutters a bunch of lawyerly words, trying to sound reassuring, but because there is so much blood beating through my eardrums I cannot hear a thing he says.

CHAPTER 42

WE CAN SEE the plume of smoke from a half mile away, but because of the prevailing winds, we don't smell it until we pull into Ted Campbell's driveway and exit the car. We follow the smoke around to the deputy sheriff's backyard and find him hoisting another clump of wet leaves onto the burn pile. It's one of the autumnal behaviors I hate most about this county. Open burning is prohibited in the city limits of both Prosperity and Gold Hills, but if you step one foot outside the red line, no one's going to stop you from throwing your leaves on the barbie. Of course, the law specifically states that only *dry* vegetation is permitted to be burned, but Ted Campbell clearly isn't a man who likes to be kept waiting for natural desiccation.

On the night we arrested Deni Rydell for the murder of Luna Rose, Tom, Vera, and I had gone to Goldy's to down a great many celebratory drinks. The solve took longer than I'd predicted, and it also took me a little by surprise. While swallowing back a shot of rye whiskey I reflected on the day she showed up at the farm—only hours after we found Luna's body. She'd seemed shocked, sure, but even back then, I remember thinking she was overplaying the role of grieving friend. I should have pushed harder at her. Should have seen she was playing us for fools when she showed us that video of Cal and Erika, as if it would prove her father's innocence in a crime we weren't even positive had been committed. Deni Rydell was far more calculating a person than I gave her credit for.

In the middle of the self-adulation, a remark made previously by Tom reemerged from the midst of my wooly brain. "Hey, Horner," I slurred. "You said someone else was probing Erika Morris's file. Who was it?"

Tom had to take a moment to focus before answering. "No idea. I was told by IT there was an alert on her. Thas' 'sall I remember."

The next morning, sporting a headache the size of Rockefeller Center, I learned that the digging was dug by Deputy Sheriff Ted Campbell from County. When I phoned him up and asked him why, what, where, when, and how, he said, "Come by my house tomorrow. We can talk there."

So now Horner and I are standing in Campbell's trash-strewn backyard surrounded by a noxious-smelling fog and trying not to hack up a lung while the man collects both the scattered leaves and his thoughts. Out of uniform, Campbell looks older and less sturdy than I've seen him. His hair is thin and his face isn't so much weathered as it is plundered by the years. Maybe it was his wife's recent passing that aged him. Grief has a bad habit of carving dark reminders into the human body. Sometimes we can see them; sometimes they're hidden away.

After a couple of minutes, he stops what he's doing and leans his heft against the rake. "She's trouble, that girl."

Tom leaps on the words. "Erika Morris, you mean? We couldn't find anything on her."

"That's because there is no Erika Morris. The woman's name is Travers. Katie Travers."

Tom and I exchange that kind of look that only lovers and partners pass between them. It's a knowing regard, one imbued with shared speculation. One eye on the ground in front of us. One on the distant horizon.

"The Coopers—Calvin and Jean—they didn't like her. Didn't trust she wasn't after their boy's money. Asked me to give her a once-over."

While Campbell slowly unveils the sordid life and times of the woman formerly known as Katie Travers, I begin to get a little disoriented, and I don't believe it's due to the haze I'm breathing in. It doesn't matter if her stepfather was feeding her dead puppy tails for breakfast: the woman was capable of stabbing a man to death.

That's not an easy skill to come by. Nor is it one easily forgotten.

With nothing but our guts leading us, Horner and I call Judge Fetterman to request a search warrant. He denies it based on the fact that all we have is hearsay from Campbell and a gut feeling. Besides which, we have another soul in custody for the crime. "Get me something solid, Torres. Then I'll grant it."

* * *

Six of us fan out across Hinsdale Road, knocking on doors and asking if anyone remembers seeing this woman in the vicinity on or around September thirtieth of this year. It's an eight by ten color photo of Erika Morris/Katie Travers. Back when we found Luna we canvassed the area, but we were shooting into the dark. Now that we've got a specific point of light, Tom and I are hoping like hell someone will recognize her and the stars will align.

Three hours is all it takes to find the winner. Leidy Childress, who greets us at the door of 65912 Hinsdale Road, and proudly informs us she regularly goes on early morning walks. To get in her steps, she says. "It's rare to see more than one or two people out here because the hill is so steep, you know. Only us diehard walkers are up to tackling it."

"And you are willing to swear in a court of law that you saw this woman walking on the road on September thirtieth?" Tom prods carefully.

"Oh, yes. Yes. I remember thinking, What a pretty girl she is. She had on a baseball hat, but I could see she had light brown hair cut short in one of those pixie styles, just like this woman," she says, gently touching the photograph. "But when we passed one another and I said hi she was so rude." Leidy tuts. "I mean, we all say hello, but this woman just turned away so fast it was like she was afraid I was going to hurt her or something. I also remember that I didn't see a car parked at the turnout, you know? That's where most people who walk the hill park. It was like she appeared out of the blue."

* * *

We find nothing in the house. But then again, it's been scrubbed clean by the substantial renovations. The guest suite, thankfully, has been left untouched, and it's there that one of the guys, while combing the rug under the bed, finds a single specimen that may hold some weight.

I'm searching the Escalade while Tom's going through the F-150 when Officer Chris Plouffe shoves the plastic bag under my nose. "I found a leaf," he declares with a gleam in his eye. It's not enough, but I have him immediately heel it down to the lab to see if there's a match to Luna's plants.

After I finish with the car I wander back over to the front of the house where I see Grant and Erika sitting side by side on the top step of the landing. Grant appears to be in his normal state of discomfiture. Erika—or rather, Katie—seems to be entirely unfazed by the events taking place around her. She doesn't know yet that Officer Plouffe is currently on his way to the lab with something that might pin the murder of Luna Rose squarely on her chest.

"You almost done?" she asks in an distinctly miffed tone, which surprises me given that she was only recently informed that she's a potential suspect in a murder case. Either she is not registering the gravity of the situation or she's a psychopath. "I need to get to my massage appointment."

"You can go," I tell her, wanting to get her off the property. "Take the Cadillac. I'm done with it."

"Awesome." She picks up her Chanel purse and walks off in a huff. I follow behind, watching her climb into the car. Tom is still searching the truck parked next to it, and I see him look up and say something. She throws him a salute before backing up and driving off.

I'm pissed we don't have anything substantial enough to bring her in for questioning. An eyewitness is flimsy. A speck of marijuana, not even close to a smoking gun. My gut, though, is gurgling with skepticism. Either that, or from too much coffee. A thought suddenly occurs to me. "Hey, Grant? Whose truck is Detective Horner searching?"

"That was Cal's."

"And the Cadillac belonged to your parents?"

"Yup."

I have my fingers metaphorically crossed when I lob the next query. "What about you? Did you have a car of your own before the accident?"

"Sure. Oh, yeah. Shit." Grant leaps up. "I completely spaced. I have an old Subaru."

"And where might that be?"

"It's been parked in the back garage," he says, walking toward it.

While Tom and I start to give the blue hatchback the once-over, Grant admits that he honestly cannot recall when it was last used. "Right after the plane crash maybe?

We must have driven it down to the airport to pick up my parents' car."

"And before the crash?" I ask, feeling around the floor under the driver's seat with my gloved hand.

"Um, let's see." I crane my neck and see him staring at the palms of his hands, as if they are a crystal ball into the past. I ignore him and shine my flashlight between the seats.

"I think it was the day my parents left for Nevada. Now I remember: Erika used it to go out for breakfast."

I'm instantly up and out of the back seat, staring at him, waiting for more. "She—yeah, she was gone a while and when I asked her where she was she said she'd gotten some food—" He wrenches the side of his mouth upward in a ghoulish expression as if his brain is overheating from the memory—"and then she said she had it washed."

"Torres!" My attention is swiftly yanked over to Tom, who's got half his body lodged inside the back of the car. "Check this out," he says, pointing his flashlight on something that he's found. Poking up in the rear section between the lower compartment that houses the spare tire and the black felt floor of the trunk is what appears to be a black sock.

* * *

After we turn the sock over to the lab, Horner and I race down to Bee Clean Self-Service Car Wash in Prosperity to speak to the manager. Yes, they have security cameras, he informs us and yes, the corporation requires all franchise owners to store their footage in the cloud for no fewer than ninety days.

Tom and I asked to see the data from September thirtieth. And now we're crushed together in the manager's tiny office, watching the feeds from the six installed cameras on a filthy Dell monitor. As Tom speeds through, I eye the nasty-looking sludge sitting in a glass coffee pot in the corner and consider pouring myself a cup, but my attention snaps back to the screen when Tom utters, "Bingo."

On camera 1 we watch Erika pull the Subaru into a stall. She gets out and hoses the car down, paying particular attention to the tires. Then she goes to the trunk and takes out what looks like a large garbage bag. She disappears, but camera 3 picks her up entering the women's bathroom. She reemerges some seven minutes later wearing different clothes. She reappears on camera 1, where she opens the trunk and puts the bag back into it, begins walking to the driver's side, then stops, returns to the trunk, removes the bag once more and throws it into the back seat. The car rolls into camera 4's field by the vacuum bay. Erika gets out, looks around before stuffing the bag from the back seat deep into the garbage bin. She then proceeds to vacuum every square inch of the car's interior. Once she's finished, she drives off.

Tom sits back in the chair and shakes his head. I attempt to steady the beating of my heart. Neither of us says anything. In front of us the footage continues to scroll by. Scene after scene of people innocently washing their cars on a typical Saturday morning in Prosperity, California.

The normality of it almost breaks me. How disturbing would it be if any of these folks knew the truth: that only minutes before they brought their grimy Hondas and Nissans and Chevrolets in for a quick cleaning, a woman in a baseball hat tried to wash away the murder of Luna Rose.

CHAPTER

43

SOON AFTER I got released from juvie and did my time on probation, I left town. My mother didn't try to stop me, even when she watched me swipe her car keys off the counter. I could almost hear her saying, "Don't let the door hit you on your way out." She loved that bastard and probably blamed me for losing another husband to that big black hole where philanderers and pedophiles go when they leave women like her.

I changed my name to Erika Morris—a totally random name that fell out of my mouth the first time someone asked me who I was. I was applying for a busser job at a Mexican restaurant in Hollywood, California, a few blocks from the hostel where I'd dropped my bags two nights previously. Orange Drive Hostel charged fifty dollars a night (plus another ten to park Mom's car) for a decently comfortable bed in a clean all-female dorm room. After the noise and stress of juvenile hall, it felt like bunking down in the Taj Mahal.

Why Hollywood? Why not? Doesn't every girl who's ever been told she's pretty want to be a movie star?

Two years in, I was co-managing Juanita's, living in my own apartment, and learning that being pretty doesn't necessarily place you on the path to stardom.

Three years in, I began hanging out with the wrong people—people who, like me, were on the fringe of Hollywood. The hangers-on. The desperate-for-attention seekers. The beggars who didn't have a chance in hell to be choosers.

That's when I discovered the joys of cocaine. And vodka. Alone, they were nice. Together, they harmonized as sweetly as a Simon and Garfunkel song.

Four years in, I was hooking up with old men who promised me a small part in their next film in exchange for a blow job. To support my coke habit, I started doing side gigs at bachelor parties. Sure, I fucked strangers, but there were rules that had to be followed. Boundaries that weren't allowed to be crossed.

Then one night in 2018 a friend of a friend of some major Hollywood player asked if I'd be a party favor. I said yes because I wanted to be inside. I wanted to be closer to the people who moved and shook.

I thought I'd be one among many playthings, but it just so happened that I was the solo blowup doll that night. I was raped, degraded, and defiled by so many men that I didn't get out of bed for a week. Peeing without being in agony took longer.

The years that followed were a blur of pain and drugs and alcohol and some more pain. My mantra became "I don't fucking care what happens to me because I am a piece of shit" until I was so close to death, I reached out to the only safety net I knew. I called my stepsister, Amelia, and begged her for help.

* * *

I met Grant Cooper in the fanciest rehab in the entire state, generously paid for by Ron Travers's extremely wealthy and utterly grateful daughter. I instantly fell for the guy's sweetness and vulnerability. His awkwardness was beyond endearing. It felt good to be adored by someone who didn't want to put a leash around my neck.

It didn't hurt that he was loaded.

Then came that day when his younger brother flew down to Santa Monica to get him. I recognized him instantly. Of all the men at that party, his was the face I remembered most clearly. Cal Cooper Jr.: the B-list movie-star wannabe. The man who liked it rough.

It took him a couple of days to recognize me, though. He first needed to sift through some of his old videos on his phone before he put two and me together. I looked different, but he still managed to remember my face (although I don't actually recall him ever looking at it—he was far too busy fucking the shit out of me from behind).

But recognize me he did, and one night he slithered into my guest suite and propositioned me. Not for sex, no. That would have been too impossible an ask. "I have a problem that needs taking care of," he'd said, holding up his phone to me. On it was a blown-up shot of my face from the party. It made me sick to see it. Before I could utter a word he went on to tell me that his lover-on-the-side was threatening to destroy his life. "She's pregnant."

"So? Make her get an abortion," I said, suggesting what I thought was an obvious choice.

"She refuses. She's obsessed with me. She's using this to trap me," he said, with zero irony in his voice. *Stupid woman*, is what I thought, but didn't say aloud. She and that Deni wench he was engaged to. How pathetically blind they were. Not that I had any intention of telling either woman what a sick fuck they were involved with.

"What's that got to do with me?" I asked, feeling as if I were a mouse with one paw stuck in a trap.

"I need you to kill her," he said as calmly as if he were asking me to fetch him a towel. "I have it all planned out." He went on to detail how to find her and what I would need to do to make it look like a marijuana robbery—a relatively common occurrence in those parts. He described where the tools were. He gave me his Buck knife, "just in case you can't just bash her head in." And then he reminded me to make sure I threw it out with my clothes after the deed was done.

By that point I figured he must have done some digging on his own and discovered my former life as Katie Travers, the girl who murdered her stepfather. I mean, why else would he think I was capable of killing someone? "Why me?" I asked, cautiously.

"Because if either my parents or my brother ever get wind of what you used to do for a living, you can bet your sweet ass—and oh yeah, was it ever sweet—" he said with such a hideous sneer I could have killed him right there, "you can kiss your dream life goodbye."

He knew nothing about Katie. He only knew he had me by the balls.

I asked him if he was worried he'd be a suspect. I mean, someone had to know they were involved, right?

"I'll have the perfect alibi. I plan to be flying to Nevada with my parents at the exact time you are killing her," he said with all the arrogance I expected. In return for my "favor," he would delete the video from his phone and never divulge to Grant or his parents that I was once a drugged-out whore.

Did I think twice about Cal's nefarious plan? Sure I did. But I was afraid. And I was alone. I needed Grant in order to breathe. To survive. I wanted to marry him and have his money. I wanted to lounge by the pool and then follow him to whatever quarry he was going to next. We would build a life together. I was desperate for that. Desperate for a normal life with a sober man I could be safe with.

I knew that if Cal showed Grant and his hard-assed parents the video, they would throw me out like the piece of trash I truly was.

* * *

It was a lot harder to kill her than I thought it'd be. But then again most things are harder to do than to think about. I just needed to get past the initial "I cannot do this." I figured I would just sneak up behind her and hit her with a rock. One and done. Although I did have a contingency plan. By that I mean I had Cal's knife in my back pocket. Just in case it was needed. And in this case it was.

What made it so hard wasn't that she put up a fight or because she was so pretty. It was because I had no reason to kill her. Other than to protect myself, that is. I'd done that before: kill to protect myself, but that was different. I knew him. But her? Didn't have an iota of background on her other than she was going to royally screw up a few other people's lives if she didn't die.

When I saw her stroll into view I almost lost my nerve. She was wearing this airy blue dress made of some material that caught every wisp of breeze. Her skin and hair were so clean she glowed like a Tesla that had just been detailed.

The moment she crouched down, her dress billowing over the dirt, I lunged at her with a sharp rock. But as soon as I raised my arm she jumped up, like she knew I was coming at her. Like she had a cat's sense, like she could hear me, which she probably could because it wasn't as if I was being stealthy.

She cinched her hand around my right wrist, which made me drop the rock. Then she kicked me in the shin, which hurt like a motherfucker, and started to run. But I reached out in time to grab a wad of that dress and yanked her back, making her lose her balance and stumble just enough for me to push her over onto the ground.

I worried it was taking too long, and I hated the way she was looking at me with her eyes full of hate and fear while continually screaming, "Who are you? What do you want?" so I decided I needed to get the whole shit plan over with ASAP.

After I slit her throat I had to make it look like a robbery. That was the plan and that part was easy. Relatively. I worked as fast as I could and by the time I finished cutting and sawing and tossing everything into the creek, my arms were burning.

As I made my way back down the road I felt like I had a 200-degree fever, I was shaking so much. I stopped when I was long clear of her property and walked off the asphalt into the trees and threw up for ten minutes on all fours, then collapsed down onto my back. I stared up at the clouds through the tall trees, trying to quiet the nightmarish pandemonium screaming through in my brain. "That was fucked up," I whispered so quietly even the chipmunk that ran past my leg probably didn't catch it.

After a while I stood, brushed the leaves and needles and dirt from my jeans and began to walk to the car, toward my new and improved life. A life that would be much easier than I'd ever imagined a life could be.

Why didn't I toss the knife as promised? Because I was going to pin the murder on Cal. I was going to get my revenge for what he did to me all those years ago.

But then the fucker crashed his plane and as much as I'm glad he died a painful death, I resent that I don't get the chance to watch him rot in jail for the rest of his miserable life.

Instead, I get to do that.

CHAPTER 44

GRANT LOOKS AWAY from the computer and rolls his head around on his neck a few times. He's spent all morning reading through the Mine Safety and Health Administration's updated Standards and Regulations report. It's a beast of a document, filled with acronyms and terms that are all new to him, but it's surprisingly interesting stuff, aspects of the mining business that as a quarry manager, he had no idea even existed.

He takes a gulp of his coffee, and before setting the mug down he glances out the window. There are Christmas lights wrapped around the C. G. Cooper & Sons Aggregates sign. For maybe the first time in his life, he feels a sense of pride in being one of those *sons* and it's an awesome feeling. He's in charge of a multimillion-dollar business that's been in his family for generations, and, if he gets this right, it will be for a few more generations to come.

He's suddenly famished. It's been three weeks since he started back to work, and Grant has yet to leave the office for lunch, given that at exactly eleven every morning Geri waltzes through his door and asks what kind of sandwich he wants from Breyer's Deli. At first he just went along with it, too nervous to shake up the routine which his father and Geri had obviously established over the years. When, this past Tuesday, he suggested that maybe they could get take-out from a different restaurant, Geri said, "Why would we do that? Danny makes the best subs in town."

But he's the boss, and today he's not going to eat a sandwich at his desk.

He leaves his office and stands in front of Geri. She's been incredibly supportive of Grant's return to the fold, almost mothering him. She tends to preface every task with, "If you prefer I handle this . . ." or "I don't want to burden you with too much too soon . . ." He appreciates the coddling, but at some point she will need to trust him.

"I'm going out to lunch," he says, zipping up his coat.

"But I ordered you a turkey bacon sandwich," she says, as if he's just personally insulted her.

"Great. I'll eat it for dinner," he replies, walking out the door.

His plan was to book it down to Mr. Lee's at the bottom of Main and order some kung pao chicken, but as Grant passes by Marvin's, he slows and gazes in. He sees Deni Rydell place a plate of food down in front of a little girl who's perched in some newfangled booster seat attached to the table. He watches as Deni leans down low and points to each item on the plate and says something. Then she straightens up and cups the kid's head in the exact same manner that she cupped his hand under his parent's dining room table all those months ago. He waits to see her smile; to know she's doing okay, but what he sees on her face saddens him so much he opens the door and walks in.

The place is mostly empty, and he takes a seat at a two-person table in the corner. A waitress comes over and puts a menu down and asks if he wants coffee. He says he does. She lists off some special that he doesn't hear because he's too busy trying to catch Deni's eye.

A second after the waitress wanders off, Deni looks over but immediately looks away. He's not too surprised by this. He's texted her a few times. Even called her once. She has yet to respond.

He's just taking another bite of a really delicious tuna melt when she's suddenly standing in front of him. "Hi, Grant," she says quietly, almost shyly.

He swallows what's in his mouth. "Hi, Deni." They look at one another for a few awkward seconds before he figures what the heck and goes for it. "Any chance you can take a quick break?" he asks.

She looks around the diner, over toward the counter, then the front door. "Sure," she says. "Let me grab some coffee."

She carries over a cup and sits down across from him. For too long, neither of them speak. He's not sure how to fill the silence between them so he holds out one of his potato chips to her and is immeasurably relieved when she snatches it out of his hand. "So, hey, thanks for, you know, reaching out and, you know, checking in and all," she says, munching it down. "Sorry I didn't reply, but . . ."

"It's cool." He doesn't want her to feel guilty for not answering him. He isn't sure he would have answered him either.

"How you been, Grant?" she asks.

"I've been good." He has been more than good, but he's not here to talk about himself. "What about you? How you holding up?"

"You know." She shrugs and takes a drink of her coffee. She doesn't meet his eyes.

He takes another bite of his sandwich. Of course he knows. Her best friend, who was pregnant by his brother, had her throat slit by none other than Grant's own girlfriend. "My family royally fucked you over," he says, instantly wishing he'd said something less dramatic. "I'm sorry about everything, Deni. I really am."

She shrugs again and looks over at a couple who's just walked through the door. Now that she's close, he doesn't want to lose her yet. "I mean, talk about dodging a bullet," he adds, grinning. "You are so lucky that wedding never happened. My brother was a total asshole, right?" He thinks by saying this she will get that he is in her corner. He wants her to know he feels badly for her. Actually, what he'd really like is to be her friend. Other than the people he sees at work and during his weekly NA meetings, he's been kind of lonely.

"Yes, your brother was an asshole, but . . ."

Grant watches her pick at something invisible on her palm. He waits.

She looks up. Her dark eyes bore into his. "Part of me wishes I'd never found out the truth and still got to—"

"What the hell?" A chunk of bread gets caught in his throat as he speaks and Grant chokes on the words. After he downs some water, he basically barks out his reply. "You would have been okay living with a man who cheated on you? Who—"

"No, Grant. You're not hearing me. If I'd married your brother, I would have . . . I would have finally had . . . Never mind. You won't understand. You could never understand." She leans back in her chair looking ten times more defeated than when she first sat down.

Grant is disappointed. He thought Deni was different. He thought she was marrying Cal because she truly loved him, and after discovering what a sick selfish prick he was, she'd want nothing more to do with the man. Turns out she's the same as the rest of them. She was a gold digger. Plain and simple.

"I've gotta go, Grant." She moves to stand, but he grabs her wrist.

"Wait," he says. He wants to hear her say it. He wants her to admit that what she was about to say was that she would have finally *had* money. Lots of money. If she'd married Cal, she would have been rich beyond her wildest dreams. And just like Erika, she would have loved spending his family's fortune. "Tell me what you would have finally *had*?"

Despite his protests, she pulls her hand away and stands up. Her face is a mashup of anger and sadness. "I would have had silence, Grant."

"What?" He was definitely not expecting that.

She takes in a deep breath and sighs it out, depleted. "My life, Grant, is nothing like yours, tucked away on that mountain, away from the chaos of the world. Me? I am constantly surrounded by it. By its noise. The noise of my neighbors. The noise of my father banging shut every door in the house. The noise of him blasting the television. I come to work and all I hear all day long is noise. The sound of people telling me what to do, telling me what to bring them, and oh that fucking bell, dinging dinging dinging." She stops for a moment and listens. Sure enough, a bell dings and someone yells out, "Order up."

She throws him a knowing smile. "Once I moved into that house in the middle of nowhere, I knew the noise was going to stop, Grant. I was going to be able to hear the sound of the wind in the trees." She reaches out and grabs his empty plate and coffee mug. "I would have finally had silence. And maybe I would have finally been able to hear myself think," she says, walking away.

CHAPTER

45

I'M JUST GETTING out of the shower when I hear the front door slam. I listen for the familiar sounds of my father tromping into the kitchen. Opening the refrigerator. Pulling out a beer, one bottle jostling another. Yet none of those sounds register. Instead, I hear his heavy footsteps coming down the hallway. I throw on my white matted bathrobe and head over to his bedroom. I find him squatting down in front of his red tool kit. It's open. He hasn't touched it since the day he was hauled away from the tarmac at Sacramento International Airport in an ambulance.

"Hi, Dad."

He jumps up and rubs his hands nervously up and down the front of his filthy black pants. "Hey, kiddo." He's smiling like he's a kid in a candy store with five bucks in his pocket.

"What's going on?"

"Manny promoted me to A&P," he announces, his eyes beaming.

"What, no way!" I walk in and sit on his bed, watching him slip one of his torque wrenches from the top tray. He holds it up to the light as if it were a piece of precious jewelry. A&P stands for Airframe and Powerplant mechanic, which means he'll get to service planes just like he used to. Sure, they won't be 737s, but it's a huge deal. I go over and hug his back. "I'm so happy for you, Daddy." I feel his body stiffen under my touch and realize, with a sad thump of my heart, that we haven't shared a tender moment together since the day we buried my mother.

I clumsily move away and direct my attention out the window. I'm about to ask him how much more money he's going to make when I see a car pull up in front of Deez Yellen's house next door. It's a fancy truck and one I'm pretty sure I recognize. It's Cal's F-150. "What the hell?" I ask the frosted glass.

"What?" my father asks, still playing with his tools.

I don't answer him and keep watching. I must be wrong. I certainly *want* to be wrong, but the moment I see Grant step out of the driver's side, I know I'm not. He's here to buy drugs.

Before I have a chance to think I race outside and down the steps in my bathrobe and bare feet. The ground is covered in snow, but I don't even notice the cold because I am so steaming angry. I rush over to the truck and begin to scream in Grant's face. "Are you freakin' kidding me? You made it through a year of rehab and now just because your life isn't all peaches and cream, you're just going to throw it all away? I am sorry your girlfriend turned out to be a psychopathic killer and I'm sorry your entire family is dead, but guess what? My life is fucked up too, but do you see me snorting shit up my nose? Do you?" I am so far gone in my furiousness that it takes me a few seconds to see that Grant is actually laughing. I swiftly bring my tirade to a dead stop. "What's so funny?"

He's grinning now. "You are. You really thought I came here to buy drugs?"

I shove my cold hands into the pocket of my robe. "Well, yeah. I mean, why else would you—"

"I came to see you!"

"Why? How did you even know I live here?"

He doesn't bother answering and reaches into the truck. I watch him lean over into the passenger seat and grab something. "I know it's not a house in the middle of nowhere, but I thought maybe these might help," he says, handing me a box.

It's a pair of Bose noise-canceling headphones. The most expensive model they make. And they're blue.

I am so beyond touched, my mouth cannot find the right words. I feel like "thank you" just won't cut it. I can't remember the last time anyone gave me such a thoughtful gift. Something that was exactly for me. I look up at him with what I hope is a look of infinite gratitude.

"You know you're not wearing any shoes," he says, looking down. It's only then that I realize I am standing ankle deep in a small snowbank and that my feet are burning.

I am also shivering, but I'm not sure if it's because I am so overcome with emotion or because it's about thirty-five degrees outside and all I've got on is a skimpy bathrobe.

"Yeah, I should probably get back inside." I step out of the snow and onto the sidewalk. My feet are bright red.

With the box gripped tightly in my trembling hands I turn to go into the house, then pause. "You wanna come in?" I ask.

* * *

After putting on a pair of fuzzy socks and getting dressed in sweatpants and a Chico State sweatshirt I go out to the kitchen. Grant is leaning up against the refrigerator holding a cup of Lipton tea in his hand. We aren't big tea drinkers, Dad and I—that was my Mom's morning drink—and I feel a tinge of embarrassment that the guy's sipping a long-expired, probably tasteless cup of hot water. Dad's drinking a beer.

"Hey," Grant says when he sees me. "How are the feet?"

"Warm," I say, smiling. It's such a disconnect to see Grant Cooper in my house, yet there's something agreeable about his presence. "What were you two talking about?" While I was in the bathroom running my feet under hot water I could hear them chatting away like old friends.

Dad motions to Grant with his bottle and says, "Grant's working on getting his pilot's license and—"

"You are?" I feel a momentary sense of unease. I have no idea why.

"Sure. I just need a couple more hours in the air. I've got a great instructor. This guy Bruce Kitt. He's awesome." Grant takes a sip of his hot tea. "I really want to do this, Deni," he says as if he's trying to convince me, as if he cares what I think.

Seeing the enthusiasm on his face, I give him what he seems to need from me. "I think it's a great idea."

"And I'm going to help him pick out a plane to buy!" Dad says, leaning forward to tap his beer against Grant's mug. "Oh, hey, let me go look for that Beechcraft article I was telling you about."

"Thanks for that," I say softly after Dad walks out of the kitchen.

"For what? Asking for your father's advice? From what I hear, that man knows planes like I know rocks."

I wander into the living room and fall onto the couch and am glad Grant follows. It's nice having him next to me. He feels familiar. "You know, you seem really, really good, Grant," I say, aware of how confident and easygoing he has become. "What's changed?"

He leans back and lets out a breath. Out of the corner of my eye I see Dad stride into the room holding a magazine, but when he sees us on the couch, he quickly backs out.

I love my father.

"Well, I've been attending NA meetings every week and that's been pretty helpful."

"Nice."

"Also, I went back to work."

"No kidding?" I sit up. "And? What's it like?"

"Pretty cool, actually. Being a boss kind of suits me." He doesn't even try to sound humble. Last week, when he came into Marvin's, I remember thinking how handsome he looked and I wondered why he was wearing such nice clothes. Everything he had on was clean and pressed. Now I know why.

"And, I, well, I joined a grief group. It meets—"

"The first Tuesday of every month at the high school," I say, finishing his sentence. "Sue Marvin tried to get me to go after Cal and Luna—well, after . . ." I let the words tumble into the space between us.

"It's a good group, Deni. The people there, they've all been through a lot of the same things I—we've been through. I'm learning how to process losing everyone in my life." He wipes his hand across his mouth as if it has suddenly gone dry. "I know I didn't get along with my parents or my brother, but they were still my family, you know? And I guess . . . I guess I'm still kind of grieving them."

I nod because it makes perfect sense. The two people I thought I loved more than anything turned out to be liars. But it doesn't mean I don't miss them. "I get it."

"Hey, you should come to next Tuesday's meeting. I'll pick you up. We can go together."

"I—ah, maybe?"

He gets up, ready to leave, and I find that I'm disappointed. I want him to stay sitting next to me on the couch. I want to keep talking. "And, just to sweeten the deal, how about I take you out to dinner beforehand?"

I look up at him, taking in the full measure of this man who has just asked me to go out on a date with him—to a grief group. I want to both laugh and cry at the absurdity of it.

I've always assumed that Grant Cooper was the lesser of Jean and Calvin Cooper's two sons. The weaker one. The man who would never be king.

The boy who was nothing like his brother, Cal, who was once upon a time the man of my dreams.

I was wrong. I see now that the man who's standing in my tiny living room next to my beat-up couch just may have been the better brother all along.

"I'd love to," I say.

CHAPTER

46

HE'S HAD TO wait until the spring for the ground to thaw, and now that the concrete footings have finally been poured, Grant will now need to wait a couple days for it to cure. Building a house requires a lot of patience, he realizes.

And help.

He was an idiot to think he could build this house on his own. As it is, he's had to hire a slew of subcontractors to get him this far in the process, but he still wants to have his hand in as much as possible. He's hoping he'll be able to at least pitch in with the framing.

He surveys the skeletal outline of the house laid out along the wooden forms. It really is a beautiful design. Cal and Deni put a lot of thought into it, and he's glad he didn't have to be the one who decided where the kitchen should go.

"We're going to get amazing sunsets from here!" Deni shouts from the far side of the foundation.

"I know!" he yells back. He observes her as she stands completely still in the center of what will someday be their large living room, one he insisted be filled with excessively comfy furniture. She's wearing a pair of baggy blue jeans and a blue and brown flannel shirt which completely clashes with the green Patagonia vest he bought her last week. Maybe he should have gotten her a black one instead. She seemed to love it, but now he's not so sure.

"Come back. I need to kiss you!" he yells, tamping down his doubt. For a few seconds he thinks she didn't hear him because she is frozen to the spot, staring off into the vast distance. "Hey, what are you doing?"

She finally acknowledges him and shuffles across the dusty ground toward him. As she gets closer a fixed-wing, single-engine plane flies overhead. They both look up and watch it as it cuts across the clear blue sky. When the sound of its loud engine finally dissipates into the air, Deni says, "I was listening to the quiet. It's a beautiful sound."

"Yup. It is."

He reaches over and takes her in his arms and puts his mouth on hers. The kiss feels effortless and familiar. When they part he sees her look up at the sky as if the plane is still lingering. "So, I've been meaning to ask you."

"Yeah?"

"How many times did you fly in the Piper?"

"I don't know. Once or twice with your parents and Cal. A few times just me and Cal," she says as she flings her arms out and holds her face up to the sun.

He knows he shouldn't push her on this. His parents and brother are dead and nothing will bring them back, but he can't help himself. He wants to put the question to rest. He wants to know what really happened the day the Piper crashed into the side of a mountain.

It was easy enough to believe the preliminary NTSB report, speculating that Cal might have gotten himself into trouble by flying into unanticipated icy conditions. His brother was both stupid enough and cocky enough to have ignored weather reports.

But then they found water in the tank and thought maybe Deni's father might have sabotaged the plane, which made no sense to anyone, even to the local cops who dragged him into the station and questioned him. Joe Rydell might have harbored some resentment toward Grant's father, but the man went out of his way to secretly *fix* the plane because he was worried about Deni flying in it.

It was when Grant received the final NTSB report two days ago that the clouds began to part. The NTSB placed the blame squarely on pilot negligence by listing the probable cause as "Water contamination in the fuel system that was not observed during the preflight inspection." Yes, there was water in one of the tanks. And yes, his father or Cal should have checked, but they didn't.

They never did.

He knew that as sure as he knew where the sun was going to set tonight.

They would have already been well into their flight when Cal switched from the left fuel tank to the right one. The water in that tank would have gotten into the carburetor, causing total loss of power. The engine would have died, causing the plane to crash.

"While I was with your dad down at the airport the other day he said I should convince you to get your pilot's license too," he says.

Deni lowers her arms. "Oh? I've never thought about it. I'm not sure I'd want—"

"He said you already know a lot about flying, and said—what'd he say? Oh, yeah, he said you could probably pass the written test with your eyes closed."

"Well, I don't know if that's—"

"You knew that both my father and my brother had a habit of using up the fuel in the Piper's left tank before switching over to the right, didn't you? You watched them do it every time you flew with them."

Instead of answering him she looks off into the forest, as if she's heard something moving through the trees. He tries to imagine what her expression is right now. What is going through her mind?

"I don't care, you know. I won't love you any less," he says to her back.

After a few seconds she turns and her eyes meet his. "You flew with them a million more times than I did."

"There had to have been a lot of water to kill the engine," he says, ignoring her statement. "Way more water than just condensation. I was wondering if someone added water to that tank."

He watches Deni pick up a stray piece of plywood out of the dirt and toss it into the trees. "Hmm," she says. "I was kind of wondering that myself."

"Is there anything you want to tell me, Deni?"

She slowly turns toward him, her expression so pointed and serious he almost doesn't recognize her. "You want me to tell you the truth, Grant?"

He takes a step back and tenses.

"The truth is I love you with my entire body and soul and will do whatever it takes to make you happy." With that, she comes toward him and pushes up on her toes, trying to kiss him, but Grant grabs her shoulders, stopping her. He peers into her face. Her dark eyes are filled with an almost violent desire. For him. Only for him.

Does the truth matter? Does he really need to know?

He looks past her, beyond the trees, toward the house on the hill. The house where his body still hesitates before he steps inside. So many bad memories linger. A childhood filled with fear. Aching to be loved by his parents. Wanting and failing, no matter how hard he tried, to be seen as competent. To be cherished and respected as much as his brother. He pictures Erika moving in, taking over the space. Demolishing all the memories, even the few sweet ones. He thought for sure that after what Erika did, the heinous crimes she committed and the ways in which she manipulated him, that she had also killed his ability to ever trust again. To ever feel love again.

He was wrong.

He takes in a deep cleansing breath, then loosens his grip on Deni's shoulder before touching his right thumb to his right forefinger. *I am enough*, he thinks as he pulls her mouth to his and kisses her deeply. After the kiss has ended, they both simultaneously turn and stand shoulder to shoulder, looking out toward the phantom living room where someday soon they will most assuredly catch some amazing sunsets.

END

ACKNOWLEDGMENTS

I AM ENORMOUSLY GRATEFUL to the team at Crooked Lane Books for introducing this book to the world. A big shout-out to Rebecca Nelson for being especially awesome. Thanks to Martin Biro for his thoughtful editing and Lunaea Weatherstone for her keen eye.

A heartfelt thank you to my agent, Stacey Donaghy, for always being my champion.

Hugs and air-kisses to all you bloggers and Bookstagrammers and readers who go all out to support authors.

Much gratitude to Mike Busch, "arguably the best-known A&P/IA in general aviation," for your expertise (and your patience). And to Corkey Harmon for the lesson on blasting rock. Any errors are my own.

Thank you to my husband, Victor, who was always up for reading yet another draft. And to the rest of my family and friends, far and wide. Your love and enthusiasm mean everything.